MORE THAN SUPERHUMAN

More Than Superhuman

A. E. VAN VOGT

NEW ENGLISH LIBRARY
TIMES MIRROR

First published in the United States of America by Dell Publishing Co. Inc., 1971
© 1971 by A. E. van Vogt

*

FIRST NEL PAPERBACK EDITION SEPTEMBER 1975

*

NEL Books are published by
New English Library Limited from Barnard's Inn, Holborn, London E.C.1.
Made and printed in Great Britain by Hunt Barnard Printing Ltd., Aylesbury, Bucks.

45002571 3

ACKNOWLEDGMENTS

'Humans Go Home!' by A. E. van Vogt. Published in *Galaxy* Science Fiction. Copyright © 1969 by Universal Publishing and Distributing Corporation.

'Reflected Men' by A. E. van Vogt. Published in *Galaxy* Science Fiction. Copyright © 1971 by Universal Publishing and Distributing Corporation.

'Laugh, Clone, Laugh' by A. E. van Vogt and Forrest J. Ackerman. Copyright © 1969 by Forrest J. Ackerman.

'Research Alpha' by A. E. van Vogt and James H. Schmitz. Published in *Worlds of IF Science Fiction*. Copyright © 1965 by Galaxy Publishing Corporation.

'Him' by A. E. van Vogt. Copyright © 1968 by Fantasy Publishing Co., Inc.; by arrangement with Wm. L. Crawford and permission of the author and his agent, Forrest J Ackerman.

Contents

Humans, Go Home!

A. E. VAN VOGT

I

'Each morning,' Miliss said, 'is the dawn of nothing.'

So she was leaving.

'No children, no future,' the woman continued. 'Every day like every other, going nowhere. The sun shines, but I'm in darkness – '

It was, Dav realized, the beginning of the death talk. He tensed his perfect muscles. His blue eyes – they could observe with a deep understanding on many levels – misted with sudden anxiety. But his lips and his infinitely adaptable tongue – which in its time, and that time was long indeed, had spoken a hundred languages – said no word.

He watched her, made no move to help her and no effort to stop her as she piled her clothes onto a powered dolly, to be wheeled into the east wing of the house. Her clothes, her jewels from a score of planets; her special pillows and other bedroom articles; the specific furniture – each piece a jewel in itself – in which she stored her possessions; her keys – plain and electronic, pushbutton-control types for energy relays and tiny combination systems for entry into the great Reservoir of the Symbols – all now were made ready to be transported with a visibly growing impatience.

Finally she snapped, 'Where is your courtesy? Where is your manliness – letting a woman do all this work?'

Dav said evenly, 'It would be foolish of me to help you leave me.'

'So all those years of politeness – I merely bought them with unalienated behavior. You have no natural respect for a woman – or for me.'

She yelled accusations at him. Dav felt a tremor stir inside him, not from her words but from the meaning of the anger that accompanied them, the unthinking automatic quality of that anger.

He said flatly, 'I am not going to help you leave me.'

It was the kind of answer one made to a stereotype. His hope had to be that these preliminaries of the death compulsion could be headed off.

His words, however, were far from effective. Her blond cheeks gradually turned to a darker color as the day – unlike other days, which were often so slow as forever – devoured itself, digesting hours in great gulps. And still her possessions, more numerous evidently than she had realized, were not shifted from the west to the east wing of the long, big house.

Late in the afternoon Dav pointed out that her act of withdrawal was a well-known phenomenon of internal female chemistry. He merely wanted from her the analytical consciousness of this fact – and her permission to give her the drugs that would rectify the condition.

She rejected the argument. From her lips poured a stream of angry rationalizations.

'The woman is always to blame. The fault is in her, not in the man. The things that I have had to put up with – they don't count – '

Long ago, when she was still in her natural state, before the administration of the first immortality injections, there might have been genuine cause for accusations which attacked male subjectiveness. But that was back in a distant time. After the body had been given chemical aids, all things were balanced by a diet of understanding drugs.

Dav located the relevant book in the library and abandoned his initial attempts to keep from her the seriousness of her condition. He walked beside her and read paragraphs detailing the emotional affliction that had led to the virtual destruction of the human race. The dark thoughts she had expressed – and was now acting on – were described so exactly that abruptly, as he walked beside her, he bent in her direction and held the book up to her face. His finger pointed out the significant sentences.

Miliss stopped. Her eyes, a deceptive gray-green, narrowed. Her lips tightly compressed, unmistakably resisting what he was doing. Yet she spoke in a mild tone.

'Let me see that.'

She reached for the book.

Dav surrendered it reluctantly. The sly purpose he detected

in her seemed even more automatic than the earlier anger. In those few hours she appeared to have become a simpler, more primitive person.

So he was not surprised when she raised the book above her head and, with a wordless vocalization, flung it to the floor behind him.

They had come to within a few yards of a door which led to her part of the house. Dave resignedly stooped to pick up the book, aware of her walking rapidly to that door. It opened and slammed shut behind her.

After silence descended, after the coming of the brilliant, purple Jana twilight, when the sun finally sank out of sight behind the slickrock mountains to the west and the sweet, soft darkness of the shining, starlit night of Jana settled, Dav tested the connecting doors between the two wings. All four resisted his pull with the rigidity of unbreakable locks.

The following morning.

The sound of a buzzer precipitated Dav into the new day. For a meager moment the hope stirred in him that Miliss was calling. But he rejected that possibility even as he formed the image in his mind that triggered the nearest thought amplifier. His dismissal of the idea turned out to be correct. The buzzing ceased. A picture formed on the ceiling screen. It showed a Jana tradesboy with groceries standing at the outer door.

Dav spoke to the boy in the Jana tongue and glided out of bed. Presently he was accepting the bag from the long-nosed youth, who said, 'There was a message to bring this to another part of the house. But I didn't understand clearly – '

Dav hesitated with the fleeting realization that the ever-present Jana spy system was probably behind those words. And that if he explained, the information would be instantly relayed to the authorities. Not that he could ever tell these beings the truth. Their time for immortality was not yet.

Nor was it their time to learn the numerous details of the final disaster – when, in a period of a few months, virtually the entire human population of the galaxy rejected life, refused the prolongation drugs. People by the billion hid themselves and died unattended and uncaring.

A few, of course, were captured by appalled survivors and had treatment forced on them. A wrong solution, it developed.

11

For the people who sympathized and helped, by those very desperate feelings, in some manner attuned themselves into the same deadly psychic state as the naturally doomed.

In the end it was established that the only real survivors were individuals who felt a scathing contempt for people who could not be persuaded to accept help. Such a disdainful survivor could sarcastically argue with someone – yes, for a while. But force him, no.

Dav stood at the door of the great house in which he and Miliss had lived these several hundred years. And he realized that this was the moment.

To save himself, he had to remember that what Miliss was doing deserved his total disgust.

He shrugged and said, 'My wife has left me. She is living alone on the other side of the house. So deliver these to the door at the far east side.'

He thrust the bag of groceries back into the hands of the Jana and motioned him away.

The boy took the big sack and backed off with visible reluctance.

'Your wife has left you?' he echoed finally.

Dav nodded. In spite of himself he felt vaguely regretful at the revelation. To these Jana males, pursuit of females began early and continued into late life, terminating approximately at the moment of death. Until now the human woman had been a forbidden and unapproachable female. But no question – there had always been a perverted Jana male interest in Miliss.

With an abrupt dismissal Dav suppressed such thoughts. What they represented was unimportant. It did not matter.

Later that day he saw her in her part of the garden, lissome, still beautiful, showing no signs of immediate deterioration. Apparently – even on this second day – she was still an immortal blond woman. Seeing her, Dav shrugged and turned away, his lip curling, and in his mind the thought that she was not really human.

She could not reason.

Still later, darkness had fallen when, after testing with the various keys the Blaze Points of the Great Reservoir of the Symbols, he came to the summit of the hill from which he could see her long, white house.

Its night lights showed the garden and the glint of the river on the far side. But around it nothing moved. Silent stood the old house, familiar, a centuries-old landmark.

Something about the stillness below disturbed him. He had a sudden feeling that no one was there. The house itself was dark – both wings.

Puzzled but not alarmed – because he was safe and Miliss did not count, for she was doomed anyway – Dav hurried down. He tried first a door to her wing. It was unlocked.

An amplified thought hit him. Miliss speaking mentally.

Dav, I have been arrested by Jaer Dorrish and am being taken to a military prison. I have the impression that this is a Dorrish clan takeover scheme and that it is connected with the fact that Rocquel has now been gone for a year. That's all...

The account was succinct, as impersonal as his own receipt of it. She had left him a communication of facts. In her message was no appeal, no request for help.

Dav stood silent. He was evoking a mental picture of the sardonic Jaer Dorrish and, more vaguely, the image of Rocquel, the hereditary leader of the Janae, who had disappeared slightly more than one Jana year ago. A year on Jana was three hundred ninety-two and a fraction days long.

He felt opposed to Jaer, of course – in a way wished the steely-minded Rocquel were back. Usurpations usually meant trouble and unrest. But if it had to be, it had to. The Janae constituted a problem for him as Guardian of the Symbols. But individuals among them were not, in one sense, important. Though he had liked Rocquel, and still liked Rocquel's – widow?

Nerda.

In the morning, I'll look into this...

II

Rocquel's senses blurred in arriving. He lay down for a few seconds on the shadowy grass. It was already day – fairly early morning; he noticed when he climbed to his feet. He could see the palace, visible among the trees of the vast garden which surrounded the building.

Rocquel stood for a moment, head thrown back, breathing deeply of the air of his native planet. A year had seemed a long absence. So much had happened. Yet the sky of Jana and these hills that he had known in his lost youth so intimately seemed unchanged. Here, during all those tremendous days of his absence, time had sculptured with a slow and exacting chisel. A gentle wind blew in Rocquel's face as he started slowly toward the road beyond the near trees, the winding road that would take him to the palace.

Incredibly, he made it to within a hundred yards of the sprawl of building before a Jana male came suddenly from around some trees, saw him, and stopped. Rocquel recognized the other at once: Jaer Dorrish. Jaer was a big fellow, bigger than Rocquel, good-looking in a swarthy way. His eyes narrowed. He seemed to brace himself.

He said arrogantly in the tone of one addressing an intruder, 'What are you doing here – stranger?'

Rocquel walked forward at a deliberate pace. He had been cautioned to take up his old position before he revealed the new facets of his personality. He didn't need the warning – it was implicit in the sly act of a person who knew him, pretending not to.

The problem of what one of the Dorrish men was doing in the Rocquel grounds so early in the morning – or ever – he would come to later. Right now the denial of his identity was surpassingly significant.

Rocquel said, 'Jaer, consider – do you want me for an enemy?'

This time Jaer Dorrish showed his understanding of the situation.

'By Dilit,' he said exultantly, 'I've caught you unarmed.'

He drew his sword in a single, continuous movement and began to circle Rocquel, apparently not quite believing that he need merely rush in and slash. His eyes speculatively sized up Rocquel's condition.

Rocquel backed and simultaneously turned. He paused where Jaer had been standing. It took him moments to locate consciously the symbol made by the invisible Tizane energy, which he had directed to the spot the instant he saw Jaer. He kicked it cautiously, leaning backward so that his body would not be attracted by the symbol. His foot tingled unpleasantly – it was a feeling of something grabbing at him, something very powerful that did not quite reach him but only clawed the outer threads of his clothing, failing to get a good hold. Twice he pulled clear of it. Presently he was able to step over the broken ground without experiencing a reaction.

He was already out of danger when Jaer laughed and replaced his sword.

The big male said arrogantly, 'If one does not threaten, one cannot show mercy. You see, Rocquel, I expected that you would return today. I have had observers watching the grounds all night so that I could have this confrontation with you.' He grimaced triumphantly. 'I analyze that you owe your return to me. Because yesterday I arrested the human woman, Miliss, and here you are this morning, exactly as I anticipated. It was a sudden intuition of mind. You have a lot of explaining to do – sir.'

Jaer was visibly jubilant. He waved at somebody behind Rocquel. Rocquel was wary of the gesture. In his careful defensive maneuvering he had gotten his back to the buildings. Finally he glanced carefully around and saw that Nerda was walking toward them.

As she came near, she said, 'You were not really in danger, were you? It showed in your manner.'

Rocquel said, 'Not from one person.'

He walked to her, and she did not resist his kiss. She might as well have. His lips were cool and unresponsive. Her passive body did not welcome his embrace.

Rocquel drew back, scowling. An old anger against this defiant young female rose to gall him.

'Damn you,' he said. 'Aren't you glad to see me?'

Nerda merely gazed at him coolly.

'I forgot,' said Rocquel, stung. 'It was a welcome period of rest for you. It's difficult for a male to remember that Jana females do not have feelings.'

His wife shrugged.

Rocquel stared at her, curious now rather than hostile. Like all Jana females, she was icily aloof. He had married her in the usual fashion by having her father bring her to his house. She had subsequently borne him a son and a daughter, but in the Jana female tradition she continued to treat him like an intruder in her life – whom she must tolerate but did not particularly care to have around.

Rocquel scowled jealously.

'What about Jaer?'

That brought a reply.

'I think he has already explained his presence. Rather than have any further words from him, I would prefer to hear your explanation of your absence.'

Rocquel rejected explanations. 'Come along,' he said gruffly. 'Let us go inside.'

There were things to do. The news of his return would spread rapidly. The men in control of the council must not be allowed too much time to decide what to do about him. There would be regents, generals, and their aides – who would be unhappy at the return of the hereditary ruler of the army. Before this night he must again be recognized as entitled by law and right to wield the scepter of his sphere.

He took Nerda's arm gently. The move was calculated. He wanted to enter the palace beside her, his identity given validity by her presence. A year was a long time on Jana. Jana males particularly had short memories. He could not have planned his arrival better if he had personally made all the arrangements in advance.

Rocquel had the tocsin sounded as soon as he reached the main guard station. Shortly the palace guard and the servants were drawn up in five lines of a hundred each. He addressed them in his deepest baritone, recalling himself to the older men, inviting the younger men to remember his face and body structure. He wanted them to be able to identify him under all circumstances.

He felt a little better when that job was done and the people had been dismissed to return to their duties. But not much better. The servants and guards could be talked to like a schoolroom full of children. But not the officers. Not the nobility.

He had a new, superior – yet not at all condescending – attitude toward these people. They were simple souls. He now understood how rapidly Dav and Miliss were rushing Janae into civilization by a trial-and-error system that attempted to take each man for what he was.

The lower classes were given easy tests. Those who showed even a modicum of mechanical ability were soon placed on assembly lines, where they performed one action, then two,

16

then several – but never many. For decades now some pretty sharp mechanics had been coming up the line, and from their ranks arose a new class – engineers.

The officers and nobility were a different breed. Quick to take insult, they were truly impervious to all but the barest elements of education. They had been persuaded that being able to read and write was a mark of distinction, but they were never entirely convinced. Why, they wanted to know grimly, were the lower classes also being taught reading and writing? The resultant, infinitely stubborn attitude had made it necessary to have a different written language for the people – one the upper classes didn't respect – before the nobles sullenly allowed their children to go to special, separate schools.

Telling the nobility of his return, it seemed to Rocquel, would have to be done at an all-male dinner in the vast dining hall adjoining the even vaster jousting room.

About midmorning Dav at last felt free to put through a call to Nerda. There was a long delay. Finally an aide came to the phone.

He said in a formal tone, 'The queen wishes me to inform you that her lord, Rocquel, has returned, and since he will in future represent the power of the armed forces, her talking to you might be misconstrued at this stage. That is all, sir.'

Dav hung up, startled. The great Rocquel was home. Where had he been?

The hereditary general had always been a male first, his every movement and the tenor of his being expressing the quiescent violence of his powerful, supermasculine breed. It seemed an unfortunate coincidence for Miliss that the deadly, narrowed-eyed Jana ruler had returned. Dav divined that, if a struggle for power took place, Miliss might be its first victim.

After some thought, Dav phoned the palace a second time and asked for Rocquel.

Once more he endured delay.

At last another aide said, 'His Excellency, the lord-general Rocquel wishes me to inform you that a new law will be promulgated tomorrow to the council. He invites you to attend the council meeting which will be held at the slick-rock rendezvous.'

2

The dinner that night shocked Rocquel. He had forgotten the extreme coarseness of his peers – at least it had become vague in his mind. An uproar of yelling and jesting began as the first males arrived. More arrivals simply added to the pandemonium. Things quieted down only to a degree when the meal was finally served. Plates clanked. Forks and knives clattered. Males yelled a peculiar type of acceptable insult at acquaintances farther along a table – insults having to do with the jester's belief that the other lacked sexual prowess. Such remarks always brought bellows of laughter, while onlookers insultingly urged the object of the attack to prove his capabilities.

Yet since humor always probed the abyss of a male's sensitivity to criticism, suddenly a word would be unacceptable. In a flash the aggrieved male was on his feet, ragefully demanding satisfaction. Moments later the two nobles, yelling furiously at each other, would stamp out to the jousting room and add the clash of their steel to the sound of the dozens that were already there.

Shortly a scream of outrage announced the first blood had been drawn. In the presence of Rocquel the custom was that the male initially blooded in any way was expected to acknowledge defeat. Such acknowledgment meant that the insult was nullified. But the loser who felt himself still aggrieved could demand a later reckoning away from the palace grounds.

It was of this assembled group of mad creatures that Rocquel demanded silence when the eating was completed. Getting it, he gave the explanation for his absence that had been suggested to him – a religious withdrawal, a year of wandering among the people as a mendicant, a time of self-searching and thorough selflessness, of deliberate, temporary abdication of power.

He concluded his fabricated account.

'I saw our people in their daily actions. I lived among them, survived on their generosity, and can report that the Jana world is indeed a worthy one.'

He received a prolonged ovation. But a bad moment came when he presently went into the jousting room, where the guests had drifted after his talk.

A voice grated beside his ear, 'Your sword, sire.'

Rocquel experienced a blank instant as he realized he was being challenged.

He swung around as of old in a swift, automatic defense action. His blade came out, weaving, before he saw that his challenger was Jaer Dorrish.

Rocquel poised, sword ready. He gazed questioningly into the dark, cynical eyes of his enemy.

From somewhere in the sea of faces surrounding them, from out of the diminishing curtain of sound – diminishing as more males grew aware of what was happening – Rocquel was aware of a top officer speaking sharply.

'Jaer – have you forgotten? You have to state your reason when you challenge the crown. And it must be a reason acceptable to the majority present.'

'My reason,' said Jaer in his deliberate fashion, 'is that story of where he said he was during the past year – '

The officer who had spoken walked forward. He was grave, fortyish, narrow-eyed.

'Is it a matter of misunderstanding the story or of rejecting it?'

Silence had settled over the room, and the words made an echo into the distances of that cavernous space. The question visibly gave Jaer pause. His expression showed his comprehension that a to-the-death had to follow any total challenge of a noble's word.

Abruptly he laughed and put away his sword.

He said, 'I think I shall ask privately for a clarification. If Rocquel decides what I have to say is truly a reason for a challenge – then we shall have our bout. Perhaps tomorrow.' He thereupon stepped close to Rocquel and said in a low, insolent voice. 'Your Excellency – the coincidence of my arresting Miliss and your prompt return needs to be explained. If the two are not related – you will, of course, have no objection to my plans for disposing of her.'

Rocquel said evenly, 'If you are operating within the frame of the law – '

'The law is what the council decides,' replied Jaer arrogantly. 'Do I have your word that you will not interfere – in view of my suspicions?'

'There will be a new law,' said Rocquel in a formal tone. 'Within the frame of that law – I shall not interfere.'

He walked away, leaving Jaer Dorrish with a black scowl

19

on his face and a query about the 'new law' unspoken on his pursed lips. In his mind Rocquel read the thought that this very night he must attend on the human woman – must force her before any protecting law was passed.

Yet Rocquel could not be sure he had read correctly even when Jaer left the party within minutes.

Nerda was waiting for Rocquel when he came in. He was late, very late. As soon as he entered – and after he had nodded to her – she retreated to her dressing room and began to get ready for bed. He watched her shadow through the translucent door. A regretful thought passed through his mind that he should have given her permission to retire without waiting for his return.

Presently he rejected the thought of such leniency. According to Jana law a wife could not undress at night to go to bed until her husband gave permission. She could lie down with her clothes on. She could even sleep, though that was frowned on. She could go to bed before his return only with his written permission or if a doctor stated in writing or in the presence of witnesses that she was ill.

The rules seemed harsh. But Rocquel had read the ancient documents containing the results of studies made of Jana female behavior prior to the passing of the stringent laws, and there was no question. Jana females would associate with males only when forced. A female, unforced, would promptly move off by herself and remain that way all her life.

The facts had been set down by amazed historians who named names and places. The truths of the long-ago experiments in allowing freedom to females were attested to by famous people of Jana history. There was no point in repeating the experience in modern times.

Jana females had no maternal instinct and particularly detested their male children. It had been a sad thing to read some of the comments made by females during the free period.

A male child will eventually become a Jana male – that most detestable being. And so any charming childlike attributes he may have are an illusion. . . .

Another female had been in favor of the race's dying out – because its continuance required that Jana males also

20

survive, to which she was 'totally opposed'.

What could males do, confronted by such females?

They had done it.

The laws were just and as kind as they could be. A female could complain if she suffered any ill-treatment – and receive an immediate hearing from a court. No expense was spared by the State to protect her from a brutal husband.

In return she must do her duty by her husband and her children. Since she had no feeling about her functions, the law prescribed her exact routine.

Obviously even the hereditary general could not lightly alter either the custom or the law. Nerda came to bed, and presently he gave her permission to sleep.

She slept – it seemed, instantly.

III

Miliss heard a key in the lock of her cell. She had not undressed. She sat up in the rough bunk and watched curiously as a manlike figure, waving a long flashlight, unlocked the door and entered.

From the vast shadowy size of him she divined his identity. But not until he deliberately raised the light and beamed it into his face did she recognize Jaer Dorrish.

His face, like that of all Jana males, was too long, too much given over to nose. But the skin was a clear reddish color and smooth.

She was not repelled.

At least, she thought, the Janae were a distinctly humanlike breed, for which – in view of the fate she sensed was in store for her – she was thankful. It did not occur to her to formulate in her mind the mental pattern that would activate a thought amplifier in the house where she and Dav lived – no help for her from that rigid mind, she decided.

But she did have a purpose of her own, adaptable to this situation. It had been growing on her all day. The male stepped briskly across the cell toward her cot.

She said hurriedly, 'I've been thinking about what you told me last night – your prediction that Rocquel would return as a consequence of my arrest. And it happened. He did come back.'

Jaer stopped his forward movement. He did not reply.

Her next words quivered on the tip of her tongue but remained unspoken.

Miliss was startled. She had an enormous sensitivity to small signals. He had been coming forward with that Jana-male arrogance, his whole manner vibrating with the message that he would not be denied.

And now he stood still. And the way he stood telegraphed uncertainty.

'Is something wrong?' Miliss asked.

More silence, a sense of darker emotions. She was astounded. Jana males were reputed to have a peculiar calm humor in the rape situation. Both humor and *savoir faire* required expression in words, not silence.

During the strange pause, like a suspension of time in the cell, she had nevertheless become aware of the night and the prison. A time had been on Jana when there had been no prisons, only a few compounds where 'enemies' were kept prior to execution.

On Jana, for more millennia than she cared to recall, people had been tolerated — or executed. No middle situation had existed. This and similar prisons were actually a great victory for less harsh attitudes.

So the sounds of a vast life around her were presently heartening to Miliss. She heard metallic clanks, distant throat raspings, Jana males snarling in their sleep, and occasional echoes of faraway voices. Sounds of many prisoners. The Nunbrid prison was large. It was filled with people who would be tried in court for their offenses and who were not subject — as had once been the case — to the compulsive masculine rage of some intolerable noble.

A feeling of peaceful accomplishment was settling over Miliss. Dav and she had civilized these people.

Jaer finally spoke.

'I had a sudden insight — and I'm having another one.'

His voice was strained, not really calm. She sensed in its tone an advantage for her. Somehow the situation was no longer as dangerous as it had been. This male was genuinely disturbed.

By what?

Miliss pressed her own purpose upon him.

'Is that all you can say about the coincidence of your prediction and Rocquel's return?'

'I'm still wondering about it myself,' was the grim answer. The threat was in his voice again. She rushed past it.

'Don't you realize the impossibility of such an unsupported insight – the odds against its baring truth?'

For a tense moment in the unyielding closeness of the cell, in the darkness broken only by a flashlight that sometimes pointed at her and sometimes at the metal bars – and occasionally, briefly, at Jaer himself – she thought that he would acknowledge reason and dismiss the subject. But Jana nobles, she shortly decided in despair, were not up to her kind of strict logic. His mien told her he was accepting his intuition.

For a long moment, while he stood there silently, her fear grew.

Then: 'There's only one explanation,' he said slowly. 'Rocquel was in hiding with you and Dav while he was gone.'

'No. That's absolutely not true. If you're acting on that assumption – you're in danger.'

'Danger?'

'There's a hidden force at work. It can strike at you if you ignore it. In fact, it probably has already struck – or how could you have had two insights?'

'You're trying to alarm me,' said Jaer harshly. 'And a Jana male cannot be frightened.'

'But he can think about how best to survive,' countered Miliss. 'At least' – she couldn't help the biting remark – 'the males I know always do.'

Again silence filled the cell. The light winked off. Into that darkness and that silence Miliss projected what seemed to her to be the only possible explanation.

'What has happened means that you've been programmed,' she said.

'Programmed? I don't understand.'

'It's impossible that you could have a second major intuition unless somebody had installed it in your mind under mechanical hypnosis.'

'I just had it. It's my own thought.'

'It's not your own thought. You're being manipulated.' She broke off. 'Don't you see, you couldn't possibly – being a Jana noble – have all by yourself predicted Rocquel's return on the basis of my arrest. It's too radical and fantastic a prediction. Yet it came true. And now another one? Impossible.'

Once more he was silent. The flashlight was on again, its beam tilted casually, showing his scowling face, narrowed eyes and lower lip pushed up. He was evidently having unpleasant, calculating thoughts.

Abruptly he asked, 'Why did you and Dav separate?'

Miliss hesitated, then said, 'He was more and more adopting the attitudes and behavior of the Jana male – and treating me as Jana males treat Jana females. I had had enough years ago – but we were alone here, two human beings, the last of our kind in this area. So I tried to make my peace with the situation as Jana females have done for so long.'

There was actually more to it than that. It had, of course, kept occurring to her that the frequent despair she had felt over Dav might in fact be the death wish that had destroyed the human race. She had fought against her growing embitterment, until, one day not too long since, she had had an insight of her own.

Human males were, had always been, exactly as vicious as the Janae. But human women, having their own maternal instinct to satisfy, had endlessly compromised with the egotistical villains. The need for motherhood had put a fortunate – for the men and the race – veil over a woman's awareness of the impossible true nature of the beasts.

Once she had recognized the thought, leaving Dav was only a matter of a brief period of rethinking her reasons, and convincing herself finally.

Jaer's voice came grimly.

He said, 'I didn't have my first insight until after I had arrested you. I've had my second one in your presence. So you're doing this to me. By Dilit, woman –'

Miliss said urgently, 'Tell me what your second insight is.'

When he had told her, she said, 'But that's ridiculous – what good does that do me?'

Jaer must have recognized her logic. He stood very still.

After a long pause he said slowly, 'But I did get both thoughts in your presence, so someone knows I'm here.'

His manner showed unease. The implication of danger was visibly penetrating his awareness. Miliss sensed her advantage.

She said, 'What is so meaningless about these insights is that I detect that your purpose in arresting me was entirely personal. You saw a possibility of challenging the throne and simultaneously obtaining me as a mistress – '

'Silence, woman.' Jaer sounded alarmed. 'I have never desired the throne – that's treason. I'd better leave before I damage you and ruin my case against you in court. But don't think I'm through with you.'

The light winked out. Quick steps sounded. A metal door clicked open and clanged shut.

She heard him retreating along a corridor. And realized that she was almost as shaken as he.

That second insight, she told herself, *is absolutely mad. . . .*
But for the first time in many years she slept poorly.

IV

The next day.

Shortly after sunrise the council members began cycling up to the meeting place at the beginning of the slickrock range, seven miles west of Nunbrid. By the time Rocquel arrived on his new motorbike, Dav and eight Jana males of high rank were already there. The human sat on his bike off to one side, but the Jana nobles were impatiently gunning their motors, visibly anxious to get started on their hazardous meeting-in-motion.

Rocquel was greeted by a number of insulting but quite good-natured comments about his overweight machine. He responded with well-placed sneers about overcautious small-bike riders. But he was curious. There had been changes in design during his absence. Wheeling around with the casual daring of an expert cyclist, he made quick, searching examination of the mount of each council member to see what time and manufacturers had wrought.

As always for slickrocking, all the motorcycles were small, tough, and light. But Rocquel noticed that three of the bikes were smaller than he remembered – not more than 100cc., perhaps even 90 or 80 – compared to his 175cc. machine.

He questioned the three owners about it. He was still getting boastful replies when Jaer Dorrish and a sly-eyed air-force officer roared up and charged their metal steeds up the first incline.

Jaer yelled, 'Meeting called to order – '

A number of nobles uttered wild cries, gunned their motors, and took off in pursuit of the latecomers.

Dav brought up the rear.

Moments later everyone was in motion, and the meeting of the supreme council of Jana was in session.

In the old days – before the machines – a king had held his council meetings while riding a tamed, high-backed Mesto-beast. The Mestos were dangerous, cunning creatures, always looking for an opportunity to upset their riders, and Mesto-riding was, accordingly, considered great fun. But a Mesto simply could not cover the distances or go over the rough and beautiful slickrock country.

At first the nobles climbed steadily, strung out unevenly, bobbing up and down over domes, knobs, and ridges, skipping at a good clip over the almost glass-smooth, steel-hard straights. Rocquel, coming up from behind, kept edging up to Jaer and finally had his bike racing along parallel to the bright green machine of the big male.

'What's on the agenda?' he yelled.

Jaer's answering cry brought up the subject of Miliss. He made a slashing gesture with one hand, cutting the air with it as if it were a blade, then showed his teeth in a grimacing smile.

He shouted, 'I propose that this woman be put to death.'

'On what grounds?' Rocquel roared back, surprised.

Jaer's suggestion was discourteous in view of the fact that Dav was at the council meeting. Or was it possible that Jaer had not yet seen Dav?

As the day dragged by, Jaer's unawareness of Dav began to seem less and less a coincidence. But Jaer's intentness on Miliss and on the new law might have accounted for his attitude toward Dav.

Dav anticipated a crisis as soon as he was told what was on the agenda, and the nature of the new law.

The law itself required no special explanation for him. It was he who had proposed the idea of a constitutional monarchy to a resistant Rocquel. The very next day – a year ago – the powerful Jana leader had gone off on a religious hegira.

Now he was back, acceptant.

Mentally, Dav triggered a thought amplifier. It in turn channeled power into a relay that blazed one of the Symbols.

The Symbol of a constitutional monarchy.

That done, he considered with mirthless good humor the proposal to execute Miliss. Ironic that Jaer was planning to put on trial a person already doomed.

Should Jaer be told?

But when Dav finally joined the group, the crisis came so rapidly that there was no time to mention anything.

The council members stopped in front of a big cave, at the 9,000-foot level. Here the great nobles of Jana sat on bikes with engines idling while they gulped breakfast.

Rocquel was aware of an ugly, throaty sound from Jaer. He spun around and saw Dav easing his bike into the clearing. Dav came to a full stop.

Beside Rocquel, Jaer let out a bellow and gunned his motor.

That night Rocquel described the day to Nerda, then asked curiously, 'What do you think happened to Jaer? You know more about what Dav can do than anyone.'

Conversations between them were not common. She was not required by law or custom to speak to him as long as she performed her wifely duties. He was not surprised when she did not reply. But he deduced from the thoughtful expression on her face that she was considering the matter and would eventually give him an answer.

Yet it was morning before she answered.

'A symbol,' she said then, 'as Dav has described it, represents a real thing or thought. It is not itself the thing or the thought – '

Rocquel waited, uneasily aware that he was being presented with a concept that might be too subtle for a Jana noble – too subtle even for himself, despite his past year of indoctrination.

Nerda continued, 'When the Symbol representing constitutional monarchy is finally a part of the thinking of millions of Janae, the force of it in all those minds will maintain such a system for decades under normal circumstances – or at least until another Symbol replaces it, which, of course, is happening very rapidly with Dav and Miliss forcing us into civilization.'

Rocquel felt helpless before her explanation. She seemed

to understand what she was saying, and he didn't.

We males of the nobility are really no longer a part of what is happening. . . .

It was discouraging, but he persisted.

'What I saw,' he said, 'was Jaer's motorcycle stop – not short – but as if it ran into an elastic wall that took the full force of his forward impetus and gently flung him back. He ended up on the ground. But he was not hurt.'

'He struck the Symbol,' said Nerda. 'These Symbols have become progressively more violent in their reaction. The most violent so far is the Symbol of a constitutional monarchy.'

He said, 'You say the Symbol. But what was the force involved?'

'The force of the Symbol.' Her expression showed her awareness of his bewilderment. 'Don't you see?' she urged. 'All those millions of people who believe.'

What Rocquel was seeing was that he had made a mistake in asking for her opinion. He wanted to say that nobody yet believed in the new law. It would not even be publicly announced until later this morning. But his awful feeling leaped past that idea to the more personal awareness that he had lowered himself in her eyes. He recalled with a sinking sensation the Jana-male conviction that if a female even once gained a genuine advantage over her husband, it was the end of their relationship. Nothing the male did after that could repair the damage.

Fighting for recovery, he nodded and said aloud, 'I see. Your many conversations with Dav have been very educational and valuable for both of us. I congratulate you. It's a difficult concept.'

He divined from an odd look in her eyes that she saw through his verbal stratagem.

She said slowly, 'We mustn't expect too much from a constitutional monarchy in terms of change in the passions. Rule of law merely regulates a society in a more orderly fashion than absolutism. An accused individual is no longer subject to arbitrary judgments but is allowed time by the courts to defend himself within the frame of the law. Yet in the end he may pay the same penalty.' She concluded: 'And so, to answer your question of last night – I believe we shall see how Jaer was affected by the way he allows the trial of Miliss to be conducted.'

Rocquel, who was still striving for recovery from his fateful error in having this discussion with her at all, said in his most matter-of-fact voice, 'What I'm curious about is the nature of the charges he intends to level against her – '

Those charges surprised Dav more than Rocquel, who still nursed memories of his year away. He had learned something about humans during his absence, and could even control a certain Symbol himself – without, he realized, really understanding it.

Miliss was accused of being an enemy alien, illegally resident on Jana; spying for an invading alien force from space; conspiring to pretend to be a member of a decadent race when in fact she was a member of a superior, dominant race set down among primitives.

She was also charged with harboring criminal intent.

Dav scanned the headlines unbelievingly, standing in the rain in front of a newsstand. Janae in colorful raincoats drifted past him as – directed by a guide sentence on page one – he turned to the editorial page. There he read in the language of Low Jana:

In an unprecedented action, the government today challenged the right to live on this planet of the two relics of an older civilization. Almost melodramatic charges of conspiracy were leveled at the couple, but only the woman has been arrested.

We propose to leave to the courts the resolution of the legal tangle implicit in this arrest, but find ourselves thoughtful about the matter on a strictly theoretical basis.

Explorers have recently found isolated tribes of Janae still living in stone-age cultures. Contact with our superior civilization was inacted as a depressant on the aspirations and mores of the backward peoples, and they have seemed unable to recover as a group.

Until today's governmental action, we have known a reverse condition with the two human beings resident on Jana. They represent an older culture – one that apparently had virtually died out for reasons never analyzed. Such a decadent culture, even though it had clearly attained heights of scientific achievement far in advance of what is available on Jana, has not acted as depressant on spirit of the Janae.

Matters to be adjudicated by the courts include the following: Are Dav and Miliss representatives of a superior culture that is merely pretending to be decadent, so that the normal depressant impact upon an inferior culture is avoided? If so, does their presence here come under the heading of an alien conspiracy? And can such a purpose be interpreted as an invasion?

The account was perceptive. It indicated the presence of a highly intelligent professional class already in existence in Nunbrid and hundreds of other cities. The lower-class Janae had clearly matured more rapidly that their hereditary rulers. Yet the tone of the editorial was neither inflammatory nor antagonistic. In fact, it showed respect for the government and awareness of the meaning of the new law.

Dav's own thought ceased at that point. He had been aware that passersby were glancing at him. Now, suddenly, one big male stopped, uttered an explosive oath, and lifted an arm threateningly, as if to strike.

Dav shrank back involuntarily. The male grew instantly contemptuous and kicked at him. Dav, alert now, dodged with easy skill but dropped his newspaper. The big fellow scooped it up from the wet sidewalk and pounded the soggy sheets.

He roared, 'You've got to be nothing. You're the last of a vanished race. A nothing! A nothing!'

Dav retreated. He found a side street, slipped into its darker, damp distances, heading for home. As he approached the edge of the city, he heard a sound in the night ahead of him, a swelling murmur of ugly voices. Then, out in the open spaces between himself and his house, he saw a huge crowd carrying torches.

Startled, Dav withdrew from the open area and headed for a small house on a nearby street. The place was actually a secret entrance to the big white mansion. Long ago, when Jana had been more primitive, unpleasant incidents had occurred. The secret access had often proved useful.

He made his way safely through the connecting tunnel to the big house, and from its interior gazed out at the crowd through a viewplate. The plate magically dissolved the night and the rain, showing a dull day-view of the large grounds in front of the house.

At first look the mob seemed even huger than he had estimated. Dav shook his head sadly. The pattern was the same as it had once been on old Earth. At the top was the hereditary hierarchy. Next came a law-abiding middle class of people. At the bottom seethed the vast mass of the unthinking.

The hierarchy was semipsychotic, murderous, subjective. And the middle class was still relatively new and unaware of its future power. The mob was completely duped.

Dav observed with relief that several hundred troops patrolled an area between him and the angry crowd. An officer spoke through a loudspeaker system, addressing the mob.

'Go home. The rule of law shall prevail. Go home. If these people are spies, they will be judged by the law. Go home – '

The frequently repeated admonition began to have its effect toward midnight. Dav saw that there were fewer people outside, and more were drifting back toward the city. But it was nearly two in the morning before, feeling that the danger was over, he went to bed.

Lying there, he rejected the accusations against Miliss and himself with little more than a moment's consideration.

It was true, as the newspaper editorial had pointed out, that primitives had in the past suffered psychic and racial disaster as a result of being exposed abruptly to a superior culture. And, conceivably, somebody might mercifully evolve a more systematic approach to the problem.

But the mentors would know. That had to be. It would be absolutely ridiculous if Miliss and he weren't aware of their own realities.

All these hundreds of years of ignorance on so vital a point? Impossible.

The truth was that simple – and obvious. Nearly four hundred empty years made a weight of time in his mind that no words and no Jana accusation could penetrate.

He had no trouble sleeping.

Rocquel had stayed in the palace communications center during the period of threat against Dav. Several times he spoke directly to the commanding officer of the troops patrolling the grounds.

At last, weary and a little guilty at having been out late again, he went to his apartment. The bedroom was dark as he entered – and he had an instant, awful intuition.

He flicked on the light and stood confused and shaken. Nerda was in bed, undressed under the sheets. Her eyes were closed. Her breathing came with the regularity of sleep.

Rocquel's thought flashed back to their conversation of the morning and to his sudden feeling that he had ruined himself with her. His inability to grasp the meaning of the Symbol idea troubled him again.

Standing beside his sleeping wife, he visualized the repercussions of her rebellion if it were ever found out. His absence had shaken the throne, and he had returned too recently to have fully recovered his power and position. He had divined an uneasiness in the nobility – it would take a little while before those suspicious, violent beings were reassured that the new law was not a direct threat.

And if they found out that he was so weak that he could not control his wife – Instantly an old impulse propelled him toward her sleeping body. His hands and jaws clenched with the automatic effort that would shove her in a single thrust out of the far side of the bed.

He poised before the act, suddenly gripped and held by a thought and feeling new to him.

He had been about to act on the Jana-male attitude. But was Nerda justified in her rebellion? Was the old way the way women should be treated? Had his analysis of her reason for what she had done been accurate?

A flash of an old male paranoia darkened his face and mind – the absolute conviction that Nerda was doing this because another male had gotten to her.

Dav, the human?

Some portion of Rocquel's mind recognized the total irrationality of the thought – recognized that if it were true, Jana females would not associate with males of their own free will, they obviously did not betray their husbands. He was also aware that Dav, who had an unlimited sense of personal responsibility, would not have taken advantage of the queen's year of 'widowhood'.

The recognition and awareness were not enough for his fevered brain, alive with brutal images.

He had to know.

He turned and walked out of the room. Within minutes he was part of a motorcycle army unit roaring through the night streets of Nunbrid toward the military prison where Miliss was confined.

The long, bleak concrete corridors of the prison echoed to his footsteps and those of his guards. The light carried by the prison's officer-of-the-night was bright enough, but it cast wavering shadows.

In that uneven brightness, Rocquel noted the gray drabness of this prison world, and some of the singleness of his purpose softened. The thought came to him that Miliss had been held here now for several days and that this was wrong.

He could no nothing about it under the new law, but within himself he felt a deep anger against Jaer.

The rage was brief. It ended as they reached Miliss' cell – and there she was. Rocquel went in alone, his guards retreating, waiting.

Their first moments together were ordinary. Miliss' surprise and pleasure when she recognized him, then her puzzlement that he should come at so late an hour, gave him his opening.

He asked her the question: Why had she and Dav separated?

The woman was startled. She sensed the dark purpose in him – who had always been so friendly to her and with whom she had communicated so well in the past.

After a moment, realizing that delay was unwise, she gave him Dav's diagnosis – that she had gone into the death thing that had destroyed man. She deemed it the best reply, considering all possibilities.

Her answer and its deadly implications for her shocked him out of his madness. She explained in greater detail.

Rocquel said, 'Then what you are saying is that you acted out of some parallel to the type of emotion used by people who actually did have the death thing. You did this consciously, knowing Dav would believe it was in fact the death thing.'

'I think that's what I did,' Miliss replied. She added quickly, 'The death thing is subtle. One can fool oneself.'

Rocquel persisted, 'But as far as you're concerned, you're not really dying?'

'As far as I know, I'm not.'

Rocquel considered that in a gathering amazement.

Finally: 'But why aren't you doing something about getting out of this prison? You shouldn't be here.'

'What can I do?'

'Don't you have any protection of your own?'

'Nothing,' she said, 'but the Symbols so far activated. Except for a few hand weapons and mobile energy units, most of which we've given to the Janae, that's all we have.'

'What about other – later – Symbols?'

'Their time is not yet,' said Miliss. 'They wouldn't work – not for Jana.'

Rocquel sighed.

But, he wanted to say, *Dav used the power of millions of believers in a constitutional monarchy before they ever believed in it – in fact, before they even knew about it. Why not use the power of millions of believers in some future Symbol before they ever believe in it?*

He did not ask the question. The concept of any Symbol was beyond his ability to grasp. He realized humbly that he was a Jana nobleman of a somewhat simple nature and that the year he had spent aboard the earth battleship – the time he had described to no one – had been really like some tribal king's being . . . entertained, if that was the right word, by traders or scientists from a superior civilization. Being kindly disposed, they had been anxious not to hurt his feelings – but to them he had been a nothing. His status had been meaningless except in so far as they had a policy of using native kings in their interplanetary welfare work.

Nonetheless, he tried again to reach understanding.

At his request Miliss explained the power of a Symbol once more. But it didn't penetrate.

We thick-skulled males. . . .

'And the ridiculous thing,' he explained his failure to Miliss, 'is that I myself actually have control of a Symbol – '

He stopped. It was an admission that he would have made

to no other living person – only to this one individual with whom he had always felt able to speak freely.

He finished lamely, 'Of course, that was given to me as a protection.'

He stopped again because of the look on her face – intent, avid, seeking, startled, unbelieving but finally believing.

Miliss whispered, 'Who gave you control of that Symbol?'

'Human beings,' Rocquel said simply.

She sank back. She seemed to cringe on the cot, as if, like a mental patient, she were wracked by a psychic disease that contracted her body, curling it, twisting her head to one side.

Finally she said, 'Then Jaer's intuitions, accusations, may be true. There are human beings out there – ' She suddenly broke off, breathless. 'Tell me exactly where you were, what you saw – '

Rocquel described his year on the battleship.

She whispered, 'There were both men and women?'

'Yes. It was a community of several thousand, I would say.'

'They never landed anywhere?'

'Not that I was aware of.' He sighed. 'But it was such a big ship. I saw only what appeared on the visual screens in the sections where I was permitted to wander. They didn't teach me the language. I only heard what the interpreting machines said to me.' He considered possibilities. 'Landing parties could have gone down to planets without my knowing it.'

'It was one of these humans that taught you control of a Symbol?'

'Yes.'

Miliss persisted: 'But what was it supposed to do? If Jaer had actually slashed at you with his sword – what would have happened to him?'

Rocquel didn't know.

He explained slowly, 'They warned me to be careful with it – because if I wasn't, it would hook onto me, too.' He added: 'When I set it up against Jaer, I could feel it tugging at me, sort of like' – he paused, groping – 'maybe like a magnet.'

'But what is it a Symbol of?' Miliss asked.

Rocquel had no idea.

She went on, baffled: 'It must be drawing its energy from some meaningful idea on another planet – since we didn't sense anything here. But what could it be?' No answer came to her, and she asked, 'You still have control of it?'

He nodded.

'Did they say they would let you maintain it permanently?'

Rocquel gazed at her unhappily. 'I can't remember. I was told something – but each time I think I'm going to recall it, it fades.'

'That sounds like close-to-the-surface programming.' Miliss nodded. 'As if whatever it relates to might happen at any time. So we must be near a crisis.' She added, obviously thinking out loud, that only a Symbol could act with subtle or powerful influence over distances. She finished: 'It must be very personal to you, which in itself is unusual. For example, if I could do what you have described – I could get out of this prison.'

Miliss' second admission of helplessness focused Rocquel's attention on her situation. Her confession that she could not protect herself was abruptly enormously significant. It placed control back in Jana hands. Janae could accept or reject a gift of knowledge from the reservoir on a self-determined basis.

We can use what they have, but we don't have to. . . .

Rocquel felt somehow stronger in his Jana identity as he had that awareness. The accusations leveled at Miliss by Jaer had had a certain truth to them. The entire populace felt a displacement as a consequence of the human presence, gentle as it was.

After a little he was able to reason out the extent of her predicament. He was appalled. Her position was very severe if she and Dav could not really protect themselves.

With an effort he pushed aside his anxiety for her, grew calm and grave.

'There will be a difficult time ahead, my dear,' he said gently. 'The new law binds me as much as it does everyone else. I cannot arbitrarily set you free. Have you an attorney?'

'Not yet,' Miliss answered.

'I'll call Dav and tell him that it is imperative he get one for you.'

'He won't do a thing.' She reminded him of the death-dive situation – how only those survived who refused to help. She finished, 'I counted on that to keep him away from me. So there can be no help from him.'

Rocquel shook his head, smiling, and pointed out that his

position in the matter was stronger than Dav's.

'I'll call him,' he said firmly. 'He'll do it because I ask him, not necessarily to help you.' He broke off. 'He's the one who should act in this matter. It will look odd if he doesn't. So he will.'

At that moment Rocquel accidentally caught a glimpse of his watch. It registered nearly four in the morning. He was instantly contrite.

'I'm sorry,' he apologized. 'I've kept you awake.'

Miliss brushed his words aside.

'I feel so much better. You've given me the first information from – out there' – she gazed upward, waved vaguely – 'that I've had in all the years Dav and I have been here. It's not clear – it's hard to decide what it means. But now I know that there are still a few other human beings.'

On that note they separated. Rocquel returned to the palace and presently slipped into bed beside the sleeping Nerda.

She was a problem to which he had no quick solution either.

VI

The Jana attorney whom Dav consulted shook his head gravely over the fourth count.

'The other accusations,' he said, 'have as yet no legal penalties. The judge could do anything, could even release her. But criminal intent has proved dangerous in the past. It can bring a capital verdict.'

Dav attended the trial as a witness, getting angrier every minute as all his 'gifts' to the Janae were used as evidence against Miliss. The argument of the State was that a superior culture was, by way of its scientific gifts, cunningly guiding the Janae away from their natural development and into a mental enslavement that was the equivalent of a takeover of one people by another. Dav's concern was with the accusations, not with Miliss.

Called to the stand by Miliss' attorney, he denied all such intent.

'Science is neutral,' he said. 'It is the truth of nature. Jana scientists would normally and in due course have discovered exactly the same truths. In giving the Janae the scientific artifacts of Earth's ancient civilization, I fulfilled a duty imposed upon me by a vanished race to hand on the torch of knowledge as rapidly as feasible in the hope that, with such a head start, the Janae would succeed in establishing a permanently growing civilization instead of one that would eventually dwindle as others, including man's, have been them – '

When he later came out on the street a troop of guards sent by Rocquel saved him from a demonstrating crowd.

KEEP YOUR FOREIGN SCIENCE . . . JANA MUST BE FREED FROM THE ALIEN YOKE . . . JANA FOR THE JANAE . . . DEATH TO THE INVADERS . . . HUMANS, GO HOME –

The crowds screamed insults as Dav was escorted to a bus that took him, accompanied by several guards, to the end of the line. From there the soldiers walked with him to his house, where other soldiers patrolled the approaches, back, front, and sides.

Miliss was found guilty on all counts and sentenced to death. Three appeals to ever higher courts failed. But Rocquel granted her a full pardon on the grounds that the Chosen had not legislated on the matters at issue.

'Prime Minister' Jaer Dorrish – and where had the title come from? – thereupon introduced amendments to criminal law. They were duly passed by the Chosen. Rocquel, to Jaer's surprise, did not veto the legislation.

He asked Rocquel about it. The hereditary ruled gestured.

'I told you I wouldn't interfere.' He paused, curious. 'Suppose all those charges you're making turn out to be true. If man is really a superior race, then presumably a fleet of total power will come to the rescue of his representatives on Jana – and we will all be degraded by having to submit, however briefly, to an occupation force. What would you gain if that were to happen?'

Jaer scowled.

'Jana honor,' he said with the traditional arrogance of the Jana male, 'demands that the truth of this matter be brought out into the open. We shall deal with this so-called total power when we see it.'

'With what weapons?' Rocquel asked derisively.

Jaer said, 'The human man is being watched night and day. At the proper moment we'll make a raid and we'll capture all man's scientific secrets and make an end of his degrading dole system on which he seems to have been operating – one secret at a time. Such doling is an unbearable insult. We want to have everything – now!'

Rocquel stared sardonically at the other's flushed face.

Finally he said skeptically, 'Your concern with such minor matters does not fit with your previous character, Jaer. I wonder what you're really up to.'

The big male stiffened. 'Do you question my loyalty, sire?'

It could have been a dangerous moment. But Rocquel merely shook his head chidingly.

'No, Jaer, I expect you will accept the new law. It is to your advantage. What is your next move?'

'You'll see.'

Jaer turned abruptly and walked away.

Later Rocquel sought out Nerda, reported Jaer's statements, and asked her opinion.

She answered at once – no longer a surprise to him. Ever since her rebellion on the matter of going to sleep without his permission – which she now did as a matter of course – she had been freer in her responses in every way, even in their personal relations.

She told him that in her opinion Jaer wanted the human woman and that therefore his real target in the trial was not Miliss but Dav.

Rocquel stared at his wife.

'But –' he began, and stopped.

Careful, he thought. *Don't give her another reason for losing respect for you. No knowing what repercussions that would have. . . .*

But he felt slightly helpless before her statement. What she suggested was an immensely tricky thing for Jaer to be doing. Presumably the head of the Dorrish clan expected that Miliss would be freed.

Rocquel's thought paused, a light dawning. Of course, in the trial of Miliss all the weaknesses of the prosecution's case – and the strength of the defense – would be revealed, whereupon all the various loopholes in the law would be rectified – at which time Dav would be tried and irrevocably convicted.

Rocquel stepped forward impulsively, and embraced Nerda.

'You're very brilliant,' he said. 'There's no question – I've got a very unusual and perceptive queen. Thank you.'

He kissed her and was aware for the barest instant that

she kissed him back. The action must have been involuntary. She broke the kiss and became passive.

Rocquel was not offended. In the back of his mind was the thought that Jana females were, perhaps, not as unemotional as was believed.

It might be worthwhile someday to conduct a deeper experiment.

Meanwhile – he had to warn Dav.

The next morning Rocquel learned that Miliss, who had been returned to custody on the formal charge of being a danger to the realm, was to be retried. Her attorney's plea at the preliminary hearing that afternoon was double jeopardy and the inapplicability of retroactive legislation.

The judge released her.

The prosecution requested and got a warrant for the arrest of Dav.

The evening paper reported that the arresting officers had failed to find the Earth man.

Dave spent the late afternoon in one of the hiding places of the Reservoir of Symbols, planning his escape.

It was time for the kind of disappearance that Miliss and he in times past had occasionally had to undertake. There had been other Janae like Jaer Dorrish. They, too, had had their own remorseless purposes. Escape in those distant times had almost always consisted of their waiting somewhere for the particular enemy to live out his short life span.

Dav left his hiding place after dark and made his way through the brush. His destination was a certain hillside where, nearly seventy years ago, he had buried a small spaceship.

In years gone by, such long-buried machinery had not always been readily located when needed – but this one had survived its seven decades totally free of unpleasant accidents. No bulldozer had nosed near it. No one had perched a building on top of it. The craft waited for him in its temporary grave.

Dav was carefully clearing away a particularly dense clump of tall shrubs when he heard a sound. Noiselessly he sank to the ground.

Too late. He heard a swift pad of footsteps in the dark. Two pairs of eyes glowed at him from beside some brush.

Then strong, lean fingers had him pinned down.

The unmistakable long nose of a Jana male was silhouetted against the haze of city lights. A Jana female stood beyond him.

The deep voice of the male said exultantly, 'Got you. Perna, quick, come over here and turn a light on this spying rascal – ' the words halted on a curse. 'By Dilit, it isn't that scoundrel suitor of yours after all. Perna, bring that light, and let's see what we've got here.'

There was silence except for the unhurrying footsteps of the female.

Dav lay unresisting. He could have taken steps. He could have reached up and, with the enormous strength that he could focus into any part of his body, with unerring fingers stabbed at the two vital nerve centers in the Jana, to send the big male sprawling in agony. Or he could simply have contemptuously and effortlessly disengaged himself by a direct muscular thrust.

He did neither. As in past times, he was prepared to act defensively according to the need.

A blaze of light cut off his thought. The light beat pitilessly down on his upturned face. And then, the female's voice came, thick with disgust.

'Why, it's the man. So this is the kind of lover you protect me from. Bah!'

'Not so fast with your criticism,' growled the male. 'There's a reward. We can get married.' His grip tightened on Dav. 'Get up, you antique. It's time you and that woman ceased hanging onto life. Your kind is dead.'

The moment for action had arrived, but Dav did nothing. He offered no resistance as he was jerked roughly to his feet.

In those moments, an astounding thing had happened.

He did not care.

His thought was: *Man's civilization is dead – why should Miliss and I be bound by the values of a society that has failed?*

The barriers he had erected against Miliss collapsed, and a great guilt overwhelmed him. Suddenly he saw how rigid he had been as the dedicated savior of a new race.

In that prolonged moment of anguish, something she had once said flashed to his memory.

I'm sure even your nose is getting a little longer. Pretty soon you'll even look like the Janae –

He had lived in a dream, he saw now, a kind of self-induced hypnotism – an ideal which had given a temporary significance to an otherwise meaningless existence.

With Miliss doomed, nothing here was worth saving.

He went wordlessly with his captor.

The news came to Rocquel in the small hours of the morning that Dav had been arrested. He left his bed, dressed, phoned Miliss.

'Have you had a visitor yet?'

'No. But I imagine he'll be here soon.'

Rocquel said, 'I'm coming right over.'

He arrived by way of the secret entrance, and walked along a narrow, dim-lit corridor until he came to a closed door.

Voices sounded from beyond it.

Rocquel drew the door toward him and stepped through. He found himself in an alcove lighted by reflections from a bright room beyond a green and gold screen. The voices came from the other side of the screen. He recognized the calm bass of Jaer Dorrish and Miliss' indignant soprano.

'I'm surprised,' Miliss was saying, 'that you continue to pursue me despite the fact that you are probably personally programmed and may be in grave danger.'

Jaer answered her with complete assurance, 'I once allowed myself to be alarmed by such words. That will not happen again.'

'What you're saying,' said Miliss sharply, 'is that you've abandoned reason.'

'The Jana male,' was the cool reply, 'knows what is important. A female is. Motivations for fear are not.' He chuckled lazily. 'Let me reason out this situation for you. If you resist me, you may be arrested again. But I may not even press charges against Dav if you give in. Who knows what privileges may continue for you two if you and I occasionally meet privately during the many, otherwise dull years ahead.'

Rocquel stood there behind the screen and shook his head. Nerda's intuition was correct. This entire action against the human beings was simply a typical Jana-male scheme in connection with a female.

He was not shocked. Or surprised, really.

Jaer said, 'It is late, my dear. Surely you do not expect any other visitors this evening.'

The remark made it the ideal moment for Rocquel to come out of his hiding place.

'What I said to him,' he told Nerda after he returned to the palace, 'was, "Jaer, if I'm going to surrender some of the prerogatives of the crown – it is because I believe you and others of the nobility, in exchange for greater political power, will give up the purely personal privileges of forcing individuals to yield to a lordly whim".'

'And what did he answer?'

'Nothing. He turned and walked out of the room and out of the house.'

Nerda made a distasteful gesture.

'If he can get rid of Dav, he'll count on eventually forcing Miliss to accept his protection.'

'Then you think he will press charges against Dav?'

'Your words didn't reach him. He's still an old-style Jana male.' She shrugged. 'So, of course.'

Dav sat apathetic throughout his trial. The defense attorney appointed by Rocquel could not even persuade him to testify on his own behalf.

He was convicted of being an alien spy and sentenced to be beheaded.

VII

By the time Rocquel's helicopter settled down on the big compound where the executions would take place, the male nobility was milling around inside, catcalling and gambling. The wagers usually consisted of someone's maintaining that he would win the chance to chop off the head of a convicted person.

Rocquel walked through the crowd of would-be executioners, hearing grumbling about the increasing shortage of criminal heads. He came to the roped-off area where the victims were guarded and saw what the problem was. Fewer than a hundred males, including Dav – and four females – were herded together at one end of an area that in the past had often held as many as five hundred.

Roughly one hundred heads were to be divided among nearly eighteen hundred eager young nobles.

Rocquel was handed the list of the doomed. Silently he scanned down it, looking for identifying comments. His attention caught two names. Their owners were classified as engineers. He scowled and turned to Jaer.

'What are valuable men like that doing on this list?'

Jaer held up a hand in a demanding way.

'Your Majesty,' he said in a formal tone. 'I must call to your attention that you are violating the procedure of the new law. The king can no longer deal directly with individual cases. As your prime minister, I will consult you or listen to your advice and, in some instances but not all, will recommend that you grant mercy. Please give me that list.'

With a sinking sensation Rocquel handed it over. He had been intent on trying to save Dav and had automatically, as in times past, taken charge. He grew aware that the big male Jana was smiling satirically.

'As for your question, sire,' Jaer said blandly, 'the new law specifies that all persons are subject to due process and to similar penalties.' He shrugged. 'They killed. They were tried. The sentence was automatic.'

'I see,' said Rocquel.

What he saw most of all was that the noisy crowd would be against Dav and that he had no solution to his problem of how to save the human.

Jaer was speaking again.

'Would you like to have me single these males out for questioning, sire?'

The Jana prime minister's tone was tantalizing. He clearly felt himself in total ascendancy in this situation and was prepared to play hard at the game of constitutional monarchy. It seemed so obviously in his favor.

Rocquel nodded yes to the question. While the two doomed males were being located, he consciously forced himself to remember his old way of dealing with one thing at a time. Presently he was able to put the fate of the human being out of the forefront of his mind and concentrate his attention on the here and now.

The scene that he was thus able to focus on was almost literally right out of old Jana. He saw everywhere the swishing silks of the nobles, a glinting ocean of changing colors.

Each male's head was an elongated red shape that was visible at about the same height above the almost solid wall of silk. Eighteen hundred such heads made a picture of – oddly enough – innocent beauty.

But it was the beauty of a beast of prey, proud, arrogant, strong, untamed. It was as if a natural state of being were on display. The primitive impulses that still moved these males from violence to violence in a never-ending madness were the product of equally primitive necessities – their truth unquestioned on Jana until Dav and Miliss had begun to force self-control on a hierarchy that lived by the bloody law of supermasculinity.

I am looking, thought Rocquel, *on the end of an era. Here, in these eighteen hundred, is embodied the last of the really feudal thing. . . .*

It had to go, of course. But how?

His thought ended as the two scientists were brought before Jaer. The Dorrish male glanced questioningly at Rocquel, who stepped forward. A moment later he was confronting their reality.

Professional scientists and all technical personnel had received special treatment from the courts for many years. They were not let off totally free, as a noble might be, but were given a preferred status. A person with an advanced degree was proclaimed to be the equal of twenty ordinary persons. Possession of a secondary degree made him the equivalent of fifteen persons. And the lowest degree, ten. Technicians started at two and went up to nine.

Thus a twenty-person engineer who killed a wholly non-professional individual suffered what was only a one-twentieth penalty – usually a fine. Only if he killed another scientist of a twenty-person status was he in serious danger of being executed. That was murder by law.

Jaer was speaking.

'Here they are, sire. I don't really see that we can do anything for them under the new regulations.'

Rocquel had the same thought. But he said nothing as Jaer turned away and ordered the males to be brought closer. The two engineers came forward and were identified as, respectively, a fifteen and a ten. The former had killed in a fit of rage, which – when his gag was removed – he earnestly protested had been a proper reaction to an insolent three.

45

And the ten had killed a unit person in a fit of typical Jana-male temper for no particular reason.

No occasion existed for favoritism. The new law must convince by its impartiality. The two were simply unlucky that they were the first examples of their class.

Racquel nodded. Jaer had the gags replaced and then read in a loud, clear voice the confirmation of the sentences.

Moments later the lottery machine drew the names of the executioners. And, to the sound of much cursing on the part of those who had lost, the grinning winners came forward, simultaneously raised their swords, and simultaneously struck at the heads on the blocks.

And missed.

A roar of amazement came from the gallery of noble Janae.

Rocquel was fighting a peculiar confusion. Something – some energy – had snatched at one side of his body, pulled at one arm, spun him slightly. At that moment the yelling started, and he realized that something was wrong.

He whirled.

The two nobles had recovered. Muttering words of outrage, they raised their swords for a second blow.

'Wait!' Rocquel roared.

The swords wavered, were sullenly grounded. Two angry, embarrassed nobles glared at their hereditary king questioningly.

'What happened?' Rocquel demanded.

Both told the same story.

Something like a wind had snatched at their swords. Or it was as if they had struck at a blast of air so strong it had diverted their slashing blows.

Catcalls were beginning among the onlookers. Rocquel glanced unhappily at the prison compound and saw that Dav had come to the gate.

Rocquel spoke to Jaer.

'Let nothing happen till I return.'

The Dorrish leader gave him a startled look but said nothing as Rocquel walked over to where Dav stood.

The human greeted him with: 'What happened?'

'That's what I was going to ask you.'

He explained what the nobles had said.

'Sounds like a Symbol,' Dav admitted, frowning. 'But I

know of none that is applicable in a situation such as this. Due process has occurred. There's nothing better on Jana right now. Why don't you have Jaer continue with the executions? Maybe it was an accident.'

Rocquel, who was remembering the grabbing sensation that had affected his right side moments before, and also on the morning of his return to Jana, silently doubted it. But he walked back to the executioners' blocks and ordered the two engineers released. That was the tradition.

'You forfeit your wagers,' he curtly told the would-be executioners.

The two males walked off, cursing.

The order of procedure now required that the females be killed. One of the four was a poor little old thing who was quite insane. She believed the crowd was present to fete her. It did not even occur to Rocquel to do anything for her. Jana had no place for insane people. They were invariably put to death if they became a burden – and a burden she was.

As Rocquel turned to consider the other females, he found his way barred by Jaer. The big male was shaking his head.

'Sire,' he said, 'you have been taking command again.'

The truth was obvious. Rocquel shook his head.

He said with a twisted smile, 'Giving up power seems to be quite a difficult process. So bear with me, Lord Jaer. I mean well.'

No answering smile moved that grim countenance.

Rocquel thought, *What a remarkable man the ancient king on earth must have been who first agreed – when there were no precedents – to limit his absolute rights under a constitutional monarchy. . . .*

At the moment he could not remember the name of that king, though Dav had told him.

What brought the historic precedent to mind was that, even now, Rocquel found it hard to adjust to the idea that what he gave up, Jaer would gain. But finally Rocquel relaxed.

He stepped back.

'Continue, Lord of the Dorrish.'

He was able then to observe the scene once more without interference from his troubled inner self.

Of the other three females, two were beyond anyone's power to help. They had been accused of adultery by their noble husbands and had been convicted. Rocquel privately doubted that the unnatural crime had occurred, but this was not the time to take issue with a court's findings.

The remaining woman had denied the truth of religion. As she was brought before them, Jaer glanced questioningly at Rocquel. He evidently expected no interference, intended the glance to be a matter of form only.

He was turning away when Rocquel caught his arm.

The Dorrish leader faced about with a tolerant expression. It became quite evident, as he listened to Rocquel, that on these minor matters he was prepared to allow the king the prerogative of granting mercy.

He finally said, 'Sire, why don't I say that in this instance a reprieve will be granted and then you state the reasons.'

That was the way it was done.

Rocquel spoke briefly to the assembled nobles, stressing the need – as Dav had urged upon him long ago – to keep religion humanitarian.

He spared her life.

He stood by then, tense, not knowing what to expect as the three overjoyed winners came forward. The two who were assigned the adulterous females uttered expressions of pleasure at having the privilege of performing so necessary a task.

All three swords whipped high and came down as one. The females had been kneeling fatalistically. They looked up after a little as if to ask what was wrong.

What was wrong was that the swords were lying a dozen feet away – Rocquel, who had watched closely, thought he had seen the glint of too much metal as the weapons had flown through the air. But he could not be sure. Something strong had grabbed at him, as with fingers of steel, and had moved him inches at the moment of attempted execution.

He saw that Jaer was lying on the ground nearby. Rocquel helped the big male to his feet.

'What happened?'

'This is magic,' Jaer muttered. 'Something hit me a terrific blow.'

He seemed uncertain and offered no objection to Rocquel's suggestion that the executions should be temporarily halted, pending an investigation.

'But what kind of investigation?' he asked in a bewildered tone.

Rocquel assured him that there was at least one person to question.

And so, after the women had been released and the second group of executioners dismissed, Rocquel had Dav brought out of the compound.

'You saw that?' he asked accusingly.

'Yes. There's no doubt. It's a Symbol, and the second time it was more violent. The power behind it is increasing very rapidly.'

'But what Symbol can it be?' Rocquel protested. 'I thought Symbols were – ' He stopped, remembering that he had no idea what Symbols were. He finished lamely: 'What do you suggest?'

Dav said, 'The next time there may be feedbacks, and the executioners may get hurt.' He seemed interested. Some of the apathy he had displayed earlier seemed to be lifting. His eyes were suddenly bright. He looked around hopefully. 'Why don't you let Jaer try to execute me? That would solve a lot of problems.'

Rocquel frowned. He shook his head. Injury to – or the death of – the head of the Dorrish clan would merely create confusion in an important segment of the Jana populace.

The catcalls were beginning again, demanding decisions. But the nobles sounded puzzled. The tone of the raised voices showed that the vocalizers were not clear as to what was going on. And only a percentage was actually yelling. It struck Rocquel that to the aristocratic onlookers the events at the focal point of the executions had probably been obscure.

Besides, no one had ever been able to explain anything, really, to Jana nobles as a group.

The fact that no help could be expected from the nobility made the situation even more difficult. Rocquel stood distracted, not knowing what to do. The yelling grew louder, more insistent. Abruptly Rocquel realized why. By bringing Dav out of the compound he had given the impression that the human was next in line for execution.

And Dav's life was what those who cried out were demanding.

Dav was pale but yelled above the bedlam almost directly into Rocquel's ear. 'Why not make the attempt? Let's see what happens.'

Rocquel tried to answer back, tried to say, *What's going*

on? What's happening? Is the Symbol I believed I had control of acting independently of my command – or any command at all?

He couldn't say it. The words wouldn't come. His face contorted with his effort to speak.

Dav asked, 'What's the matter, sire?'

Rocquel tried again to speak, could not. A degrading awareness overwhelmed him.

I'm programmed. I could tell Miliss about the Symbol I controlled, but I can't tell Dav. . . .

Not – the realization suddenly was strong – that he had ever really controlled it. It had been attached to him somehow – but in the manner of a Symbol it had reacted in this situation because this was what it related to.

'I feel,' said Rocquel – and now the words came easily – 'that these executions are not being allowed.'

So he could speak if he made no direct reference to his Symbol.

Dav was shaking his head.

'I don't understand it. The time is not yet on Jana for the end of capital punishment. In fact – ' He sounded appalled. He waved vaguely, his gesture taking in the horizon. 'If a few million of those paranoid males out there ever get the idea that they cannot be executed, all hell will break loose.'

The picture of total disaster – of pillage, rape, and mayhem – evoked by the man's words sent a chill through Rocquel. He visualized vast armies of criminals rioting in the streets, swarming in gangs through the country. Something had to be done at once.

Belatedly, again he remembered that the Dorrish leader was in charge here and should be consulted. He swung about and became aware that the big male was standing off to one side, watching Dav from narrowed eyes.

Rocquel had time for only a glance – the seconds were flying by, and the noise from the gallery was rising to such a crescendo that further conversation was impossible. Rocquel signaled the royal drummers to beat for silence.

Moments later he explained to a startled audience what Dav had said about a Symbol's being involved.

When he had finished, a loud voice cried from somewhere in the crowd, 'If we mob that so-and-so, it'll end the nonsense.'

Whoever spoke must have tried to push forward. A movement started. A dozen, then dozens, then hundreds surged forward.

A voice yelled in Rocquel's ear, 'Run for your life – '

The tone was so urgent that Rocquel was a score of feet toward safety before he realized that it was Dav who had yelled at him. He stopped and turned – and was barely in time to see the disaster.

VIII

Male bodies were being spun as if in a whirlpool. A fountain was already up in the air, being held and twisted by an invisible force.

From the corner of one eye he saw Dav frantically pushing through the retreating crowd toward him. The human broke through abruptly.

'Quick!' he yelled. 'If they're whirled any higher, they may be hurt or killed when they fall.'

Rocquel said blankly, 'What do you mean – quick? Quick what?'

Dav's eyes, so bright for a moment, misted. A puzzled look came to his face.

He muttered, 'What's the matter with me? I don't know why I said that.'

But the real message of his reaction had penetrated. Rocquel was thinking, *He's programmed, also. . . .*

He felt the truth grow in him. It bothered him. Bothered him a lot. But the truth was that he was unquestionably watching the Symbol over which he had been given control.

What was reassuring was the fact that in this decisive hour the ultimate decision had been left to the hereditary general of Jana – himself.

As he hastily evoked within his mind the mental pattern that would bring the Tizane energy to bear on the Symbol, Rocquel thought, *It really doesn't take very much direct interference with individuals to control a planet with Symbols. Only a few key persons. . . .*

In the entire sequence of events, the most unique facet was that both of the mentors – Dav and Miliss – had also not been allowed free will.

*

After the whirlpool of noble males of Jana began to drop to the ground – where some lay for a long time – Rocquel suggested to Jaer that the executions continue.

The big male stared at him blankly.

'Your Majesty,' he said finally in amazement. 'I doubt we could find a single person at this moment willing to act the role of executioner.'

Rocquel was convinced of it. He worded his reply blandly. The decision to suspend executions must be made by the government and not by the constitutional monarch.

He added, watching Jaer closely: 'I have a feeling that the government should also grant a pardon to Dav.'

Those words got him, first, a dark, darting look. Slowly a crooked smile stretched across that normally grim face.

'Your Majesty,' said Jaer Dorrish, 'let me refer to an earlier remark of yours. I have realized today that you do mean well and that it is hard to give up power. Apparently it is almost as hard for a person like myself to accept an accretion of power gracefully – but I should like to assure you that it is my intention to try. I see the role of prime minister as one that will involve a great deal of integrity. So – ' He made a gesture with one hand, said in a formal tone, 'To prove to you that I have the intent of living up to that level of integrity, I hereby request in my capacity as leader of the government until the first election under the new law that you grant a reprieve and full pardon to Dav, the human.'

'I grant it,' said Rocquel.

It was a great victory – yet he experienced a sudden drop in spirits on the way home. He rode nearly a hundred yards with his motorcycle guard before he realized that he was having a more severe recurrence of an earlier feeling.

I'm programmed, and that degrades me. . . .

Back in the palace, he told Nerda his feeling. All the rest of that afternoon and part of the evening, she argued with him.

Programming, she pointed out, was like a drop of chemical which might give to a flowing stream a slightly bluish tinge. Nothing but a dam could stop or divert the stream – yet after the injection of the chemical it was colored in a specific way.

Her analogy triggered a thought in Rocquel. His programming had taken the form of accelerated civilizing of a paranoid male – himself. He was still hereditary general, still married to Nerda, with no intention of giving up either the position or the wife. Yet he had tolerated a change in the form by which he exercised his power, and he had accepted less total control over his wife.

And in neither instance did he feel a real loss.

Nerda suggested to him that the long-term programming of Miliss and Dav had been designed to make it possible for them to accept the unendurable existence of a lovely human couple marooned on an alien planet. And because the stream of life flowed immortally through them, they were separately programmed as a man and a woman to survive periodic crises. So the great civilization out there controlled even its own emissaries.

In this generation, Nerda continued, perhaps only she and Rocquel would know the truth and, to a lesser extent, Jaer. The hereditary general and his wife, and the hereditary leader of the principal subordinate group, the Dorrish. But their own personalities remained overwhelmingly private. The stream of Jana identity flowed on in them – but it was now a more civilized being that felt the flow.

She must have realized from the accepting expression of his face and body that she could finally change the subject.

'Do you still have control of the Symbol?' she asked.

It was night, and they were standing at a huge window looking toward the slickrock mountains.

Rocquel imaged the first three stages of the Tizane pattern. Something grazed his leg. He knew a hackles-raising sensation – a sense of an energy field of enormous power.

Hastily he turned his thoughts aside.

'Yes,' he said. 'It's still there.'

'In your presence,' said Nerda, 'no one can be killed – as long as you control that Symbol. Did they say when they would take it away from you?'

Rocquel was about to make the same reply he had given to Miliss – when he realized that there was quite a different awareness in him. A barrier had lifted from his memory. He recalled exactly what he had been told.

'No,' he said simply, 'they just gave it to me. It's a lifetime gift.'

He began to feel better.

In my presence, no one can be killed. . . .

Suddenly he divined that his was a very advanced Symbol indeed. He stood at a nearly unthinkable height of understanding and power.

Deep inside him something that was almost infinitely savage was mollified. Possessing what was surely one of the ultimate human Symbols – he accepted his lesser than human status.

For Dav it felt strange to be free. He walked slowly to a nearby restaurant and sat down at a table. He was eating almost mindlessly when he heard the radio announce that he had been pardoned. The news struck him with an odd impact. The life force within him quickened.

He grew aware that the Janae in the restaurant were staring at him curiously. No one showed hostility.

He had no place that he wanted to go – so later he walked the streets. Finally he began to wonder.

Am I trying to solve a problem – and if so, what?

He could not decide. Everything seemed very far away.

He had a feeling that there was something he should be doing. But he did not know what.

Night came.

He waved a surface car to a halt. It drew up, its lights glittering, its bells clanging. No one said anything to him as he swung aboard.

Some younger Janae climbed on at the next stop. They sat giggling at him. But they rushed off into a brilliantly lighted park where hundreds of youthful Janae were dancing to the rhythm of a low, fast-tempo, sobbing music.

He continued his public exposure until almost midnight, without any untoward incidents. He returned to the white house by the river. As he entered the west wing, he presumed Miliss was in her part of the residence. But he made no effort to contact her.

He slept the special deep sleep which triggered long-ago programming deep in his brain. Still asleep, he went to a room that was deceptively equipped with what seemed to be ordinary Jana-level electronic equipment. But by pressing certain buttons and turning certain dials in a specific sequence, Dav activated a communications system hidden in a remote part of the Jana planet.

54

Subspace radio waves thereupon transmitted a message to a receiver many light-years away.

The message was: 'The crisis of the last stage of kings has passed –'

The message completed automatically, then repeated and repeated. Finally a relay was closed on the receiving planet by an accepting mind.

A voice – or a thought – said, 'Message received, recorded.'

A light flashed on in an instrument in front of Dav and, still asleep, he returned to bed.

Miliss had watched him first through scanners and then – as she realized his catatonic unawareness of his surroundings – by following him closely.

So that, as he turned away from the equipment, she stepped up to it and spoke to the distant listener. It was almost as if her communication were expected.

The voice answered, 'We have come to a time when the woman – you – must know something of the truth.'

'What is the truth?' Miliss asked. She did not wait for the reply, but rushed on: Was there a universal death, or was the idea the result of early programming?

'At the next crisis,' was the reply, 'you will be allowed to visit – and see for yourself. Meanwhile, the man – Dav – must not be told. In fact, you will discover if you try that you cannot tell him.'

'Why not tell him?'

It seemed that the reasons for that were deeply bound up in the godlike cravings of masculinity in the male and related idealistic motivations.

'And that's all we are allowed to say,' concluded the faraway voice.

When the connection had been broken, Miliss – feeling suddenly much better, even lighthearted, as if she were again somebody and not a living artifact of a dead culture; feeling strangely tender toward that poor, programmed superbeing, her husband – began the long task of moving back into the west wing.

By morning she had most of her beautiful things in their proper locations. And so, when Dav awakened and turned over, he saw a blonde woman with a smile on her face – and

55

a faint look of innocence, as if everything she had done, including this return, had been totally rational.

This vision said to him, 'I hope you'll be glad to know that you have a wife again.'

On a planet where there is only one woman, and that woman beautiful, what could the only man say to that?

Dav said he was glad.

'Come over here,' he said.

The Reflected Men

A. E. VAN VOGT

I

Time, 5:10 P.M. The crystal was less than fifteen minutes from reactivation.

To Edith Price, the well-dressed young man, who came into her library was typical of the summer visitors to Hark-dale. They lived apart from the townspeople, of whom she was now one. She wrote down his name – Seth Mitchell. And, assuming he wanted a temporary library card, she pushed the application form across the counter toward him.

It was only when he thrust it back, impatiently, that she actually for the first time listened to what he was saying.

Then she said, 'Oh, what you want is a piece of crystal!'

'Exactly,' he said. 'I want returned to me a small stone which I presented to the museum part of the library some years ago.'

Edith shook her head. 'I'm sorry. The museum room is being reorganized. It's closed to the public. I'm sure no action will be taken about anything in it until the job is done, and even then Miss Davis, the librarian, will have to authorize it. And it's her day off today, so you can't even talk to her.'

'How long will it take – to reorganize?'

'Oh, several weeks,' said Edith casually.

The effect of her words on the man – so clean-cut, so typical of the well-dressed, successful men she had known in New York – startled her. He became very pale, mumbled something indistinguishable, and when he turned away, it was as if some of the life had gone out of him.

Staring at the retreating figures of library patrons was not something Edith was normally motivated to do. But his reaction was so extreme that she watched him as he walked unsteadily off toward the main entrance of the library. At the door a squat, thick-built man joined him. The two men conversed briefly, then went out together. Moments later

Edith caught a glimpse of them through a window, getting into a brand-new Cadillac. Seth Mitchell slid in behind the wheel.

The costly automobile, and the fact that another man was involved, gave importance to an otherwise minor incident. Edith slipped off her stool, making suitable gestures to Miss Tilsit. Very openly she secured the key to the women's rest room as she covertly palmed the key to the museum room – and went off.

A few moments later she was examining the display of stones.

There were about thirty altogether. According to the sign beside them, they had long ago been the result of a drive among local boys to find valuable minerals and gems. Edith had no difficulty in locating the one the young man had wanted. It was the one under which a faded card announced: 'Donated by Seth Mitchell and Billy Bingham'.

She slid back the side of the case, reached in carefully, and took it out. It was obvious to her that very little discrimination had been used in the selection. The forces that had fashioned this stone seemed to have been too impatient. The craftsmanship was uneven. The result was a stone about two and a half inches long by one and a half inches wide at its thickest; a brownish, rocklike stuff which, though faceted, did not reflect light well. It was by far the dullest-looking of the stones in the display.

Gazing down at the drab, worthless stone, Edith thought: Why don't I just take it to his hotel after work tonight, and bypass all the red tape?

Meaning Miss Davis, her enemy.

Decisively, she removed the names of the two donors from the case. After all these years, the label was stuck on poorly, and the yellowed paper tore to shreds. She was about to slip the stone into her pocket, when she sadly realized she was wearing *that* dress – the one without pockets.

Oh, damn! she thought cheerfully.

Since the stone was too big to conceal in her hand, she carried it through the back stack corridors, and was about to toss it into the special wastebasket which was used for heavy debris, when she noticed that a broken flowerpot half full of dirt was also in the basket. Beside the dirt was a paper bag.

It required only seconds to slip the crystal into the bag, empty the dirt on top of it, and shove the bag down into the basket. She usually had the job of locking up the building, so it would be no problem to pick up the bag at that time and take it with her.

Edith returned to her desk. . . .

And the stone began at once to utilize the sand in the dirt on top of it, thus resuming a pattern that had been suspended for twenty-five years. During the rest of the evening, and in fact all through that night, all the possible Seth Mitchells on earth remembered their childhood. The majority merely smiled, or shrugged, or stirred in their sleep. Most of those who lived outside the Western Hemisphere in distant time zones presently resumed their normal activities.

But a few, everywhere, recalling the crystal, could not quite let the memory go.

At the first slack period after filching the stone, Edith leaned over and asked Miss Tilsit, 'Who is Seth Mitchell?'

Tilsit was a tall, too-thin blond with horn-rimmed glasses behind which gleamed unusually small but very alert gray eyes. Edith had discovered that Tilsit had a vast, even though superficial, knowledge of everything that had ever happened in Harkdale.

'There were two of them,' said Tilsit. 'Two boys, Billy Bingham and Seth Mitchell.'

Thereupon, with visible relish, Tilsit told the story of the disappearance of Billy twenty-five years before, when he and his chum, Seth Mitchell, were only twelve years old.

Tilsit finished, 'Seth claimed they had been fighting over a piece of bright stone that they had found. And he swore that they were at least fifty feet from the cliff that overlooks the lake at that point, and so he always insisted Billy didn't drown – which is what everyone else believed. What confused the situation was that Billy's body was never recovered.'

As she listened to the account, Edith tried to put together the past and the present. She couldn't imagine why an adult Seth Mitchell would want a reminder of such an unhappy experience. Still, men were funny. That she knew, after waiting five years for a worthwhile male to come along and find her. So far she seemed to be as well hidden and unsearched for in Harkdale as she had been in New York.

Tilsit was speaking again. 'Kind of odd, what happens to people. Seth Mitchell was so crushed by his friend's death that he just became a sort of shadow human being. He's got a farm out toward Abbotsville.'

Edith said sharply, 'You mean Seth Mitchell became a farmer?'

'That's the story.'

Edith said nothing more, but made a mental note that perhaps Tilsit was not as good a source of local information as she had formerly believed. Whatever Mitchell was, he hadn't looked like a farmer!

She had to go and check out some books at that point, and so the thought and the conversation ended.

II

A few minutes after nine-thirty, Edith parked her car across the street from the entrance to the motel in which – after some cruising around – she had spotted Seth Mitchell's distinctive gold Cadillac.

It was quite dark under the tree where she waited, and that was greatly relieving. But even in the secure darkness, she could feel her heart thumping and the hot flush in her cheeks. She asked herself, 'What am I doing this for?'

She had the self-critical belief that she was hoping this would end up in a summer romance. Which was pretty ridiculous for a woman twenty-seven years old, who – if she shifted her tactic from waiting the pursuing – ought to concentrate on genuine husband material.

Her thought ended abruptly. From where she sat, she could see the door of the cabin beside which the Cadillac was parked. The door had opened. Silhouetted in the light from the interior was the short, squat man she had seen with Mitchell that afternoon. As Edith involuntarily held her breath, the man came out and closed the door behind him.

He emerged from the main motel entrance, stood for a moment, and then walked rapidly off toward the business section of Harkdale, only minutes away.

And only minutes back, she thought glumly.

Watching him, her motivation dimmed. Somehow, she

had not considered the short, heavy-set man as being *really* associated with Seth Mitchell.

Defeated, she started her motor. As she drove home, she suddenly felt degraded, not by what she had done, but by what she suspected she had intended to do.

What her future path should be was not clear to her. But not this way, she told herself firmly.

Arrived at her apartment, Edith shoved the bag containing the crystal into the cupboard under her sink, ate apathetically, and went to bed.

And in the motel, the squat man returned, scowling. 'The stone wasn't there. I searched the whole museum,' he told Seth Mitchell, who lay on one of the beds, gagged and bound hand and foot.

Seth Mitchell watched uneasily as the other untied his feet. The man said impatiently, 'I've been thinking about you. Maybe the best thing is just to drive you back to New York. Once I get away, the police'll never find me again.'

He removed the gag. The younger man drew a deep breath. 'Look,' he protested, 'I won't even go near the police.'

He stopped, blank and afraid, and choked back a surge of grief. The possibility that he might be killed was an idea that his brain could contemplate only for a few moments. Not Seth Mitchell, who had all those good things going for him, finally, after years of finagling around the edges of success!

The squat man had come up to him in his office parking lot at noon that day, smiling deceptively, a short man – not more than five-feet-four – and stocky. He looked, in his grayness, like an Arab. A well-dressed Arab in an American business suit. As he came up, he said, 'Where is the crystal you and Billy Bingham found?'

What might have happened if Seth had instantly answered was, of course, now impossible to analyze. But he did not immediately remember the crystal, so he had shaken his head.

Whereupon the man took his hand out of his coat pocket. A pistol glittered in it. Under the threat of that gun, Seth had driven to Harkdale, had shown the stranger the ledge beside Lake Naragang where he and Billy had fought. And it was there, on the spot, that he recalled the crystal; and so he had reluctantly gone to the library, aware of the weapon behind him all the time that he talked to the young woman at the desk.

Abruptly remembering that conversation, Seth said desperately, 'Maybe that woman librarian – '

'Maybe!' said the other noncommittally.

He untied Seth's hands, and then stepped back, motioning with the gun. They went out to the car and drove off.

As they came opposite the lake, the man said, 'Pull over!' After Seth complied, the shot rang out, and the murder was done.

The killer dragged the body to a cliff overlooking the lake, tied rocks to it, and dumped it into the deep water below.

He actually drove on to New York, left the car in Seth's parking lot, and after spending the night in New York, prepared to return to Harkdale.

During that night Edith slept restlessly, and dreamed that all possible Edith Prices marched past her bed. Only half a dozen of those Ediths were married, and even in her dream that shocked her.

Worse, there was a long line of Edith Prices who ranged from fat to blowsy to downright shifty-eyed and mentally ill. However, several of the Ediths had a remarkable high-energy look, and that was reassuring.

Edith woke to the sound of the phone ringing. It was the library caretaker. 'Hey, Miss Price, better get down here. Somebody broke in last night.'

Edith had a strange, unreal feeling. 'Broke into the library?' she asked.

'Yep. Biggest mess is in the museum. Whoever it was musta thought some of the stones in there were the real stuff, because they're scattered all over the floor.'

III

To Edith Price, the lean young man in overalls was just another inarticulate farmer.

She wrote down his name – Seth Mitchell. A moment went by, and then the name hit her. She looked up, startled.

The haunted face that stared back at her was sun- and wind-burned, with gaunt cheeks and sick eyes. Nevertheless, the man bore a sensational resemblance to the Seth Mitchell of yesterday, it seemed to Edith.

She thought, a light dawning: This is the Seth Mitchell that Tilsit knew about! There must be a Mitchell clan, with cousins and such, who were look-alikes.

Her mind was still fumbling over the possibilities when she realized the import of the words he had mumbled. Edith echoed, 'A stone! A crystal that you presented to the library museum twenty-five years ago!'

He nodded.

Edith, compressing her lips, thought: All right, let's get to the bottom of this!

During the moments of her confusion, the man had gotten a bill out of his billfold. As he held it out to her, she saw that it was twenty dollars.

She had recovered her self-control, and said now, conversationally, 'That's a lot of money for a worthless rock.'

'It's the one I want,' he muttered. She didn't hear several of the words that followed, but then she said clearly, '. . . the time Billy disappeared.'

There was silence while Edith absorbed the impact of the notion that here indeed was the original Seth Mitchell.

She encouraged him, finally, 'I've heard about Billy A very unusual incident.'

Seth Mitchell said, 'I yelled at him to get away, and he vanished.' He spoke tautly. His eyes were an odd, discolored gray from remembered shock. He spoke again: 'We both grabbed at it. Then he was gone.'

He seemed only dimly aware of her presence. He went on, and it was as if he were half-talking to himself, 'It was so shiny. Not like it became later. It went all drab, and nobody would believe me.'

He paused. Then, intently, 'All these years I've been thinking. I've been awful slow to see the truth. But last night it came to me. What else could have made Billy disappear when I called him? What else but the stone?'

Edith decided uneasily that this was a problem for a psychiatrist, not a librarian. It struck her that the simplest solution would be to give this Seth Mitchell the worthless rock he wanted.

But of course that would have to be carefully done. Her one indiscretion so far had been her questioning of Tilsit the day before – asking about Seth Mitchell. Throughout the police investigation of the breaking and entering of the library museum, she had maintained a careful silence about her own involvement.

So the sooner she got rid of the stone in her kitchen, the better.

'If you'll give me your address,' she requested gently, 'I'll ask the head librarian, and perhaps she'll get in touch with you.'

The address he reluctantly gave her was a rural route out of Abbotsville.

She watched him then, wondering a little, as she shuffled off to the door and outside.

On her way home that night, Edith drove by way of the motel. The gold Cadillac was gone.

So that little madness was over, she thought, relieved.

She had her usual late dinner. Then, after making sure the apartment door was locked, she took the paper bag from under the sink – and noticed at once, uneasily, that there was less dirt in the bag.

A momentary fear came that the stone would be gone. She spread a newspaper and hastily emptied the bag, dirt and all, onto it. As the earth tumbled out, a brilliance of color flashed at her.

Wonderingly, she picked up the beautiful gem.

'But it's impossible,' she whispered. 'That was dull. This is – beautiful!'

It glittered in her hand. The purple color was all alive, as if thousands of moving parts turned and twisted inside it. Here and there in its depths a finger of light stirred up a nest of scarlet fire. The crisscross of color and flame flickered so brightly that Edith felt visually stunned.

She held it up against the light – and saw that there was a design inside.

Somebody had cut a relief map of the solar system into the interior of the stone, and had colored it. It was quite a good example – it seemed to Edith – of the cutter's art. The purple-and-red overall effect seemed to derive from the play of light through the coloring of the tiny 'sun' and its family of planets.

She took the stone back to the sink. There was a fantasy in her mind, she realized, in which she pictured the jewel as having magical powers. Remembering what the farmer Seth Mitchell had said, about yelling at Billy Bingham in the

64

presence of the stone . . . maybe the sound of a human voice would have an effect. . . .

She tried that right away, speaking words.

Nothing happened. The picture remained unchanged. She spelled words, articulating each letter.

Nothing.

She ran the gamut of sounds possible in her own voice from a low contralto to a ridiculously piercing soprano – nothing!

Once more, she noticed the design inside, and held the stone up against the light to see it better. And she was visually tracing the outline of the solar system in the crystal when she had a sudden thought and, with abrupt determination, said in a clear voice: 'Billy Bingham – the boy – I want him back . . . now!'

After she had spoken, during the silent moments that followed, she felt progressively foolish.

Of the long-missing Billy, there was no sign.

Thank God! she thought, breathless.

Edith rose early the next morning; her mind was made up. It was time she got rid of something that was threatening to undermine her good sense.

As she looked at the crystal, she saw that the interior scene had changed. It was now a human body outlined in purple and red points of light.

The outline, she saw presently, was actually extremely detailed, showing the bone structure and the principal organs. There was even a faint flow which suffused the shape, suggesting a fine mask of nerves and blood vessels.

She was examining it, absorbed, when abruptly she realized what she was doing.

Firmly, she put the stone into a small box, filled it with new soil – crystals, she had read, needed nutrients – wrapped it, and addressed it to Seth Mitchell, Rural Route 4, Abbotsville.

Shortly, she was driving to the post office. It was not until after she had mailed the package that her first realization came that she had done it again. Once more she had acted on impulse.

Too late, the cautioning thought came: Suppose Seth Mitchell wrote the library a note of thanks. Unhappily, she contemplated Miss Davis' joy at the discomfiture of the college graduate who had been forced upon her by the library board. It would be impossible to explain how the flame of romantic compulsion had motivated her to steal the crystal . . . and how once that possibility faded, her only desire had been to dispose of the evidence; which she had now done.

Edith had a sudden grieving thought: Why don't I just get on the next bus to New York and leave this crazy little town forever?

It was an extremely depressing moment. The feeling she had was of an endless series of similar wrong decisions in her life. She sat there in her car at the curb, and thought of that first young man at college. A long-hidden memory burst into view, of how she had actually lost him through an impulse, she had been caught by the God-is-dead-so-now-you're-God movement, in which what you did to other people no longer mattered; you didn't have to feel guilty.

In her self-pitying mood, it struck her with abrupt anguish: If I hadn't joined the guilt-free generation, right now I would be Mrs Richard Staples.

The realization reminded her of her dream, and that unique remembrance escalated her out of her apathy. What an odd concept. Involuntarily, she laughed, and thought: Sending the crystal to the least of all possible Seth Mitchells had not been good sense.

Thinking about that, her fear faded. How funny! And what an odd dream to have had.

How could one ever know what way was best, what decision, what philosophy, how much exercise? And, best for what?

Edith was already at her desk in the library when Tilsit came in with the look on her face. In her six months in Harkdale, Edith had come to recognize Tilsit's expression of 'I've-got-special-information'.

'Did you see the paper?' Tilsit asked triumphantly.

Edith presumed the paper referred to was the Harkdale *Inquirer*, a daily of four pages. She herself still read the *Times*, though she loyally subscribed to the local sheet.

'Remember you asking me the other day about a man called Seth Mitchell?' Tilsit asked.

Edith remembered only too well, but she put on a blank face.

Tilsit unfolded the paper in her hands and held it up. The headline was: BILLY BINGHAM FOUND?

Edith reached automatically, and Tilsit handed the paper to her. Edith read:

'A twelve-year-old boy staggered out of the brush near Lake Naragang shortly after ten o'clock last night and tried to enter the house where Billy Bingham lived twenty-five years ago. The present tenant, John Hildeck, a carpenter, took the bewildered youngster to the police station. From there he was transported to the hospital.

That was as far as Edith read. Her body bent to one side, her arms flopped limply. She stooped over, and the floor crashed into her.

When she came out of her faint on the cot in the rest room, the remembrance was still there, bright and hard and improbable, of how she had commanded the crystal to bring back Billy Bingham, somewhere between nine and ten the previous night.

IV

In Miami.

The Seth Mitchell in that singing city had a private vocabulary in which he called God (or, as he sometimes thought of Him, Nature or Fate) the 'Musician'. In this exclusive terminology, his life had been tuneful, and the music a symphony, or at least a concerto.

Somebody up there evidently regarded him as a suitable instrument.

For he had money, girl friends, a fabulous career as a gambler on the edge of the underworld – all without restrictions, for his orchestra was well disciplined and responsive to his baton. Not bad for a small-town boy who had not learned the melodies of city life till he was over twenty.

But now, suddenly, the Musician had sounded a sour note.

Mitchell had in his hand the Harkdale *Inquirer*, in which was the account of the return of Billy Bingham.

He studied the newspaper's photograph of a frightened-looking boy who did seem to be about twelve years old. It looked like Billy Bingham, and it didn't. Mitchell was surprised that he wasn't sure. The *Inquirer* apologized for having lost its photocut of the real Billy, and explained that Billy's parents had moved to Texas – it was believed. No one knew where.

The news story concluded: 'The only other person who could likely identify the claimant is Seth Mitchell, Billy's boyhood chum. Mitchell's present address is unknown.'

Mitchell though, sarcastically: The *Inquirer* ought to examine its out-of-state subscription list.

The next day.

As he walked into room 312 of the Harkdale hospital, he saw that the youngster in the bed to the right of him was putting down his magazine, and looking frightened. Mitchell said with a reassuring smile, 'Billy, you don't have to worry about me. I'm here as your friend.'

The boy said uneasily, 'That's what the big man told me, and then he got nasty.'

Mitchell didn't ask who the big man was. There was a chair near the bed. He drew it up, and said gently, 'Billy, what seems to have happened to you is almost like a fairy story. But the most important thing is that you mustn't worry.'

Billy bit his lip, and a tear rolled down his cheek. 'They're treating me as if I'm lying. The big man said I'd be put in jail if I didn't tell the truth.'

Mitchell's mind leaped back to the days when he had been questioned by just such impatient individuals about the disappearance of Billy. His lips tightened. He said, 'Nothing is going to happen if I can help it. But I'd like to ask you a few questions that maybe nobody else thought of. You don't have to answer if you don't want to. How does that strike you?'

'Okay.'

Mitchell took that for a go-ahead signal. 'What kind of clothes was Seth wearing?'

'Brown corduroy pants and a gray shirt.'

The reality gave Mitchell his first disappointment. He had hoped the description would jog his memory. It didn't. Of all the reality of that distant day, he had not been able

68

to recall what particular pair of ragged trousers he had had on.

'You wore corduroys also?' It was a shot in the dark.

'They're in there.' The boy pointed at the chest in one corner.

Mitchell stood up, opened the indicated drawer, and lifted out a skimpy pair of cheap corduroys. He examined them shamefacedly, but with an eye to detail. He put them back, finally, disappointed. The identifying label had been torn off. He couldn't remember ever having seen them before.

Twenty-five years, he thought drearily. The time was like a thick veil with a few tattered holes in it. Through the holes, he could catch glimpses of his past, mere instants out of his life, each one illuminated because of a particular momentary impact, and none actually fully visible.

'Billy.' Mitchell was back in the chair, intent. 'You mentioned trying to grab a shining stone. Where did you first see it?'

'On the ledge. There's a path that come up from the lake.'

'Had you come up that way before?'

The other shook his head. 'A few times, when it was cold. Usually Seth and I liked to stay near the water.'

Mitchell nodded. He remembered that. 'This bright stone you saw – how big was it?'

'Oh, it was big.'

'An inch?'

'Bigger. Five inches, I'll betcha.' Billy's face was bright with certainty.

Mitchell paused to argue out the error of that with himself. The stone had been roughly two and a half inches at its longest, and somewhat narrower and thinner. A boy who had had only a glimpse would not be the best judge of its size.

The reasoning made Mitchell uneasy. He was making excuses where there should be none allowed. He hesitated. He wanted to find out if Billy had actually touched the crystal, but he didn't quite know how he should lead up to the question. He began, 'According to what you told the paper, you admitted that your chum – what's his name?' He waited.

'Seth. Seth Mitchell.'

' – Seth Mitchell saw the stone first. But you still tried to get it, didn't you?'

The boy swallowed. 'I didn't mean any harm.'

Mitchell had not intended to imply moral disapproval. He said hastily, 'It's all right, Billy. When I was a boy, it was the guy who got a thing that owned it. None of this seeing-first stuff for us.' He smiled.

Billy said, 'I only wanted to be the one who gave it to the museum.'

The thunder of that vibrated through Mitchell's mind. 'Of course,' he thought, 'now I remember.'

He even realized why he had forgotten. The museum-library had accepted the stone, which had become dull during the days he had carried it in his pocket, with reluctance. The librarian had murmured something about not discouraging small boys. With those words she had discouraged him so completely that he had needed an actual naming of the fact to remember it.

It was hard to believe an impostor would have such detailed recollections. And yet, that meant that Billy Bingham, when he disappeared, had —

His brain poised, stopped by the impossibility of this situation. His own doctor had already told him that mental disturbances, such as this boy had, were usually traced to an overactive imagination.

Mitchell drew a deep breath. 'All right. Now, two more questions. What time of day was it?'

'Seth and I went swimming after school,' said Billy. 'So it was late afternoon.'

'Okay. According to the paper, it wasn't until nearly ten when you got back to your house. Where were you from four-thirty in the afternoon till ten o'clock at night?'

'I wasn't anywhere,' said Billy. 'Seth and I were fighting over the stone. I fell. And when I picked myself up, it was pitch dark.' He was suddenly tearful. 'I don't know what happened. I guess he just left me lying there, somehow.'

Mitchell climbed to his feet, thinking suddenly: This is ridiculous. I ought to have my head examined.

Nevertheless, he paused at the door and flung one more question toward the bed, 'Has anyone else called you — besides the police, I mean, and the big man, and me?'

'Just a woman from the library.'

'Library?' Mitchell echoed blankly.

'She wanted to know the exact time I woke up beside the

lake. Her name is Edith Price, and she works in the library. Of course, I didn't know.'

It seemed meaningless. Mitchell said quickly, simulating a friendliness he no longer felt, 'Well, Billy, I guess I'd better let you get back to your comicbook. Thanks a lot.'

He went out of the room and out of the hospital. He paid his bill at the hotel, got into his rented car, drove to the airport, and flew back to Miami. But the time the plane landed, the old, disturbing music from his childhood had faded from his mind.

It seemed to Mitchell that the Musician had let him down. To ensure that it never happened again, he resolved to cancel his subscription to the Harkdale *Inquirer.*

In Chicago.

Seth Mitchell (of the Seth Mitchell Detective Agency) stared at the man who had just walked into his office as if he was seeing a hallucination. Finally he blinked and said: 'Am I crazy?'

The stranger, a well-set-up young man in his mid-thirties, sat down in the visitor's chair, and said with an enigmatic smile, 'The resemblance is remarkable, isn't it?'

He spoke in a firm baritone; and except that Mitchell knew better, he would have sworn it was his own voice.

In fact, afterward, in telling Marge Aikens about the visitor, he confessed, 'I keep feeling that it was me sitting there.'

'But what did he want?' Marge asked. She was a slim blond, taking her first look at thirty, and taking it well; Mitchell intended to marry her someday when he could find another associate as efficient. 'What did he look like?'

'Me. That's what I'm trying to tell you. He was my spitting image. He even wore a suit that reminded me of one I've got at home.' He pleaded uneasily, 'Don't be too hard on me, Marge. I went to pieces. It's all vague.'

'Did he give you his address?'

Mitchell looked down unhappily at the interview sheet. 'It's not written down!'

'Did he say if he intended to come to the office again?'

'No, but he gave me this thousand dollars in bills, and I gave him a receipt. So we're committed.'

'To what?'

'That's the silliest part of it. He wants me to find an onyx

71

crystal. He says he saw it quite a while back in a small-town museum south of New York. He can't remember just where.'

'That's going to be either very hard or very easy.' Marge was thoughtful; she seemed to be considering the problem involved.

'Let me finish,' said Mitchell grimly. 'I know where that crystal is. Just think of what I said. I know that region like a book. I was born there, remember?'

'It had slipped my mind,' said Marge. 'You think you can locate the crystal because –'

Mitchell said, 'It's in the museum annex of the public library in the town of Harkdale, where I was born. And now – get this. I presented that crystal to the library, and, what's even more amazing, I dreamed about that stone the other night.'

Marge did not let him get off the subject. 'And he came to you? Out of the scores of detective agencies in Chicago, he came to the one man in the world who looks like him and who knows where that crystal is?'

'He came to me.'

Marge was pursing her beautiful lips. 'Seth, this is fantastic. You shouldn't have let him get away. You're usually so sharp.'

'Thanks.' Dryly.

'Why didn't you tell him where it is?'

'And lose a thousand dollars? My dear, a detective is sometimes like a doctor. People pay him for information he already has.'

Marge held out her hand. 'Let me see that interview sheet.'

As she read it, she said without looking up, 'What are you going to do?'

'Well, I told him the truth, that I've got several days of workload to get rid of; and then –'

He fell silent, and the silence grew so long, the woman finally looked up. She was relieved at the expression she saw on his face, for it was the shrewd, reasoning look that was always there when he was at his detective best.

He caught her glance, said, 'It would be a mistake to appear in Harkdale until three or four mysteries have been cleared up. Like, how come there's two of us.'

'You have no relations?'

'Some cousins.'

'Ever see them?'

He shook his head. 'Not since I was around nineteen, when my mother died.' He smiled grimly. 'Harkdale is not a town one goes back to. But scotch that thought you've got. None of my cousins looked like me.' He shuddered. 'Ugh, no.'

Marge said firmly, 'I think when you do finally go, you ought to be disguised.'

'You may count on it!' was the steely reply. 'This calls for all our ingenuity.'

Elsewhere on earth, about two dozen of the total of 1,811 Seth Mitchells — among whom was the best of all possible Seth Mitchells — also considered the crystal, remembered their dreams of a few nights earlier, and had a strange, tense conviction of an imminent crisis.

As the Seth Mitchell in Montreal, Canada, described it to his French-Canadian wife, 'I can't get over the feeling that I'm going to have to measure up. Remember, I mentioned that to you when I awakened the other morning.'

His wife, a pretty blond who had a French-Canadian woman's practical contempt for such fantasies, remembered it well, and wanted to know, measure up to what?

Her husband said unhappily, 'I have a feeling I could have made better decisions, made more of myself. I am not the man I could have been.'

'So what?' she wanted to know. 'Who is? And what of it?'

'Kaput. That's what's of it.'

'How do you mean?' sharply.

'Kaput.' He shrugged. 'I'm sorry to be so negative, my dear. But that's the feeling. Since I didn't measure up, I'm through.'

His wife sighed. 'My mother warned me that all men get crazy ideas as they approach forty. And here you are.'

'I should have been braver, or something,' he moaned.

'What's wrong with being a tax consultant?' she demanded.

Her husband seemed not to hear. 'I have a feeling I ought to visit my hometown.' He spoke in an anxious tone.

She grabbed his arm. 'You're going straight to Dr Ledoux,' she said. 'You need a checkup.'

Dr Ledoux could find nothing wrong. 'In fact, you seem to be in exceptionally good health.'

The Seth Mitchell of Montreal had to concede that his sudden alarm was pretty ridiculous.

But he decided to visit Harkdale as soon as he cleared up certain business.

V

The man's voice came suddenly, with a slight foreign accent. 'Miss Price, I want to talk to you.'

In the darkness, Edith saw the speaker, and saw that he stood in the shadows between the garage and the rooming house where she lived, barring her way.

Seeing him, she stopped short.

Before she could speak, the voice continued, 'What did you do with the crystal?'

'I – don't – understand.'

She spoke the words automatically. She could see her interrogator more clearly now. He was short and broad of build. Abruptly, she recognized him as the man who had been with the Seth Mitchell look-alike in the gold Cadillac.

'Miss Price, you removed that crystal from the display cabinet. Either give it to me or tell me what you did with it, and that'll be the end of the matter.'

Edith had the tense feeling of a person who has acted unwisely and who therefore cannot possibly make any admissions, not even to a stranger.

'I don't know what you're talking about,' she half-whispered.

'Look, Miss Price.' The man stepped out of the shadows. His tone was conciliatory. 'Let's go into your apartment and talk this over.'

His proposal was relieving. For her apartment was only a little suite in a rooming house in which the other tenants were never more than a wall away.

Incredibly – afterward she thought of it as incredible – she was instantly trusting, and started past him, unsuspecting. And so the surprise as he grabbed her was total. One of his arms engulfed both her arms and body. Simultaneously, he put a hard, unyielding palm over her mouth and whispered, 'I've got a gun!'

Half-paralyzed by that threat, she was aware of her captor carrying her toward the back alley. And she allowed him to shove her into a car that was parked against a fence.

He climbed in beside her, and sat there in the almost dark

of the night, gazing at her. It was too dark to see the expression on his face. But as the seconds went by, and he made no threatening move, her heart slowed in its rapid beating, and she finally gasped, 'Who are you? What do you want?'

The man chuckled satirically and said, 'I'm the worst of all possible Athtars from the thirty-fifth century.' He chuckled again, more grimly. 'But I turned out to have a high survival faculty.'

His voice tightened. 'Where I come from, I'm a physicist. I sensed my danger, and I analyzed a key aspect of the nature of the crystal in record time. In dealing with human beings, it operates on the vibrations a body puts forth from all its cells. In re-creating that vibration, it creates the person. Conversely, in canceling the vibration, it uncreates him. Recognizing this – and since I was not its orientation in my era – I simply put up a barrier on the total vibration level of my own body, and thus saved my life when it uncreated all the lesser Athtars.'

The man added somberly, 'But evidently, by defeating it, I remained attached to it on some other level. As it fell back through time to the twentieth century, I fell with it. Not – unfortunately – to where and when it went. Instead, I arrived last week beside that ledge overlooking Lake Naragang.'

He finished in a wondering tone, 'What a remarkable, intricate internal energy-flow system it must have. Imagine! In passing through time it must have detected this twenty-five-year inactive period, and its reawakening, and dropped me off within days of its own reactivation.'

The voice became silent; and there was the darkness again. Edith ventured a small movement; she changed her position on the seat to ease a growing discomfort in one leg. When there was no countermovement from him, she whispered, 'Why are you telling me this? It all sounds perfectly mad!'

Even as she uttered the stereotype, she realized that a quality of equal madness in herself believed every word that he had spoken. She thought in a spasm of self-criticism: I really must be one of the lesser Edith Prices. She had to fight to suppress an outburst of hysterical laughter.

'From you,' said the worst of all possible Athtars, 'I want information.'

'I don't know anything about a crystal.'

'The information I want,' said the man in an inexorable

voice, 'is this: At any time recently have you had a thought about wishing you had taken a different path in life instead of ending up in Harkdale as a librarian?'

Edith's mind flashed back to her series of impulses after she had mailed the crystal – and back farther to some of the times she had thought about in that moment. 'Why, yes,' she breathed.

'Tell me about one of them,' said the man.

She told him of the thoughts she had had of just getting on a bus or train and leaving.

In the darkness the man leaned back in the seat. He seemed surprisingly relaxed. He said with a chuckle, 'Are you the best of all possible Edith Prices?'

Edith made no reply. She was beginning to have the feeling that perhaps she could confide in this man; *should* tell him where the crystal was.

Athtar was speaking again: 'I have a conviction that the Edith Price who is the twentieth-century orientation for the crystal is on that bus, or is heading for safety somewhere else. And that therefore you are under the same threat as I am – of being uncreated as soon as the crystal selects the perfect Edith Price.'

For Edith, terror began at that moment.

During the minutes that followed, she was only vaguely aware of words mumbling out of her mouth.

Listening to her revelation, Athtar suppressed an impulse to murder her out of hand. He played it cautiously, thinking that if anything went wrong, this Edith was all he had to help him to trace the other Ediths.

So he spoke reassuring words, put her out of the car, and watched her as she staggered off . . . safe . . . she thought.

VI

The note read: 'He wasn't there. It wasn't there. The farm was deserted. Did you lie to me? Athtar.'

Edith felt a chill the first time she read the words; particularly she reacted to the last line with fear. But on her tenth of twelfth reading, she was more determined. She thought: If this whole crazy business is real, I'd better – what? Be brave? Consider the problem? Act with decisiveness?

It was Saturday.

Before going to work, she bought a small Browning automatic at the Harkdale Hardware. She had often gone target-practicing with the second of her two college boyfriends, the one who had a gay philosophy that God was dead, and that therefore one need only avoid jail – and otherwise do anything one pleased. Eventually, he departed without marrying her, presumably feeling guiltless about having lured her away from a man who might have offered her a wedding ring.

But this man did show her how to shoot an automatic firearm, and so she put the little pistol into her purse – and felt a hardening of her conviction that it was time *this* Edith started measuring up.

One doubt remained: Was willingness to shoot in self-defense a step forward, or a step away, from being the best of all possible Edith Prices?

At the library that day, Tilsit was waiting for her with another news item:

YOUNG FARMER MISSING

Seth Mitchell, Abbotsville farmer, has not been at his farm for several days. A neighbor, Carey Grayson, who called on Mitchell yesterday to buy seed grain, found his cows unmilked, a horse in the stable starving, chickens unfed, and no sign of life around the house. Grayson fed the animals, then contacted Mitchell's cousin in a neighboring county and notified the sheriff's office. An investigation is under way.

Edith handed the paper back with a meaningless comment. But she was thinking: So that's what Athtar had discovered.

In spite of her resolve, she trembled. It seemed to her that there was no turning back; she must carry forward inexorably with all the thoughts that she had had.

Sunday.

She had driven to New York and parked two blocks from the little hotel for women only where she had formerly lived. Surely, she told herself, that was where at least one Edith duplicate would have gone.

From a phone booth she called the hotel and asked for Edith Price. There was a pause, then, 'I'm ringing,' said the woman desk clerk's voice.

Instantly breathless, Edith hung up. She sagged limply inside the booth, eyes closed. It was not clear to her even now what she had expected. But the only hopeful thought in her mind was: Can it be that I'm the only Edith who knows that there are others? And does that give me an advantage over the unknowing ones?

Or was there already somewhere an Edith Price who had naturally become the best of them all?

Her thought ended. She realized that a short, stocky man was standing beside the booth, partly out of her line of vision. There was something familiar about him.

The familiarity instantly grew sensational. She straightened and she turned.

Athtar!

The Edith Price who stepped out of the phone booth was still shaky and still not brave. But in two days fear and threat and gulps of terror had transformed her. She had been a vaguely sad, wish-my-mistakes-won't-doom-me young woman. Now, at times she trembled with anxiety, but at other times she compressed her lips and had thoughts that were tough and realistic.

The sight of Athtar caromed her into anxiety.

Which was just as well, the tough part of her analyzed realistically. She didn't trust the worst of all possible Athtars. And he would feel safer with a frightened Edith, she was sure.

Seen close in broad daylight on a deserted New York street on Sunday morning, Athtar – short, broad, with a thick face and gray cheeks – was surprisingly as she remembered him. Totally unprepossessing.

He said softly, 'Why don't you let me talk to her?'

Edith scarcely heard. The first question of her forty-eight-hour, stop-only-for-sleep, stream of consciousness siphoned through her voice. 'Are you really from the thirty-fifth century?'

He gave her a quick, shrewd look, must have realized how wound up she was, and said receptively, 'Yes.'

'Are they all like you? Your height, your complexion?'

'It was decided,' said Athtar in a formal tone, 'that a body built thicker and closer to the ground has more utility. That was several hundred years before I was born. And so, yes. No one is over 177 centimeters. That is, five feet, six inches.'

'How do you know you're the worst of all possible Athtars?'

'In my time,' was the reply, 'it is a felony for anyone but a member of the Scientists' Guild to have a weapon. Hence, political and economic power is part of the prize of the struggle for position in the Guild. On my way to becoming a tougher member, I wished many times to be there, relatively safe, among the faceless, unarmed masses. And the crystal, in creating other Athtars, solidified those wishes.'

There was an implication here that getting tougher was not the answer; not the way. Edith sighed her disappointment, and remembered her other questions. She told him, then, about the two pictures she had seen in the crystal, the one of the solar system and the other of the outline of a human body. Did he know what the pictures meant?

'When I first saw it,' said Athtar, 'the scene inside was of our galaxy. Later, it became the solar system. So what you saw was probably a carry-over from my time, where we occupy all the planets. And what I saw must derive from a time when man has moved out to the galaxy. It could mean that the crystal adjusts to the era in which it finds itself. Though why a human being, instead of the planet Earth in this era, is not obvious. Was the outline that of a woman or a man?'

Edith couldn't remember it that clearly.

Standing there in the bright, sunny day and on the dirty, narrow street, Athtar shook his head. There was awe in his ugly face. He said wonderingly, 'Such a small object; such a comprehensive ability.' He added, half to himself, 'It's got to be potential flow patterns. There are not enough atoms in such a crystal to act as a control board for so much.'

He had already, by implication, answered her next question, but she asked it anyway.

Athtar sighed, 'No, the crystal is definitely not from the thirty-fifth century. It appeared suddenly. I picture it as having fallen backward through time from some future era in drops of fifteen hundred years.'

'But why would they have sent it back?' Edith asked, bewildered. 'What are they after?'

The chunky little man gave her a startled look. 'The idea

of the crystal having been *sent* back for a purpose had not previously occurred to me. It's such a colossally valuable machine, we assumed it got away from them accidentally,' he said. He was silent; then, finally: 'Why don't you let me go and see this second Edith Price? And you go back to Harkdale? If I find the crystal, I'll report with it to you there.'

The implication seemed to be that he planned to cooperate with her. What he meant was that the crystal would be no good to him until he had found and murdered the Edith to whom it was oriented.

The tough part of Edith hesitated at the idea of trusting this man. But it occurred to her that he might have thirty-fifth-century weapons and that therefore he was being generous from a position of total strength in offering to cooperate.

With such fear thoughts in her mind, and having no plans of her own, she agreed.

She watched him get into a shining new automobile and drive off down the narrow street. It was a middle-sized car, she noted absently. She had never been one who kept track of auto designs, so by the time she wondered what make it was, it was too late. Equally belatedly, it struck her that she ought to have looked at the license-plate numbers.

She stood there, and she thought sarcastically: What a third-rate Edith Price I am!

She was vaguely aware of a car pulling up at the near-by curb. A young woman climbed out of it and casually walked toward her as if to go into the phone booth.

She stopped suddenly, stepped over beside Edith, and said, 'You're Miss Price?'

Edith turned.

The other woman was a bright, alert, thirty-year-old blond, and Edith had never seen her before. She had no sense of being threatened, but involuntarily she backed away several steps.

'Y-yes,' she said.

The woman turned toward the car and called, 'Okay, Seth.'

Seth Mitchell climbed from the car and came rapidly toward them. He was well dressed, like the Seth Mitchell in the gold Cadillac, but there was a subtle difference. His face had a firmer, more determined expression.

He said, 'I'm a detective. Who is that man you were talking to?'

And thus the story, as well as Edith knew it, was presently shared.

They had gone into a coffee shop for their tense discussion. To Edith it was both relieving and disturbing to realize that these detectives had been in Harkdale for two days and had traced her down as a result of her call to the hospital, inquiring about Billy Bingham. Having thus spotted her, they had become aware that the squat man was also keeping track of her movements. And so that morning, not one but three cars had headed for New York – Edith's, Athtar's, and theirs.

The exchange of information took time and several cups of coffee – though Edith rejected the final cup, with the sudden realization that coffee was probably not good for people, and that the crystal might judge her on it at some later time. She smiled wanly at how many restraints she was placing on herself. Exactly as if God was no longer dead.

When they came out of the restaurant, Seth Mitchell phoned the other Edith Price. He emerged from the phone booth uneasy.

'The switchboard operator says that Miss Price went with a man about twenty minutes ago. I'm afraid we're too late.'

From Edith's description, he had already come to the conclusion that Athtar was a dangerous man. They decided to wait for the second Edith to return. But though they remained in New York until after eleven that night, the young woman did not come back to her hotel.

She never would return. For some hours, a bullet in her brain, her body, weighed down by stones, had been lying at the bottom of the East River.

And Athtar had the crystal.

To his intense disappointment, that Edith was not the crystal's orientation.

Accordingly, he spent the evening and a portion of the night fitting together parts in the construction of a special weapon. He had a peculiar prescience that he would need its superfine power the following day against the Edith who, he believed, was back in Harkdale.

VII

Since it was late, and since, after all, they could phone the second Edith again by long distance, in the morning – shortly after eleven – the three of them, Edith and the detectives, set out for Harkdale in the two cars. Seth Mitchell, at Edith's request, drove her car. Marge Aikens followed in the larger machine.

En route, Detective Mitchell told Edith that he believed she was the original Edith, and that it was to her that the crystal was still oriented. He considered also that her analysis of Seth Mitchell, the farmer, as the worst Seth, had doomed that unfortunate Mitchell duplicate. The crystal accepted her judgment and probably uncreated Seth, the farmer, when the package with the crystal addressed to him had barely been deposited in the post office.

Edith was taken aback by the detective's logic. 'But,' she stammered, 'I didn't mean it that way.' Tears streamed down her cheeks. 'Oh, that poor man!'

'Of course you didn't mean it,' was the reply. 'And so just to make sure that I heard you correctly, tell me again in what sequence that judgment of yours came. Was it before or after your various impulses to leave Harkdale?'

'Oh, after.'

'And did I hear you correctly, that you thought of going into the post office, and asking for the package you had mailed to be returned to you?'

'Yes, I had that thought.' She added, 'But I didn't do it.'

'I would analyze that at least one other Edith did go back in,' said Mitchell.

'But it's all so complicated,' Edith said. 'How would any Edith just go, leaving clothes, money, car?'

'I've been thinking of my own background on that,' said Mitchell. 'Evidently the crystal can excise all confusions like that. For example, I never again even thought of going back to Harkdale. It didn't even cross my mind.'

He broke off. 'But there are no blanks like that in your mind?'

'None that I can think of.'

Seth Mitchell nodded. 'That's what I heard. So I think I've got the solution to this whole crazy business – and we don't even have to know where the crystal is.'

What he analyzed was simple. In bringing back Billy Bingham at her command, the crystal had deposited the boy nearly two miles away. True, at the time, she had been holding the crystal in her hand. But that didn't apply to her negative thought about farmer Seth Mitchell, which had occurred after she had mailed the crystal and was approximately a hundred yards from the post office.

So if she had indeed uncreated the mentally ill farmer, then the distance of the crystal's human orientation – in this instance one of the Edith Prices – from the crystal was not a factor.

When he had finished, Edith did not speak at once.

'You don't agree?' said the detective.

'I'm thinking,' Edith said. 'Maybe I'm not really the orientation.'

'We'll test that tomorrow.'

'What about Athtar?' Edith asked. 'I keep feeling he may have special weapons. And besides, the crystal cannot affect him. What about that?'

'Let me think about Athtar,' said the man.

While she waited, Edith was reminded of what Athtar had asked about the figure in the crystal: Was it of a man or a woman?

It was her first time for trying to remember, and so she sat there in the darkness next to the man, and was aware of two separate lines of thought in her mind.

The first: She attempted to visualize the human design in the crystal.

The second –

VIII

She watched his profile, as he drove in silence. And she thought: How brilliant he is! Yet surely a mere detective, no matter how keen his logic, cannot be the best of all possible Seth Mitchells. A man in such a profession has got to be somewhere in the middle – which in this competition is the same as the worst.

And he disappeared.

For many seconds after she had that thought, the suddenly driverless car held to its straight direction. Its speed, which had been around seventy, naturally started to let up the instant there was no longer a foot on the accelerator.

The only error was when Edith uttered a scream, and grabbed at the wheel, turning it. The machine careened wildly. The next second she grasped it in a more steadying way; and, holding it, slid along the seat into a position where presently she could apply the brake. She pulled over to the side of the road and stopped. She sat there, dazed.

The detective's aide, Marge, had slowed as soon as she saw that there was a problem. She now drew up behind Edith, got out of the car, and walked to the driver's side of the other machine.

'Seth,' she began, 'what – '

Edith pushed the door open and climbed, trembling, out onto the road. She had a mad impulse to run somewhere. Her body felt strange, her mind encased in a blank anguish. She was vaguely aware of herself babbling about what had happened.

It must have taken a while for the incoherent words to reach through to the blond woman. But suddenly Marge gasped, and Edith felt herself grabbed by the shoulders. She was being shaken; a breathless voice was yelling at her, 'You stupid fool! You stupid fool!'

Edith tried to pull away, but Marge's fingers seemed embedded in the shoulders of her dress.

The shaking became pain. Her neck hurt, then her arms. Edith thought for the first time: I must be careful. I mustn't do or say anything that will affect her.

With that thought, sanity returned. For the first time she saw that Marge was in a state of hysteria. The shaking was actually an automatic act of a person almost out of her mind with grief.

Pity came. She was able to free herself by a simple action. She slapped Marge lightly on the cheek, once, twice, three times. The third time, the woman let go of her and leaned against the car, sobbing. 'Oh, my God!' she said.

A wind was blowing out of the darkness from the west. Car headlights kept glaring past them, lighting the scene briefly. The two women were now in a relatively normal state, and they discussed the problem. Edith tried to recreate Marge's employer with the same command that she had used for Billy Bingham.

'*Seth Mitchell, the detective, back here, now!*'

She had had a feeling that it wouldn't work – the Seth Mitchells were undoubtedly due to be eliminated one by one – and it didn't. The minutes ticked by. Though she yelled the command in many variations into the night, there was no sign of the vanished Seth, whose presence had for a long half-day brought to the whole situation the reassurance that derives from a highly intelligent and determined mind.

In the end, defeated, the two women in their separate cars drove on to Harkdale. Since Marge had a room reserved at the Harkdale Hotel, she went there, and Edith drove wearily to the rooming house where she lived.

It was nearly four o'clock when she finally limped into her little suite. She lay down without undressing. As she was drifting off to sleep, she had a tense fear: Would the best of all possible Ediths be this sloppy about personal cleanliness?

Literally hurting with exhaustion, she rolled off the bed, undressed, bathed, brushed her teeth, combed her hair, changed the linens and climbed into a clean pair of pajamas.

She awakened with a horrible start shortly after 5:30 with the thought that conformism might not be it. Such toiletry amenities as she had performed were products of early training and did not necessarily have anything to do with life and living as it should be.

She fell asleep imagining a series of rebel Ediths, each one of whom had some special characteristic that was noble and worthy.

The next time she awakened, it was light outside. It occurred to her that all of her concepts, so compulsively visualized, where probably being created somewhere by the crystal. And so undoubtedly there were already beatnik and hippie Ediths as well as rougher, tougher types.

For the first time she realized what a mad whirl of possibilities she had considered in the previous thirty-six hours. Ediths who were hard-boiled and could coldly shoot to kill, or, conversely, were superfeminine, sweet, tantalizing temptresses.

'And it's all unnecessary,' she whispered, lying there. 'The decision will probably be made as arbitrarily as my own impulsive condemnation of the inarticulate farmer and the courageous – but presumably not perfect – detective.'

Having no standards that applied to the twentieth century, the crystal had uncreated a powerful and good man on the passing judgment of the person to whom it had by chance become oriented. Accordingly, the future looked grim for all Seth Mitchells and Edith Prices, including the original.

When she next awakened, it was time to get up and go to work – and think some more about what the perfect Edith would be like.

As she dressed, she looked out of her window with its distant view of the blue waters of Lake Naragang, and the nearby downtown section that at one place, opposite the Harkdale Hotel, crowded the water's edge. Pretty little town, Harkdale. She remembered that on her arrival she had thought that at least here she could be more casual in her dress than in New York.

Edith gave a curt, rueful laugh as that thought struck her. She had come full circle during the night, back to the notion that appearance would count. Trying to think feminine – 'After all, I am a woman' – she put on her frilliest dress.

Yet in some back closet of her brain there was a fearful conviction that all this was in vain. The crisis was imminent; she might be dead – uncreated – before this day was out.

It seemed ridiculous to go to work on the day you were going to die. But she went.

As she moved about her duties, Edith was conscious of her subdued manner. Twice, when she unthinkingly looked into the rest-room mirror, she was startled by the pale face and sick eyes that looked back at her.

'This is not really me,' she told herself. 'I can't be judged on this.'

Surely the crystal wouldn't reject her because she was in a daze. Every passing minute, fleeting images of other Ediths passed before her mind's eye; each one had in it the momentary hope that maybe *it* held the key to the best. There was an Edith living out her life as a nun; another chaste Edith, married but holding sex to a minimum, placing all her attention on her children; and an Edith who was a follower of Zen Buddhism.

She had, earlier, put through a call to Marge Aiken at

the Harkdale Hotel. About two o'clock Marge called back. She reported that she had phoned New York and discovered that the second Edith had not returned to her hotel at all the previous night.

After imparting this grim news, Marge said, 'And so, if Athtar contacts you, don't be alone with him under any circumstances until he produces the Seth Mitchell in the gold Cadillac and the Edith in New York.'

After that call, more images, mostly of saintly and good-hearted, unsophisticated Ediths, now haunted her. Somehow, they stemmed from her childhood conditioning, against which she had rebelled in college, as seen through a child's unnoticing eyes.

Into this haze of thoughts, Tilsit's voice suddenly intruded: 'Phone call for you, Edith.'

As she picked up the phone, Edith was vaguely aware of Miss Davis' disapproving face in the background. Though it was the first day she had received personal calls in her six months in the library, the chief librarian had the outraged expression of an employer whose patience has been tried beyond reason.

Edith forgot that as she heard the familiar voice on the phone – Athtar's.

The man said, 'I want to see you right after work.'

Edith said, in a suddenly faint voice, 'At the Harkdale Hotel – in the lobby.'

IX

Athtar stepped out of the phone booth from which he had called. A cruel smile twisted his broad face. For him there were two possibilities of victory, now that he had the crystal.

The first solution was to kill its current orientation – Edith. He intended to take no chances with that. She would never, he was resolved, reach the Harkdale Hotel.

However, murder of his only Edith had one unpleasant possibility. Though he had analyzed that she was the orientation, if it should happen that she was not, then, in destroying her he would remove his source of information for tracing other Ediths.

It was a chance he was resolved to take. But, as a precaution, he had already removed the crystal from the nutrient soil on which it fed. He was not certain how long it would be before the stone was deactivated by starvation, but he deduced not more than two weeks. Whereupon it would orient to whoever reactivated it. To himself, of course.

Now that he had a special barrier-penetrating weapon, he firmly believed that before this day was over he would be in sole possession of the remarkable machine of all time and space – the crystal.

The Harkdale Hotel was a summer resort hostelry. Its prices were high, and as a result it had made money. Wisely, some of the money had been spent on decoration, fine furniture, and a sophisticated staff.

The clerk on day duty had his own definition of a sophisticated desk clerk: a person with a memory so good that he can forget with discretion.

He was such a clerk. He described himself as an import from fine hotels. His name, he said, was Derek Slade. He had – he always explained – asked for an assignment to a small resort town, because he had a certain childhood nostalgia for village life. So discreet, however, was Derek, that on this fateful day he allowed four Seth Mitchells to register. Each time he believed it was the same man but with a different woman; and he was just beginning, he told himself, to enjoy the situation, when Seth Mitchell arrived for the fifth time; only this time he had no woman with him.

Yet it took Derek only a moment to figure it out. This smooth male, Seth Mitchell, had four women in different rooms, and evidently he wanted a separate room for himself. Why? Derek didn't try to analyze the matter further. Life – he had often said – was full of surprises. He would observe the fact, not speculate about it.

Derek spoke in a low tone, 'You may count on my discretion, Mr Mitchell.'

The Seth Mitchell across the desk from him raised his eyebrows, then nodded with a faint smile.

Derek was pleased. The remark ought to be good for a twenty-dollar tip.

He was still congratulating himself when the elevator door opened and another Seth Mitchell stepped out and walked toward the desk. As he came up, the Seth Mitchell who had just registered turned to follow the bellboy carrying his bags to the elevator.

The two Seth Mitchells almost bumped into each other. Both took evasive action. Both murmured polite nothings, and were about to pass each other when Derek recovered.

It was one of his perfect moments. He raised his voice, spoke with that exact right note of authority: '*Mister* Mitchell.'

The two Seth Mitchells were already in a mildly confused state. Their name, uttered in that peremptory tone, stopped them.

Derek said, 'Mr Seth Mitchell, I want you to meet Mr Seth Mitchell. Gentlemen, please wait there a moment.'

He let them kill their own time – one of them seemed to recover quickly, the other remaining bewildered – while he phoned the rooms of the previously registered Seth Mitchells. He had to call all four rooms, but presently there in front of him stood five Seth Mitchells.

Of all the people present, the one most completely unnoticed was Derek Slade. He wouldn't have had it any other way, for he could watch.

Four of the five Seths were gulping and stuttering at each other. The fifth had stepped off to one side with a faint smile. Almost as one, the four suddenly became embarrassed, and so Derek's cool voice caught them again at the right moment: 'Gentlemen, why don't you go into the conference room over here and talk this whole matter over?'

As they started for the conference room, Marge Aiken entered the hotel – in time to catch a profile view of the last Seth Mitchell to enter the room. She became very pale and then rushed forward.

'Seth!' she cried out tearfully. 'For God's sake, I thought you were dead!'

She stopped. She had grabbed the nearest man by the arm. He turned, and the something different about him flustered her.

Afterward, when everybody had been told what Marge knew, and after they had heard about Edith, the woman detective suggested that she call Edith at the library and have her come over at once, instead of later.

Three of the Seth Mitchells objected. Listening to each

in turn, Marge glanced along the line of sensationally familiar faces, and saw in all but one man's eyes a haunting apprehension. Yet there was in all of them the same bright intelligence that she had seen so often in her own employer.

The Seth from Montreal said, 'Our first act must be to protect ourselves from that young woman's automatic judgments, such as she rendered on farmer Mitchell and detective Mitchell.'

A second, slightly deeper-voiced Seth was concerned about Athtar. 'In killing Edith Price Number Two, Athtar must have got the crystal, and then discovered that the dead Edith was not the orientation. Therefore,' he said, 'our initial act must be to protect the Edith who *is* the orientation.'

So the first real problem was getting her safely to the hotel, not what she would do when she got here.

The third Seth said the problem was not so much Edith's judgment of men; it was her stereotyped thoughts about how a woman should be. Presumably, the crystal had dutifully created a long list of Edith Prices who were simply ordinary human beings with varying moral standards, or with slightly different beliefs about how to get along in the drab world of the twentieth century.

'As an example of how differently I would want her to handle her control of the crystal, one of the first Edith Prices I wish her to create is one that has ESP. Why? So that she can understand this whole situation and what to do about it.'

His words brought a hopeful reaction. It was an obviously good idea – if it could be done.

A fourth Seth, who had sat gray and silent, now spoke up: 'It would be interesting if such ESP ability included being able to spot the Seth Mitchell who' – he nodded at Marge – 'paid your boss a thousand dollars to locate the crystal.'

The Seth who had arrived at the hotel without a wife – and who had reflected none of the fear that the others felt – stirred, and smiled cheerfully. 'You need look no further. I'm he.'

When the chorus of questions and excitement finally died down, he continued, 'To answer your basic question, I also dreamed, as you all did. And just as the worst Athtar found himself with the address of one of the Seth Mitchells in his

90

mind, in the same way the morning after the dream the address of detective Mitchell was in mine.'

'But why didn't you come for the crystal yourself? Why pay a thousand dollars?'

The bachelor Mitchell smiled again. 'I hate to tell you people this, and it is to your advantage not to let Miss Price know, but according to the thoughts I had after my dream, I am the best of all possible Seth Mitchells.'

Many minutes chattered by before his audience was again calmed down, and he was able to answer the substance of all the words they had projected: 'I don't know why I'm best. But I hired someone to come here in my place because I sensed danger, and I came here today believing that this was the crisis. I can't tell you what I'll do about it. I don't even have the feeling that my role is decisive. I simply believe that something will present itself, and I'll do it.'

He finished simply, 'I don't think we should devote any more time to me. We have many vital things to do, and only until Edith Price comes off the job to do them. Let's get started.'

They were law-abiding people; so they now contacted the police, who checked the motel where the Seth Mitchell of the gold Cadillac had registered. Then they phoned his office in New York on the basis of his license-plate number and found that the car was there, the man missing for many days. A warrant was accordingly issued against a squat man whose only known name was Athtar.

Since the police of Harkdale were few in number, after dark Athtar was able to drive into town and into the library parking lot without being observed. He had timed his arrival for about a minute after the library officially closed.

Dimness. A lingering twilight that had barely transformed into night. A few library patrons were still maneuvering in the library parking lot when Edith emerged from the rear door.

She noted with a vague surprise that a town fire truck, engine running, was standing near the door. But she was already having qualms about the forthcoming journey to the hotel – so far away, it seemed to her suddenly. And so the sight of the big truck was reassuring instead of astonishing.

To get to her own car, she had to go around the fire truck. As she started forward to do so, the big machine surged into motion with a gigantic thunder of its engine. Edith stopped, teetered, then leapt back out of the way — barely in time.

As it came abreast of her, the truck jammed on its brakes and screeched to a halt directly in front of her.

Somewhere beyond the big machine, a purple flash lighted the sky.

X

Though Edith did not see it, the purple light had its origin in one of the maneuvering cars. Like a tracer bullet, the light flashed from the auto to the fire truck. As it hit, it made a sound of a pitch never before heard on earth: a deep, sustained, continuing spat of chemical bonds by the quadrillion snapping in metal.

The tiny bullet penetrated the thick steel frame of the fire truck, and reformed itself a micromillimeter at a time from the steel molecules. It did not slow as it passed through the heavy machine. Indeed, there was no thickness of metal of the twentieth century that could have held it back by even one foot a minute of its forward speed. Not the armor plate of a battleship, nor the solid mass of the earth itself.

It was a rifle bullet, and so its path was straight — through air and through metal. It also would have been straight through Edith, except that its speed *was* that of a bullet, immense but finite.

And so it transited the fire truck while the truck was still in motion. The bullet carried along inside the moving vehicle during a measurable time of several split seconds and missed Edith by twenty inches.

Unchecked, it struck the library wall, moved on through, emerged from the far side, and zipped off into the night. Its kinetic energy being a precise quality, it bored forward another hundred yards, and then rapidly fell.

Moments later, two plainclothes police officers discharged their rifles at the figure that was dimly visible inside the car from which the purple-glowing bullet had been fired.

The screech of bullets striking his own machine, startled Athtar. But he had a molecular reinforcing unit putting out a field that hardened the glass and the metal of the auto; and so the bullets failed to penetrate.

What bothered him was that he had only a few bullets, and in the dark he couldn't gauge the extent of the trap that had been set for him. So now, hastily, he put his car into drive, stepped on the gas, and drove rapidly out of the parking lot.

A police car fell in behind him, flashing its red lights at him. Though it or its weapons were no danger to him, he feared a roadblock. He turned up several side streets, and in only a few minutes of driving lured the police car onto a street near the lake on the far side of the Harkdale Hotel, an approach that he had thoroughly explored on foot earlier.

Satisfied, he opened the car window on the driver's side, slowed, leaned out, looked back, took quick aim at the engine of the other machine, and put a purple-glowing bullet through the crankcase. There was a shattering crash. The stricken motor almost tore itself apart, screaming metallically. The auto itself came to a bumpy halt.

Athtar hurriedly circled back to the Harkdale Hotel. A first queasy doubt had come that for a reason that was not clear his time was running out. Yet it still seemed true to him that all he need do was sneak into the hotel and discharge a single bullet at one, and only one, beating heart.

Minutes later, after squeezing through a kitchen window of the hotel, he found himself in a shadowy storeroom on a concrete floor. As he fumbled his way to a door, he had a fleeting mental image of his colleagues of the great Science Guild viewing him in such a lowly action. Of course, Athtar told himself scornfully, what they thought would not matter after he got control of the crystal. There would be dramatic changes after he got back to his own time: a few hundred Guild members were scheduled for extermination.

Cautiously he pulled open the door. It was as he started through the hallway beyond that he became aware of a faint sound behind him. He spun around and jerked up his gun.

Instant, unbearable pain in his arm forced the gun back down and his finger away from the trigger. Almost at once the gun dropped from his nerveless hand, clattering to the floor. Even as he recognized that thirty-fifth-century technology was being used against him, he saw that a short, squat man was standing in the doorway of the storeroom from which he himself had just emerged.

Athtar's arm and hand were now inexorably forced by intolerable pain to reach into his inside breast pocket, take out the crystal, and hold it out to the other man.

The second Athtar did not speak. He drew the door behind him shut, accepted the crystal, and bending down, picked the gun up from the floor. Then he edged past his prisoner, stepped through the door beyond, and closed it behind him also.

At once, all the muscle pressures let go of the worst Athtar. Instantly desperate, he tried to jerk open the storeroom door, intending to escape by the same window he had entered. The door was locked, and it had an unnervingly solid feel to it. Athtar whirled toward the other door.

When he found it locked also, and with that same solid resistance to his tug, he now finally recognized that he was trapped by molecular forces from his own era. There was nothing to do, as the minutes lengthened, but to sit down on the concrete floor and wait.

Sitting there, he had the partly mixed reaction that the drama of the crystal would now play on without him. What seemed good about it was the distinct conviction that perhaps he was well out of it; perhaps this was a more dangerous situation than he had let himself be aware of. Would it have been dangerous for him? The intuition wasn't that definite.

He had recognized his assailant as the best of all possible Athtars. So now he told himself he was glad it was the best Athtar and not himself who would be present while these twentieth-century human beings tried to save themselves.

The Price woman was being cleverer than he had anticipated. Which meant that the automatic programming of the crystal to uncreate all but the best would force her to the most desperate actions. Or so it seemed to the worst Athtar.

Better not to be around when such extreme events were transpiring.

The best of all possible Athtars walked through the hotel lobby to the conference room. The five Seth Mitchells were grouped outside the door, out of the line of vision of Edith, who was inside. Athtar gave the agreed-on signal and handed the worst Athtar's automatic pistol to one of the Seths. They were thorough. They searched him, and then passed him on

94

to Marge Aikens, who stood in the doorway.

To Marge, Athtar gave another agreed-on signal. Having thus established his identity as the friendly Athtar, whom Edith had re-created as a first step, he was now admitted inside the room.

Athtar placed the crystal on the conference table in front of Edith. As her fingers automatically reached toward it, he placed a restraining hand on her wrist.

'I have a feeling,' he admonished, 'that this time when you pick it up – when the true orientation, *you*, picks it up – that will be the moment of crisis.'

His voice, and his words, seemed far away. She had – it seemed to her – considered those thoughts, and had those feelings, in approaching the decision to re-create *him* – the best Athtar. That, also, had been a crisis.

As she nevertheless hesitated out of respect for his knowledge and awareness, Edith noticed two impulses within herself. One was to go into a kind of exhaustion, in which she would act on the basis that she was too tired to think all that through again.

The second impulse was a clearer, sharper awareness, which had come to her suddenly at the library after she realized that the worst Athtar had tried to kill her.

Abruptly, then, the problems that had disturbed her earlier faded. Whether it was better to be tough and be able to shoot, or be soft and feminine, had no meaning. The real solution was infinite flexibility, backed by unvarying intention.

One handled situations. That was all there was to it.

As she remembered that perfect thought, the impulse toward exhaustion went away. She turned to Marge and said matter-of-factly, 'Shall I tell him what we discussed while he was down in the storeroom?'

Marge nodded tensely.

Athtar listened with what appeared to be an expression of doubt, then said, 'Having the crystal re-create one of its makers could be exactly what those makers are waiting for you to do.'

'That's exactly what we thought,' said Edith. And still she felt no fear. She explained, 'Our thought is that, since the crystal is programmed to find the best of each person, and the best Athtar turned out to be a reasonable person and not a criminal, then the makers of the crystal understand

95

the difference. We may therefore assume that the society of the future is normal and will not harm us.'

She added, 'That's why we re-created you – as a check.'

'Good reasoning,' said Athtar, cautioning, 'but I sense there's something wrong with it.'

'But you have no specific thought?' she asked.

'No.' He hesitated, then shrugged. 'As a start,' he said, 'why not pick up the crystal – just pick it up – and see if my feeling about that being sufficient has any substance?' He explained, 'If I'm wrong there, then we can dismiss my doubts.'

'You don't want me to look at the design?'

The Seths had discovered that that was the key to her control of the stone. By questioning her closely, by eliciting from her the thoughts she had had on the three occasions that it had performed its miracle for her, it had become apparent that when she mentally or visually traced the interior picture and gave a command, it happened – literally.

Athtar answered, 'No, I sense that they're ready.'

His words, the implication of ultraperception that reached over, perhaps, thousands of years, startled Edith, and held her unmoving, but only momentarily.

'The truth is,' said Edith aloud, completing her thought, 'we all feel that we have no alternative.'

Without any further delay, she reached forward and picked up the crystal.

Then she gasped.

The man who walked out of the corner of the room, where he had materialized, was a giant. Seven, eight, nine feet – her mind kept reassessing the height, as she strove to adjust to the enormous reality.

The size, the blue harness clothing – like a Roman centurion guard in summer uniform – the bronze body, the large face with eyes as black as coal, unsmiling and firm; and in his bearing, conscious power unqualified by doubt or fear.

He said in a bass voice, in English, 'I am Shalil, the best of all possible.'

XI

For a long moment Edith waited for him to complete the sentence. She presumed that the final word would be his name. At last, with a shock, she realized the sentence *was* finished. The crystal makers had sent the most qualified individual of their entire race to handle this situation.

In the doorway, Marge cringed away from the monster with a moan. At the sound, two of the Seth Mitchells leaped into view from where they had been standing. As they caught the blonde woman's half-fainting body, they also saw the apparition, and froze with glaring eyes. That brought the other three Seths crowding into the doorway.

As of one accord, obviously unwisely and therefore – as Edith realized later – under unnoticed control, they moved into the room, bringing Marge with them. The Seth who brought up the rear pulled the door shut behind him.

And there they were, as the best Athtar stirred and said in a sharp tone, 'Miss Price – uncreate him! He does not mean well.'

The giant grimaced. 'You cannot uncreate men.' He spoke again a perfect English in the same bass voice. 'Naturally, I, and only I, now control the crystal. The term "mean well" is relative. I mean well for my own time and my own group.'

His eyes, like black pools of dark shiningness, glanced over the five Seths and the two women, and then settled on Athtar. 'Which of you are the biologically original human beings?' he asked.

There was a speed to him and a purposefulness that was disturbing all by itself. Edith clutched the crystal, and then she glanced uncertainly over at the Seths, silently appealing for suggestions. But they were staring at the giant and seemed unaware of her seeking gaze.

Yet it was one of the Seths who said abruptly, 'Athtar, in what way doesn't he mean well?'

Athtar shook his head. 'I don't sense the details,' he said unhappily. 'It's a feeling. They sent the crystal back here for their purpose. His question about original human beings points a very significant direction. But don't answer it – or any other question.'

It seemed a small, useless denial. Even as it was uttered, the huge man strode toward the door. The little group of Seths separated before him automatically. The giant opened the door and peered out into the hotel lobby. After a single, swift survey, he pushed the door shut, and faced about.

7.

'I deduce,' he said, 'that the people of this era are the originals. That's who we want for our experiments.'

Athtar said tautly to the Seths, 'One of you has the worst Athtar's gun. Shoot him!'

The instant the words were spoken, the pistol floated into view, avoided the fingers of the two Seths who tried to grab it, and darted over to Shalil's palm. He slipped the weapon into a pocket of his simple blue garment.

The best Athtar glanced at Edith. 'Well,' he said glumly, 'I've done my best.' He faced the monster. 'What happens to me?'

Those wonderful black eyes studied him again, more carefully. 'The crystal is communicating data to me,' he said. 'You and the other Athtar are from an era where the people have already been biologically altered?'

Athtar was silent. The giant grimaced, and thereupon analyzed substantially what the worst Athtar had told Edith in New York, adding only that he had the impression that vast amounts of bodily organ transplants for medical purposes had preceded the first big decision to chance the race itself.

Athtar glanced apologetically at Edith. 'He has it so accurately,' he said, 'that I see no additional danger in asking him a question.'

Without waiting for a reply he addressed the huge man: 'The decision made in the thirty-first century, nearly four hundred years before my time, was that small, heavy bodies had more survival potentiality than tall, thin ones. I see that in your era a much taller, bigger, more powerful man than any we have even imagined is the norm. What is the rationale?'

'Different problems,' answered Shalil. 'In my era, which by your reckoning would correlate to the ninety-third century, we are space people.' He broke off. 'Since we have no interest in you at present, I propose to send you and the other Athtars back to your own time.'

'Wait!' The best Athtar spoke urgently. 'What do you intend to do with these people?' He waved toward Edith and the Seths.

Again there was a grimace on the huge face. 'They are crystal patterns now,' was the stern reply. 'But all we actually want for our experiments are the best Seth Mitchell and the best Edith Price. The other 1810 Seths and' – he hesitated, then – '723 Ediths are free to go. We set the crystal to find the best specimens.'

'But why?'

'Something has gone wrong. We need to restudy human origins.'

'Do you need these specific persons, or will you merely have the crystal duplicate them in your own era?'

'There's only one of each. If any of them is created in any other time, he becomes uncreated here.'

'What will you do? Dissect them?'

'In the end, perhaps. The experimenters will decide.' Sharply. 'Never mind that. The program is laid out on a crash basis, and the subjects are urgently needed.' His voice grew imperious. 'Miss Price, give me the crystal. We're not needlessly cruel, so I wish to send the Athtars home.'

Athtar urged, 'Miss Price, don't give it to him. His statement that he totally controls the crystal may not be true yet, but it may become true the moment he has possession of it. These far-future beings must be persuaded to accept another, less arbitrary solution to their problem.'

Edith had been standing, watching the fantastic giant, listening to the infinite threat that was developing out of his blunt words. Suddenly, what had seemed an utterly desirable goal – to be the best – had become the most undesirable.

But she observed that she was still not afraid. Her mind was clear. And she realized that the millions of tumbling thoughts and feelings of all these days, which had suddenly fallen into an exact order in her mind earlier that night, remained orderly.

Her own reaction was that Athtar was wrong and that she had, in fact, lost control of the crystal.

Obvious that they would have had some preemptive system, by which they could regain its use at a key moment.

But she intended to test that.

She glanced at and into the crystal, and said firmly, 'Whoever can defeat this giant – be here now!'

Moments after she spoke, the crystal was snatched from her fingers by the same kind of unseen force as had taken the automatic pistol from one of the Seths earlier. She looked up and watched helplessly as it also floated over to the giant's palm. The huge man's black eyes gleamed triumphantly at her, as he said: 'That was a good try. But all your allies are in this room. There's nobody else.'

'In that case,' said a man's voice quietly, 'I imagine that, regardless of consequences, my moment has come.'

Whereupon the bachelor Seth Mitchell walked forward and stood in front of the giant.

For some reason the monster man merely regarded him. There was a long pause. Edith had time to gaze at the Seth and to savor the mere humanness that he represented. She saw that he was well dressed in a dark gray suit, that his lean face was firm, his gray eyes calm and fearless. At some deep of her mind, she was proud that at this key moment such a Seth Mitchell existed. Yet, though she was still not afraid herself, she was aware of her hopes sinking.

The silence ended.

The great being from the far future said in a deliberate tone, 'I hope you realize that you are condemning the other Seths in thus forcing your identity on me. In this era the crystal has no alternative but to uncreate them.'

Behind Edith, Marge cried out faintly.

Edith whirled. For several seconds, then, she was blank, not knowing what ailed the young blond woman. Marge seemed to be choking, and after a moment Edith ran over to her, and caught her arm, and put one arm around her waist.

'What's the matter?' she cried.

Marge continued to choke, and the words when they finally came were almost inaudible: 'They're gone, the other Seths!'

Edith looked around, and it was then that the reality finally penetrated her blankness. Where the four Seths had been standing near the door, there was no one. She had an impulse to run to the door and glance out of it. The feeling was, surely, that they had stepped outside for a moment.

Abruptly, she realized.

They had been uncreated.

'Oh, my God!' she said, and it was a sob.

She caught herself, for the giant was speaking again: 'Other than that,' he said, 'the best of all possible Seth Mitchells merely seemed a good specimen, and not dangerous.'

Seth Mitchell spoke in the same quiet tone as before, 'I said, regardless of consequences.'

He glanced back toward the two women. 'Since the Seths

remain crystal patterns, they're no more in danger now than they would be if this creature is able to carry out his threat. That probably even applies to the Seth of the gold Cadillac and the Edith who presumably was killed in New York.'

To Shalil he said, 'I think you'd better put the Athtars up in their own time.'

There was an ever so slight pause; the giant's eyes changed slightly, as if he were thinking. Then: 'It's done,' he said.

Edith glanced to where Athtar had been, with the same automatic second look as before, and the same gasping intake of her breath. . . . And then with a conscious effort she had control once more.

Athtar had disappeared.

With a grimace, Shalil surveyed the best of all possible Seth Mitchells, said, 'You really benefited from the crystal, didn't you?' He spoke in his softest bass. The intent expression, as if he were listening, came into his face. 'You own . . . one . . . three, four corporations.'

'I stopped when I was worth ten million,' said the best Seth. He turned to look at Edith apologetically. 'I couldn't imagine having use for even that much money. But I had set it as a goal, so that's what I did.'

Without waiting for her reply, he once more faced the gigantic enemy. 'All the Seth Mitchells,' he said, 'are the results of a boy's dreams based on what information he had. He undoubtedly observed that there are tax experts, and lawyers, and doctors, and tramps, and policemen. And in a town like Harkdale it would include being aware of summer and resort visitors, many of them highly personable people from New York. And on the level of a boy's daydreams it would mean that until they were uncreated just now there was a cowboy Seth Mitchell, an African hunter Seth, a sea captain, an airline pilot, and probably even a few glamorous criminals.'

He broke off. 'I have a feeling you wouldn't understand that, because you don't have any boys anymore where you are, do you?'

The giant's eyes did an odd thing. They shifted uncertainly. Then he said, 'We are crystal duplicates. Thus we shall presumably live forever – if we can solve the present tendency of the cells to be tired.'

He added reluctantly, 'What's a boy?'

'Maybe there's your problem,' said Seth Mitchell. 'You've forgotten about children. Gene variation.'

The best Seth continued to gaze up at the great being. 'I'm the creation,' he said gently, 'of a boy who for a long time after Billy Bingham disappeared, was under exceptional adult pressure and criticism, and as a result had many escape fantasies.'

The steady, determined voice went on, 'Picture that boy's fantasy of total power: somebody who would handle mean adults who acted as if you were lying and who treated you nasty . . . and someday you'd show them all. How? It may not have been clear to the boy Seth who felt that resentment. But when the time came, you'd just know, and of course you wouldn't be mean about it the way they had been. There'd be a kind of nobleness about you and your total power.'

The two men, the best of all possible Seth Mitchells from the twentieth century and the best of all possibles from the ninety-third century, were standing within a few feet of each other as these words were spoken.

'Perhaps,' the best Seth addressed the giant softly, 'you can tell better than I what the crystal would create out of such a command.'

'Since nobleness is involved,' was the harsh reply, 'I feel that I can safely test that boy's fantasy to the uttermost limit.'

Whereupon he spoke sharp, commanding words in a strange language.

Edith had listened to the deadly interchange, thinking in a wondering dismay: God really is dead! These far future people had never even heard of Him.

Her thought ended. For the giant's deep bass tones had suddenly ceased.

Something hit Edith deep inside of her body. Around her the room dimmed. As from a vast distance, she heard Seth Mitchell's voice say apologetically, 'Only thing I know, Miss Price, is to send you along with him. Seems you've got the solution in what you just thought, whatever that was. The crystal will make that real. Hope it works.'

A moment after that she was falling into infinity.

XII

The body of Edith lay unconscious on a contour rest-space in one corner of the crystal administrative center. Periodically, a giant walked over to her and routinely checked the instruments that both watched over her and monitored the invisible force lines that held her.

A slow night went by. A new day finally dawned. The sunlight that suffused the translucent walls also revealed half a dozen giants, including Shalil, gathered around the slowly breathing – but otherwise unmoving – body of the young woman from the twentieth century.

To wake or not to wake her?

They discussed the problem in low, rumbling voices. Since they were all scientists, capable of appreciating the most subtle nuances of logic, what bothered them was that the small female being presented an improbable paradox.

Outward appearance said she was helpless. At the instant of the best Seth's command to the crystal, Shalil had been able to put Edith into a coma, and she had arrived in that degraded condition in the ninety-third century.

Or rather, she had been uncreated in her own time, and had been re-created by the crystal in their time, already unconscious.

Accordingly, she herself had not for even a split instant had any control of her own destiny.

What disturbed her captors was that there now radiated from her, and had ever since her re-creation, an undefinable power. The power was not merely ordinary. It was total.

Total power! Absolute and unqualified! How could that be?

Once more they gave attention on both hearing and tele-pathic levels, as Shalil repeated his accurate account of what had transpired while he was in the twentieth century. The story, already familiar, reiterated the same peak moments: the ordinariness, the unthreatening aspect, of all the people of the past that Shalil had confronted.

Again they were told the climax, when the best Seth assumed that the crystal would evolve an unusual energy configuration out of a boy's fantasies of power. Clearly – at least, it was clear to the huge men – the crystal's response to that command established that it had originally been oriented to the best Seth, and its energies mobilized for later expression, when Seth Mitchell was a boy. From that energy response by the crystal alone, the giants reasoned unhappily: 'There is more potential in these crystals than we have hitherto analyzed.'

And how could *that* be?

But there was even worse.

In giving his command to Edith, the best of all possible Seth Mitchells had implied that he had received a feed-back message from her, presumably by way of the crystal, indicating that she would all by herself now be able to defeat the entire science of the ninety-third century.

Once Shalil took control of the crystal, such a feedback of information – whether true or false – should not have occurred. And Seth's command, by any known scientific analysis, was impossible.

True, they did not know all there was to know about the crystals. There were several unexplained areas of phenomena, which were still being researched. But it had long been argued that nothing major remained to be discovered.

Furthermore, they believed that, under strict scientific control, the crystals had created the supreme possibilities of the biologically manipulated beings of their own time period. Every conceivable potentiality of the cells, and of the total gestalt of those cells, had been reasoned through. And the crystal had dutifully created each possibility for them: levitation, telepathy, control of distant matter on a thought level, and so on.

The only other implication: Original, unmanipulated human beings might have special qualities that had been lost to their biologically manipulated descendants.

Unquestionably, that culminative decision had made her the best of all possible Edith Prices. But such a person would have been meaningless in the twentieth century. And since she hadn't visualized the scene inside the crystal when she made it, *that* was not the source of her present power.

That was something else. Something fantastic, unheard of, beyond all their science.

XIII

A giant grunted, 'I think we should kill her.'

A second huge man growled an objection. He argued: 'If the attempt to destroy her brought a reaction from the absolute power that radiated from her, the power would be uncontrolled. Much better to deduce on the basis of Shalil's report the low-level ways in which her mind functions, awaken her, and inexorably force responses from her.'

Everybody thought that was a good idea. Accordingly, they made their deductions. Each new one added to their growing conviction that they could retain complete mastery of the situation.

'And if something goes wrong,' one giant bubbled, 'we can always render her unconscious again by instantaneous uncreation and re-creation by the crystal.'

Shalil reminded gruffly, 'What about that odd decision she had reached, in her attempt to be the best of all possible Ediths, to handle situations with infinite flexibility?'

A groan of contempt greeted the remark. 'With *her* lifetime conditioning,' one huge scientist rumbled despisingly, 'she couldn't possibly deal with each situation according to its merits.'

Edith, they criticized, would never even know what the real issues of a situation were.

They completed their increasingly confident consideration by deciding that when Edith awakened she should appear to herself to be completely free. . . .

She was lying on grass. It touched her fingers and her face. The fresh smell of it was in her nostrils.

Edith opened her eyes, and simultaneously raised her head.

Wilderness. A primeval forest. A small brown animal with a bushy tail scurried off into the brush, as she climbed hastily to her feet, remembering.

She saw the giant in the act of picking himself up fifteen feet to her left. He seemed to be slow about it, as if he were groggy.

It was a misty day, the sun still high in the sky. To her right, partly visible through foliage, was a great, gray hill of soil. To her left, the land fell away, and the mist was thicker. After a hundred yards it was an almost impenetrable fog.

Almost, but not quite, impenetrable. Vaguely visible in the mist was a building.

Edith barely glanced in that direction. Instead, she faced the giant squarely and said, 'Where are we?'

Shalil gazed at her warily. It was hard for him to realize that she did not intuitively know. Almost unacceptable that alongside her infinite power was such nadir thinking.

Yet she continued to stand there, facing him. He sensed her concern. And so, reluctantly, he decided that the analysis by his colleagues and himself continued to apply. They had perceived her to be motivated by unnoticed attitudes and forgotten memories, each psychically as solid as a bar of steel. All her life she had followed rules, gone along with group-think behavior.

To school and to college; these were the early norms, adhered to while she was still under the control of her parents. Basically those norms had been unquestioned.

Shalil noticed in her memory an awareness that millions of people had somehow failed to achieve higher education. That was astonishing to him; yet somehow, they had been veered away, by a variety of accidental circumstances.

So in those areas of personal development Edith had gone farther, better, straighter than the average. Yet in college, first time away from her family, she had swiftly been caught up in a group movement of nonconformism. Whatever the motives of the other persons involved, Edith's had been solely an intense inner need to belong to the group.

So, for her, it had been the beginning of aberration, which her behavior ever afterward reflected. Thus, Shalil observed, like a person struggling against invisible force lines, she had fought to return to an inner norm. More study, different jobs, different places to live, association with different men – the confusion was immense, and it was difficult to determine which of these numerous actions represented a real goal.

Adding to the jumble, everything she did was modified by a very large, though finite, number of small, endlessly repeated actions – eating habits, dressing habits, working, sleeping, walking, reacting, communicating, thinking: stereotypes.

What bothered Shalil was that he could not find a single point of entry that would not instantly trigger one of the stereotypes. The others had assumed that something would presently come into view in a conscious mind; they had taken it for granted that he would locate it. His instruction was to uncreate her into unconsciousness if he failed to make such an entry, whereupon there would be another consultation.

The possibility of such a quick failure disturbed Shalil. Temporizing, he said aloud, 'This is the Garden of the Crystals in the ninety-third century. Here, in the most virgin wilderness left on our planet, the crystals lie buried in the soil tended by guardian scientists.'

Having spoken, having had that tiny bit of extra time to consider, he decided that the problem she presented would be solvable with a steady pressure of verbal maneuvering by which *she* was motivated to express one after the other the endless stereotypes that had been detected in her, while *he* waited alertly for the one through which the crystal – on his command – would divest her of the power with which it had (through a factor that the others and he did not know) invested her.

Her primary concern, he saw, was that she would never get back to her own era. Since he knew she could return at once simply by thinking the correct positive thought, his problem was to keep her worried, negative, unaware, deceived, misled.

Shalil became aware that his anxiety about how to proceed was causing a hasty telepathic consultation among his colleagues. Moments later the suggestion was made: 'Divert her letting her win some minor victories, and believe that they are gifts from you.'

It seemed like a good idea, and Shalil carried it out as if it were a directive.

XIV

At the Harkdale Hotel, it was another morning. Marge Aikens came downstairs, bleary-eyed from lack of sleep. Almost automatically, she walked over and peered into the conference room. The lights in it had been turned off, the drapes were still drawn; and so the dim emptiness of it was an instant weight on her spirits.

Heavy-hearted, she turned away – and became aware that

a man had come up beside her. She turned about, and faced him with a start.

The hotel day clerk, Derek Slade, stood there, as usual the very mirror of New York male fashion. 'Madame,' he said courteously.

He continued to speak, and after a while his meaning penetrated her dulled mind. He thought he had recognized her as the young woman who had late the previous afternoon gone into the conference room with the five Seth Mitchells.

Where – Derek wanted to know – were the four married Seths? The wives had been phoning all night, according to a note on his desk from the night clerk. And a police officer was on the way over, because three Mrs Mitchells had finally called the authorities.

Marge had an impulse to deny that she was the woman he thought he had seen. But his failure to mention the bachelor Seth captured her attention, and she asked about him.

Derek shook his head, 'Not in his room. Went out early, I'm told.'

Marge stood in the doorway, somewhat blankly considering what might have happened to the best Seth. Why would he have gone out when he had said the previous night that he would have breakfast with her? Then she became aware that Derek Slade's gaze had gone past her shoulder and was seeking the darkened interior of the room behind her.

His jaw grew lax, his eyes grew round.

Inside the room, a man's baritone voice uttered an exclamation.

Marge turned.

The four Seths, who had been uncreated the previous night, were standing near the door. Their backs were to her.

She realized that it was one of the Seths who had exclaimed and that what he had said was, 'Hey, who turned out the lights?'

Marge had an immediate and totally perceptive awareness of the implications of those words. Her mind leaped back to how Billy Bingham had explained the transition in time: no impression at all of time having passed.

This was the same.

Almost involuntarily she reached into the room to the light switch beside the door, and pressed it. As she did so, a fifth Seth walked forward from one corner of the room, where he had suddenly appeared. He seemed bewildered. Many minutes would go by before he was identified as the Seth of the gold Cadillac, somehow re-created without a bullet in his brain or a drop of lake water on his immaculate suit.

At the moment, Marge had only a fleeting glance for him, for a sixth Seth was suddenly standing on the far side of the conference table. The way he held himself, his quick alertness as he looked around the room, saw the other Seths – and then flicked his gaze to her with a relieved recognition . . .

Seeing him, and receiving so many familiar signals that identified Detective Seth Mitchell for her, she became emotionally unglued. Without any of her usual discretion, she let out a scream.

'Seth – my darling!'

Exactly how she got to him, and he to her, could undoubtedly be reasoned out from the fact that they met at the halfway point around the big table, and desisted in their embrace only when Marge grew aware that Edith Price was standing a few feet away, glancing around very timidly.

Close behind Edith, another Seth appeared. He was dressed in work clothes, and Marge surmised that he therefore must be the farmer.

Marge scarcely more than glanced at him. As she released herself from Detective Seth's embrace, she saw that Edith wore a different dress and had her hair done differently. Despite those swift noticings, it would take a while before Marge clearly, and the others in any way at all, understood that this was the Edith Price who had been murdered in New York by the worst Athtar.

Of the Athtars there was no sign.

And though the minutes fled by – and finally the bachelor Seth walked into the doorway – Edith Price, the crystal orientation, did not reappear.

The best Seth explained that he had gone for a walk, and in thinking over all that had happened, had decided that things would work out. He finished hopefully, 'And here, when I get back, you all are. Each of you is a living proof that Edith has found out something of what she can do. Or' – he paused – 'someone has, and is willing.'

'But what *can* she do?' One of the Seths asked that, bewildered.

The bachelor Seth smiled his friendly smile. 'I'm rather

fond of that young lady. In a way, a total reflection of our own age, yet she thought her way to some kind of best.' He broke off, glanced from one to another of the numerous duplicate faces, and said softly, 'You want to know what she can do. I didn't dare speak of it at the time, but, now, well . . . If God is dead, then what can replace Him?'

'Then you are God,' parroted Marge. She put her hand over her mouth, exclaimed, 'Oh, my lord – Edith!'

The best Seth said slowly, 'I wonder what the crystal and Edith are doing with that concept?'

Shalil was in deep trouble. The giant had continued to wait for the purely personal, restrictive thought that, he and his colleagues believed, would presently end any control Edith had of the crystal's future.

But the moments had gone by, and she had kept on uttering her idealistic words, so binding on him and his kind in relation to the people of the past. All the Seths and the Ediths re-created. A cooperative solution for the severe threat to the giant human beings of the ninety-third century – between the giants, on the one hand, and the Ediths and Seths on the other.

Edith in an outburst of imagination visualized a time corridor between the twentieth and ninety-third centuries. Thriftily she retained control of that corridor for her own group.

It was as she established that enormous connection, and control, that Shalil – desperate – had her uncreated. He re-created her, unconscious, on the contour rest-place. The huge scientists gathered around her comatose body and gloomily evaluated the extent of their defeat.

One grudged, 'But let's face it. We *can* live with what's happened so far.'

The problem was that they had made no headway. Edith still radiated total power; somehow, she continued to evoke from the crystal an energy output that no one had ever analyzed to be potential in it.

Shalil had a tremendous insight. 'Perhaps that's what we need to examine – our own limitations. Perhaps the real problem is that, in our scientific zeal, we have rejected the enigma.'

After he had spoken, there was a dead silence. He saw that they were shaken. The enigma was the forbidden – because unscientific – area of thought: the enigma that is the universe. Why does it exist? Where did it come from?

Since science began, scientists had concentrated on how things worked and what they did.

Never *why*. Never ever *how* in the meaning of *why*.

The thrall of shocked silence ended, as a giant laughed a harsh, determined laugh. 'I don't know anything about the enigma, and do not plan to,' he said, 'but as a scientist I do know my duty – *our* duty. We must bring this small female being to consciousness, inform her of the unqualified extent of her power, and see what she does with it.'

'B-but she may kill us all,' protested another. He added, almost plaintively, 'I've never been killed.'

'It will be an interesting experience for you,' replied the first man. 'Quite different from uncreation.'

Shalil interjected matter-of-factly, 'Edith is not a killer.' He broke off. Shrewdly, 'I think this is an excellent plan. I see it as being totally in our favor.'

They perceived what he meant, and accordingly sanctioned the awakening.

Lying there, Edith was brought awake.

After she had calmed herself – after she was told about her absolute ability, exactly as they had anticipated, she had a first automatic response to the possibility. For prolonged seconds a wild hope suffused her entire being. She wanted, most urgently, to undo the errors of judgment which had led her down the empty road of numerous boyfriends, none of whom took responsibility for her and her capacity to bear children. In a single overwhelm of earnest desire, all the years of frustration since college found their way first to her eyes in the form of quick tears, and then, when she could speak, to the words: 'Aside from what I've just told you' – she spoke the qualifying phrase, which retained for her control of access to the twentieth century without even noticing it – '*all* I really want is to be happily married.'

The giants perceived that the person she had in mind for a husband was the bachelor Seth Mitchell.

They accordingly commanded the crystal that the wish she had expressed be carried out forthwith in its exact and limited meaning. And then, safe and relieved, they stood marveling at the difficult concept of marriage.

In an era where everybody lived forever by a process of

crystal duplication, they would never, left to themselves, have been able to ask the right question to produce such an answer.

'It is just possible,' Shalil cautiously summed up, 'that the interaction between the unmanipulated human beings of the twentieth century and the manipulated of the ninety-third will actually bring about a lessening of the rigidities of both groups.'

His stern, black gaze dared a denial. After a long moment, he was surprised to realize that no one was offended. Indeed, a colleague murmured reflectively, 'If that should happen, we may even find out what the crystal is.'

But, of course, that was impossible.

The crystal was a space phenomenon. The energy flows in that space, and around it, and out of it, involved individual events, things, persons. But that was a subordinate function – like the motor center of a human brain that moves a muscle in the tip of the little finger.

The muscle should be movable. Unfortunate if it wouldn't, or couldn't. Yet truth is, if that muscle were permanently incapacitated, it would be unnoticed by the vast brain on the conscious level.

On the flow level of existence, the patterned *interactions* in and around and out of the crystal exceeded 10 to the 27,000th power times the number of atoms in the universe – enough interactions for all the life configurations of all the people who ever lived; perhaps enough even for all those who ever would live on Earth.

But, for the crystal, that was minor. As a pattern of time and life flows, it had suspended those flows during twenty-five years in the Harkdale museum. That didn't matter. That was almost-nothing. As a shape of space, its existence was continuous. As space, it occupied a location, and was related. Though it had no flows during the quarter-century, made no recordings, and had no memory and no doing, it nevertheless knew, it was, it had, and it could.

In finding it and tens of thousands of crystals like it, human beings of the eighth and ninth millennia made use of the interactions and flows; never of the space ability. They discovered the principal 'laws' – the how and the what – by which the crystals operated, and were determined to find out eventually the rules that would 'explain' certain unknowns in the wave behavior in and around and out of the crystals.

Someday all the interactions of all life and all time would be evenly divided among the crystals. It would then become its true form: one crystal shape, one space. It would then be complete, its intention achieved.

There was no hurry.

And so it waited. And, waiting, fulfilled other goals than its own, minor, unimportant goals involving flows and interactions; reflecting the illusions of motion: events, things, persons, involving nothing, really. . . .

In consequence, in Harkdale today there is a one-story building of unusual design. The building stands on the exact spot were Billy Bingham one disappeared, on the shore overlooking Lake Naragang. It is a solidly built structure and has a certain beauty. On a gold plaque beside the ornate front door are the words:

CRYSTAL, INC.
Owned and Managed by
SETH MITCHELLS AND EDITH PRICES
Not Open to the Public

Resort visitors who stop to look at the sign are often puzzled by the plural names. And long-time residents, when asked, offer the impression that Crystal, Inc., actually deals in the numerous crystals to be found in the rock formations in and around the hills and lake.

There is a large, pretty house with spacious grounds located near the building. In this house dwell Seth and Edith Mitchell.

To the puzzlement of their neighbors, Mr and Mrs Seth Mitchell (née Edith Price) started their married life by legally adopting a thirteen-year-old boy whom they called Billy Bingham Mitchell.

All The Loving Androids

A. E. VAN VOGT

The police came in answer to the android's emergency call, and an ambulance bore away the unconscious body of Anita Copeland, who had taken an overdose of a sleeping potion.

Police Officer A. Sutter noted in his report that this android – who had telephoned for help – seemed to be unusually human in his mannerisms and conditioning. 'Even the slight forward tilt,' he wrote, 'which is the main recognizable characteristic of the mass-produced androids, appears to have been rectified in this model, suggesting costly custom design. I do not recall ever having been informed that such masterful androids were being manufactured.'

After he and his companion had the story of what had happened, they were briefly nonplussed. 'Well-l-l,' said Officer J. Black doubtfully, while Sutter wrote furiously, 'it doesn't sound illegal, but it sure was a dirty trick to turn his wife over to an android image of himself without her knowing it.'

It was Sutter who addressed the android. 'Does she have any relatives?'

'A brother,' was the reply. 'But he won't be much help. He thinks his sister is a nut.'

'But you do have information about him?' Officer Sutter persisted.

'Yes. His name is Dan Thaler. He's a physicist in government employ.'

He had the address and phone number, and so Officer Black put through a call, which fortunately connected at once.

Dan, as he entered his sister's living room, saw waiting for him two police officers and his brother-in-law, Peter Copeland.

At least, it seemed to be his brother-in-law until Dan said, 'Hello, Peter.'

Peter bowed and smiled a faint, cynical smile, but said nothing.

One of the officers came forward and addressed Peter sternly. 'You realize that you have just given the impression that you are in fact Peter Copeland?'

'I am Peter II,' was the calm reply. 'I am programmed to act as if I am Peter I. I cannot cancel that out of myself.'

Utter surprise!

His first real clue.

Dan stood very still, trying not to give away what a fantastic piece of good luck this was for him.

For more than a year he had been on a secret assignment, his task to find out exactly what was going on among the androids.

Something was – the government knew that. But what?

Neither he nor his superiors had had any suspicion that such perfect androids existed.

Ordinary androids in their tens of millions had face, body, limbs, artificial flesh, skin that was in appearance undistinguishable from that of human beings. But they had a way of standing, walking, turning, that everybody had learned to recognize.

This android did not have such identifying characteristics.

Instants after he realized the astonishing reality of what was here, Dan had a labeling thought: superandroid!

He presumed, of course, that this one *was* an android and therefore underneath all the outward paraphernalia of humanness was a basic mechanical-electronic structure.

'What's all this about?' he said as he arrived at that point in his reaction.

When he had heard the details of what had happened to his sister, Dan's somewhat pale face became spotted with angry color. His lean body stiffened. And his voice went way up.

'Does anybody know where this so-and-so is? I'm going to beat his brains out.'

The android, who had been standing off to one side, came courteously forward. 'You are referring to Anita's husband, Peter – where is he?' He drew a billfold from his pocket and produced a card. 'My orders from Peter are to not reveal this address, but naturally police can preempt such a programming.'

He handed the card to Officer Sutter. Dan Thaler attempted to snatch it, but the policeman held it away from him.

'Not in your state of mind, Mr Thaler,' he said judicially.

Dan had actually been thinking rapidly while he acted out the role of indignant brother. What decided him finally on a course of action was the presence of the police. He took down the names of both officers and secured their identification numbers with the intention of using his influence to have one of them forced to be his companion for the next few days.

With the data safe in his pocket, Dan turned to the android, said, 'Since I am a responsible relative, and you are a valuable property, I think you should be stored until all this is settled.'

The duplicate Peter bowed politely. 'My box is in the basement,' he said. 'Shall I accompany you down there?'

Dan took the precaution of having Officer A. Sutter go along. A few minutes later, the two men stood by as the android fumbled with a remote-control device, clicked it, and sank back into the coffinlike box.

Officer A. Sutter helped Dan lower the lid. Whereupon the policeman went upstairs. Dan drew a tiny instrument from an assortment he carried and studied the dials on it.

The little meters indicated that the superandroid was not turned off at all but was lying quietly in his case, waiting.

Smiling grimly, Dan went up to the main floor, accompanied the officers outside, and locked the door. He walked with them to their combo-cruiser, watched them take off, then went to his own combo and zoomed up into the night sky – but came down again, this time landing on the street a hundred yards away.

An hour went by, and then the door opened and the Peter android came out. Dan identified the humanlike figure as an electronic unit on his highly sensitive instrument panel – and, aiming carefully, shot the creature with a high-powered energy gun.

His combo glided toward the still body at high speed, and stopped. Swiftly Dan leaped out, dragged the body into the combo, and took off.

In terms of communication, he was many places the balance of that night. But as a person he spent the long darkness in his combo-air-ground unit outside the hospital to which his sister had been transported for emergency treatment. About noon the next day, when he made his nth inquiry, the receptionist sighed, dialed a number, and presently pointed to a phone on the desk.

'Pick that up. Her psychiatrist will talk to you.'

Dan did so. A man's voice said, 'At Anita's request, I have agreed to bar all visitors for the time being.'

'I'm her brother.'

'She specifically doesn't want to see any relatives.'

Since he was her only relative, other than her husband, somewhere inside Dan Thaler's head a tiny spot of brotherly rage, connected since babyhood to his sister by emotional circuitry, expanded in size. Fortunately, the brain-nerve complex involved had long-suffering inhibiting mechanisms associated with it. And so Dan was presently able to remind the apoplectic spot in his brain that Anita was probably quite sick and needed consideration.

He said aloud, 'When do you think – ?'

'She said she'll call you – '

Policeman A. Sutter was considerably exhilarated that same afternoon when he was told by Inspector Ingrath, 'Uh, stay on this case, Constable, until, uh, this matter of the brother's threats is resolved.' Ingrath went on, 'Make a point of seeing this rat, uh, Peter Copeland, and warn him of his possible danger from his brother-in-law.'

What Sutter did was phone the private number he had been given, and he was put through to somewhere; and a man's voice said, 'Yes, officer, this is Peter Copeland.'

After Sutter had told his story, the voice said, 'I think the best solution would be for me to have Dan come and hear my side of this matter and for you to be present; so why don't you bring him over, Officer?'

The two men – Dan Thaler and Officer A. Sutter – flew to the Copeland factory together, and were at once ushered into the inner sanctum.

'I found myself,' wrote Sutter later, 'in the presence of a man of about five-feet-ten who was, naturally, of very familiar appearance to me, since he was an exact duplicate of the android I had seen the night before in Anita Copeland's home.'

Officer Sutter drew a chair off to one side and, as he wrote it, 'prepared to act as a mediator'.

Peter Copeland broke the silence with what was clearly

intended to be an appeasing statement, 'I'm very glad you came, Dan. I realize I owe you an explanation.'

Peter continued, 'It's a little difficult to talk to a brother about his sister, because it is unlikely that he'll ever realize how unreasonable a woman can be.'

Dan Thaler said grimly, 'If a man and woman don't get along, they should get divorced.'

Peter Copeland laughed curtly. 'Are you kidding?' he said.

The verbal picture he now drew of Anita – as Sutter recorded it – 'was of a hysterical woman who figuratively held a gun to her heard and threatened to fire it at the slightest indication that her husband would not do exactly as she required.'

Some of the statements which Sutter noted down verbatim were: 'She insisted on possessing me body and soul. She demanded the shadow as well as the substance. She phoned me at the office a dozen times a day. It seemed as if I had barely time to think before there she was again. One day, when her call interrupted an important conference for the third time, I realized I had to do something. At first I merely had in mind having an android that would answer the phone for me when she called. The rest – letting the android play my part at home also – came later.'

'The rest,' Dan said, 'is absolutely unforgivable.'

'Hear me out –'

Exactly when the change had taken place, Anita had no recollection afterward.

Somehow, life became – normal.

She would find herself starting to fret with Peter. On occasion she actually spoke irritably. And then a realization would come that he had not resisted her, as she had expected he would; had not asserted any thought of his own; not objected to her plan; was willing.

'Anything your little heart desires,' he would say lightly.

One day she flared at that. 'You say those words as if you're speaking to a child!' she yelled.

'So,' said Peter Copeland to Dan Thaler, 'when the android reported that remark – if you can call a shriek that – to me, I accepted it as a challenge. That's when I decided I would become infinitely flexible and change the programming of the robot to conform to her desires. It became a matter of mild interest to me to discover how much a neurotic woman

118

required of her husband – and of course I knew by this time that I had the worst neurotic of all time and space on my hands.'

He paused. His face worked; he seemed to be fighting grief. He mumbled, 'How could a woman like that have happened to a good guy like me!'

Abruptly he braced himself, continued. 'To solve this particular problem – of Peter II just using one now-suspect sentence – I recalled a line I had seen somewhere in a story, or heard in a play: "Your slightest wish is my command". Later I added three more sentences, leaving it to my android to decide which one fitted the occasion. The three sentences were: "You always think of interesting things to do"; "That's what we'll do"; "I'm very happy to go along with that". What astonished me, as I proceeded with my conformance plan, was that not once did it seem to cross her mind that I never expressed a wish, myself. She seemed to take it completely for granted that what she liked I liked.'

Peter I went on in an amazed tone, 'If I were to tell you all the things that happened during this period, you wouldn't believe me. She began to give me errands to do during the daytime; it took the android all day just to carry out these instructions. But – get this! – she continued her twelve calls to the office, and there I was answering the phone again. I ordered another android duplicate.'

Officer wrote in his notebook: 'At this point Mr Copeland rose to his feet, went to a door behind his desk, opened it, and said, 'Peter III, will you come out here?' Whereupon his exact duplicate walked out, bowed with a faint, mocking smile on his face, and said, 'At your service, gentlemen.'

Peter I addressed the android: 'Will you tell Mr Thaler and Mr Sutter what your duties were?'

'For the most part,' was the reply, 'I simply sat in the adjoining room and answered the phone to Mrs Copeland.'

'Will you give an estimate of how long on average you were kept on the phone?'

'Between seven and seven and a half hours each day.'

'What is our work day? Office hours, I mean?'

'Including time out for lunch, seven and a half hours.'

'During this time, where was Peter II?'

'He was out shopping for Mrs Copeland.'

'Where was I?'

'Here at this desk working, except for those occasions when – '

'Never mind those occasions!' said Peter I hastily.

'Very well, sir,' said Peter II with a meaningful smile.

Dan Thaler interjected stridently, 'I think that was a very important slip. Now, I'm beginning to see this whole picture. There's another woman.'

Peter I sighed. 'All right, so it came out. But that didn't happen until much later. I swear it.'

It was the moment Dan Thaler had been waiting for; what he believed might be the psychologically locked mental door in Peter could probably be opened by the exact right emotion.

He stood up and said in a venomous tone, 'I don't want to listen to any more of this rat talk.'

Peter said, 'For heaven's sake, Dan, be reasonable. You're a scientist. Surely I've presented a logical case.'

Dan hissed, 'Where did you get these special androids? I've seen people with one – but you've got two!'

He saw that Peter's face had on it a sheepish smile.

'Each one of these,' said Peter, 'cost me eighteen thousand dollars. Boy, I had to be sincere. I tell you, Dan, it was a real problem.'

'But who sells them?'

'Oh, some outfit. An android salesman comes to your office. You think it's a human being until he reveals the truth. I could hardly believe it at first.'

'But how do they know you're in the market? Nobody's ever come to sell me one.'

'Oh!' Peter was silent, frowning. 'Well, I really can't answer that. There he was one morning, and did I ever welcome him. I think he did say something about it being illegal. I suppose you being a government physicist puts you off bounds for him.'

'But what about the second one?' Dan asked. 'Did the salesman just drop by?'

'As a matter of fact, yes. Checking, he said.'

'And he arrived when you were contemplating buying another one?'

'That's right.'

'Had you let some hint drop?'

'Don't be a nut. To whom?'

Abruptly Dan realized that that was Peter's full information.

'Never mind all this!' he snapped. 'Don't think you can get around my feelings by changing the subject.'

'But it was you who changed it!' Peter protested.

Dan snarled, 'I'm going to talk to my sister. That rotten hide of yours is safe until then.'

With that, he stalked out of the room, feeling pleased with his handling of the key questions.

Officer Sutter subsequently added to his account: 'I remained behind and discussed with Peter the possible danger to him of these threats. He would not take them seriously, and he also refused to comment on the other woman in his life, saying only that he didn't love her and that therefore she didn't count.'

During the two days that Dan waited for word from or about his sister, he dismantled and studied the 'dead' android, then put it back together again and replaced it in the box in Peter's house.

Before leaving, he concealed a camera overlooking the box and set to operate automatically if someone came into its range.

On the morning of the third day, he was told that his sister had been discharged. Outraged, Dan demanded to be put in touch with Anita's psychiatrist.

'Just a moment,' said the woman's voice. A pause. Finally, 'I'm sorry. Dr Schneiter does not feel that a communication with you would serve any useful purpose.'

'Schneiter-Schweiter!' snarled Dan. 'You tell Dr Schneiter that I'm coming up there for a quart of his blood for letting that girl out on the street without consulting me.'

He smashed the receiver down on the phone.

Immediately after this bit of acting, he called Officer Sutter, and was put through to that individual, who, on the phone screen, was revealed as being in his police cruiser somewhere over the city.

Dan said, 'Am I right in thinking that everybody has to show a change of address immediately, and that when an apartment or room is leased anywhere in the zone the name of the new occupant is recorded in a police computer? And if so, can you get it for me?'

It was a purely rhetorical question. Dan was perfectly aware that such a record system existed, and – given time – he could undoubtedly get the information through his own agency. But he preferred to appear unofficial. Anita was the hottest lead he'd had so far on this assignment.

As he had expected, Sutter admitted that the system existed, and that under the circumstances he could probably secure the information, given a little time.

During the twenty-four hours that passed before Inspector Ingrath bent his long-necked head over a desk and signed the address release authorization for Sutter, Dan Thaler sought his sister in department stores and other haunts of hers – in vain. And when he finally had the address, she was not there. The room receptionist at the building said, 'She's seldom in – there's a bar down the street that I think she goes to.' She had a round face, on which was shown her disapproval.

Anita was nervously sipping at a tall green drink when Dan sank onto the stool beside her. At first she did not see him, and when she finally became aware that someone had taken the adjoining seat, she said without glancing around, 'Did you do that on purpose – sit next to me?'

Her voice was tense; she had a flushed look; she was visibly under a strain and probably had drunk too much. And she did not seem to realize who it was she was talking to.

Dan Thaler nodded; he could not trust himself to speak. All in a flash, his acceptance of what Peter had said – for he had believed Peter – yielded to his first real emotional pity for his sister.

Still without looking at him, Anita said, 'Did you come over to pick me up? You want a woman? All right – any time you're ready.'

Dan gasped, '*Anita!*'

At that she turned and looked at him. Her eyes widened. Then she flung her arms around him.

'Oh, my God, Dan!' she sobbed. 'I needed you so. Where have you been?'

After a little, Dan gently disengaged himself. Her words had unfortunately reminded him of one of Peter's complaints: that in the course of a sentence or two Anita always turned blame away from herself.

He sat there, remembering her refusal to see him at the hospital, her departure from the hospital without notifying him, her disappearance, his subsequent attempts to find her – and now these words making *him* totally responsible for *his* failure to comfort her, when, as a matter of fact, she had behaved like a maniac throughout.

There was a time – before Peter's story – when he might not have considered the significance of what she had done so swiftly; would simply have tucked it away with the scores of other times when she had somehow irritated or enraged him.

Now he felt a heated sensation rising up from some choleric depth. But, remembering, he restrained himself – remembering that Anita, his only sister, had proved herself an easy pickup. For any man. Absolutely any.

He recalled how she hadn't even glanced at him, had herself made all the moves; had shown no interest in who the man was or what he looked like.

The bloodcurdling recollection of her manner and approach had an abrupt, subduing effect on him.

'Anita, you need help.'

'I'll be all right.'

'Don't be a stupe!' he said with a brother's privileged rudeness. 'You ought to see a psychiatrist.'

'I've already seen one,' said Anita. 'Dr Schneiter. He's a cute little man. He thinks Peter is a rat, too.'

The picture her words evoked of the doctor confirmed Dan's previous low opinion. By agreeing with her, the psychiatrist had barred her from the need to question her own madness.

So it was up to him. So he would have to drum some sense into her. So be it.

Sitting there, he told her Peter's complaints. He was aware of her blue eyes staring at him. When he had finished, tears suddenly misted the blue: her eyes took on a dark, mottled look.

She said with a sob, 'So you're on his side? You've turned against me, too.'

Dan was impatiently convinced that she had not heard most of what he had said.

'Look,' he argued, 'let's just take one item of Peter's complaint: is it true that you phoned him twelve or more times a day at his office?'

'I never phoned him at all.' Her tone was angry. The tears had dried, and her eyes flashed with blue sparks. 'I hate him. Why would I phone a man I hate?'

'You didn't hate him then,' Dan pointed out.

'I've always hated him. I never liked him.'

Dan looked into her eyes. They were sky blue again, but staring. He thought: There's nobody home.

He remembered an android at college physics class that had been deliberately damaged. It's basic stability gone, it began to answer questions with partially associated answers only. Anita's response resembled *that*.

Dan had half-turned away as he had these disturbing thoughts. Before he could face her again, or deduce her intention, she was gone. He saw her hurrying among the tables. Then she was at the table of a man who had come in moments before; Dan recalled observing his entrance with an idle glance.

As he watched in dismay, Anita tried to pick up the man.

But the man shook his head. She argued with him and tried to sit in his lap. As he continued to resist, abruptly she left him, made a wide turn around the far end of the room, and a moment later settled back beside Dan.

And, as if the interlude had not occurred, said, 'There's another woman, isn't there?'

Since Dan felt no obligation to Peter, he answered without thinking, 'Yes.'

'I thought so,' she said. A vindictive look came into her face. 'So *that's* it.'

'Just a minute,' said Dan in a groping tone.

He made a vague gesture with his hand. And then he sat there, stunned. He thought: The truth is, I believe Peter, that the woman came later. What struck him was that now the whole thing would be twisted even more in Anita's mind.

'Hey, wait a minute,' he said hoarsely. 'That isn't it. That isn't it at all.'

He saw that she was not listening. The vindictive look was still on her face.

He said, 'What about these men you've been picking up?'

'Oh, that!' she said. A shrug of her slender shoulder dismissed his question. She added, 'What a woman does, doesn't count. Women are just objects.'

The vindictive look had complete possession of her face as she uttered these words.

Dan gulped, and decided that this was the moment for the real questions he wanted to ask.

'Maybe we can find out who this woman is,' he said. 'Listen, when you were with that android who played Peter – '

'I don't want to talk about it!'

' – Did you ever go with him anyplace that struck you as unusual?'

The question seemed to penetrate. 'Just once,' said Anita. 'It was the street with those queer places.'

'What queer places?' said Dan, who suspected that that was key information and that his idiot sister was going to spoil things by not remembering.

'You know!' said Anita, waving vaguely. 'I was there once before to a meeting.'

'With whom? What kind of a meeting?'

'Ohhh!' she said, and yawned.

Whereupon she put her arms on the bar, lowered her head onto them, and went to sleep.

The barkeeper came over. ''You'll have to get her out of here,' he said. 'We can't have anybody as drunk as her in here.'

Dan said, 'Give me a hand.'

The man promptly helped him carry her into a seat in the cabin of his combo-cruiser. Dan landed on the roof of her apartment building and took her down to her room on a dolly that he had.

Then, thoughtful, he departed.

At three o'clock in the morning, Dan's phone rang.

He grabbed it, and after a little made out from what the man was saying that Anita was being held at the police station.

'For what?' he yelled into the mouthpiece.

'For trying to destroy an android with a hammer.'

'I'll be over in a few minutes!' Dan yelled.

And he was.

Anita and the handsome duplicate android of Peter were

brought into the anteroom where Dan waited. It took a little while to get the story.

It seemed the android had turned Anita in for trying to damage someone else's property: himself.

The android, who identified himself as Peter II, said with dignity, 'I was lying in my box and I felt this blow on my shoulder padding, I opened my eyes, and there was Anita with a hammer raised for a second blow. Naturally, I removed the destructive instrument from her hand and called the police at once.'

Quietly Dan bailed her out and took her off to his combo. As he headed, groundside, for the apartment building where she had her room, he was aware of Anita sprawled beside him, head back, eyes closed. Her body seemed limp and helpless; her hair and clothes were disheveled. It seemed useless to upbraid her in her present state.

'What happened?' he asked finally, glumly. 'What was all that about?'

After what must have been a minute, a tired voice answered him. 'I followed him,' she said.

'Who?'

'Peter, of course.'

It still made no sense.

'Do you know who he's living with?' Anita asked.

Dan's mind grappled now with a developing feeling that the conversation was getting away from him. 'Why would you follow an android?' he asked peevishly. 'A robot under present law cannot be guilty of a crime, and it doesn't matter who it lives with.'

Silence greeted his words. Dan took his eyes off the street to glance at her. He nearly went off the road at what he saw.

Her eyes were open. They were glaring at him with a blue rage. 'Still my stupid little brother,' she hissed. 'I'm talking about Peter. Who else?'

Her hand came up and slapped him in the face. It was like childhood days. Dan swung about and grabbed at her neck with both hands, and was choking her – when a grinding sound snapped him out of his passion.

He caught at the wheel. But it was unnecessary.

The combo's automatic control mechanism had brought the machine to a halt.

The bright, deserted street was almost like day around them, as brother and sister sat there glaring at each other.

'All right, who is he living with?' Dan shouted.

'Me. An android that looks like me.'

The anger went out of Dan. He recalled what Sutter had told him, that Peter had said that he didn't love the woman he was living with. And, of course, that was now obviously true.

Dan was patient. 'Now, look, Anita. You can't be jealous of an android.'

She sat sullen, staring past him; the way the light fell on her eyes, they seemed slate blue.

'An android,' said Dan, 'is – well' – he groped – 'it's an android, that's all.'

Those perfect lips parted and spoke: 'Then why does she have to resemble me? That's degrading.'

For Dan, hers was an unhappy choice of words. He remembered her behavior at the bar.

'But just a minute,' he said. 'Why take a hammer to Peter II because Peter I is living with Anita II?'

'Oh, you men!' said Anita. 'Take me home.'

Her brother did so, silently.

Officer A. Sutter, while cruising on duty the following morning, wrote in his daybook: 'Presumably, during the night, Peter I, II, and III Copeland, Peter I's estranged wife, Anita Copeland, and his brother-in-law, Dan Thaler, continued their various reactions to each other. But I have no additional reports. It is a beautiful day this 1/23/2287.'

As Sutter finished his account, he grew aware that Inspector Ingrath's face was forming on the screen in front of him. Seeing the man, Sutter wrote mentally, 'On a small screen, he looks almost human.'

'Uh, Sutter.'

'Yes, sir.'

'The Copeland matter.'

'Yes, Inspector.'

'I have two reports, uh, before me. The first states that Anita Copeland was in police custody during the night for attempting to, uh, destroy an android – with a hammer.'

Officer Sutter felt a strange guilt, as if he should have anticipated and prevented such an attack. He said, 'Has the, uh, brother been informed, Inspector?'

Later he wrote: 'He'll have me, uh, communicating that way, uh, soon.'

At the moment, Ingrath said, 'Yes, uh, he obtained her release during the night. However, I have a feeling that you should contact Mr Thaler now that another interview with the real Peter Copeland is indicated.'

'Very well, sir. Now, what is the second report?'

'It says here that Anita Copeland is again in custody.'

'Uh – ' said Officer Sutter. 'You mean, again.'

'Yes, uh!'

'What is the charge?'

'Attacking an android with a hammer.'

Officer Sutter's face must have shown bewilderment, because Inspector Ingrath said hastily, 'I think you and Mr Thaler should straighten out this confusion, because I am not clear as to whether it's the same android or another. Will you, uh, attend to the matter?'

'Of course, sir.'

As Sutter and Dan Thaler entered the police waiting room, Dan saw Anita sitting in a chair in a corner.

He hurried over to her. 'You nut!' he said rudely. 'What's the idea this time?'

The blue eyes gazed up at him, puzzled. 'Do you know me, sir?'

Dan felt a chill.

'I – I – Anita, don't be an idiot!' he stuttered.

Officer Sutter touched his arm. He had been studying a report. 'Just a moment, Mr Thaler. I think you've jumped to a false conclusion.'

'Eh?'

Sutter addressed Anita. 'Will you describe the attack?'

The seated woman said, 'Shall I stand up?'

'No, no.'

'Very well. Shortly after Peter left for work this morning, the doorbell rang. When I answered it, this woman with the hammer, in whose image I have apparently been constructed, rushed in and attacked me. Naturally, I took the instrument away from her and called the police.'

Dan Thaler was staring at the perfect duplicate of his sister. 'You – you're the other woman!'

He turned to Sutter, 'Where's my sister?'

Sutter indicated the paper he held. 'According to this, she's in custody.'

Dan's eyes lighted hopefully. 'Look, Officer,' he said, 'This is the one bright feature. This could well be the frame in which we can solve the entire problem.'

'How do you mean?'

'Before I get Anita I released, why don't we go see Peter I.'

Peter I was in his office, and he listened with a faraway expression on his face. Finally he said, 'I can guess what is now going on in that woman's noodle. And she's all wrong. The duplication of her body in Anita II doesn't mean that I am constantly longing for her. No person in his right mind would involve himself with Anita I. She is completely impossible. You must make that absolutely clear to her. Impossible.'

Dan persisted, and as Sutter reported it, stated that 'I must have your explanation.'

Peter Copeland spread his hands in a dismissing gesture.

'It's very simple,' he said quietly. 'Physically, I was always attracted to Anita. So I just had an android made to look like her, but otherwise to act like a normal woman should.'

His eyes grew dreamy.

'There she is, waiting for me when I get home. Anita II always has my slippers and robe laid out. Dinner is cooking and is served just right at exactly the proper time without histrionics. After dinner, I have brandy, while she washes the dishes without argument. If I want to read or watch TV, I do. And if presently I realize that she's in the bedroom, and I retire, there's still no argument. Now, it happens that I'm a real man with strong needs, and so if I wake up three times during the night, do I get the story about being tired or sleepy? Not at all.' His expression hardened. 'Why should a woman be tired? If she would have a little consideration for her husband, she would naturally conserve her energies during the day instead of expending them on useless activities. All I ever wanted is just a normal wife behaving in a normal fashion. That's the truth, Dan.'

He sighed, and reaching into his pocket, drew out a key ring. He removed a key from it and handed it to Dan.

'I wish you'd check on Peter II. I'm kind of worried. Did he go back to his box after he was released last night?'

'Why don't you check it yourself?' asked Dan, merely curious.

9

Peter shook his head. 'I'm staying away from there. I have a feeling if Anita were to pot me with her .38 – yes, she's got one – it would be considered justifiable homicide.'

Dan took the key; and Sutter and he cruised over and found the android box empty.

Eagerly, Dan examined his camera. The film had of course developed itself. As he ran it over the spool and peered at it through an opening he saw on the film a small man enter the shot from the direction of the stairway and open the case containing Peter II. There was Peter, much as Dan had left him.

The little man reached down, turned Peter II on, and said, 'What happened to you? You were to report.'

Peter II climbed with dignity out of the box and said, 'Dr Schneiter, I have no programming to that effect.'

The little man stared at him with a frown; then, thoughtfully: 'Tell me what's happened to you since that first night.'

Peter II described the arrival of the police and of Anita's brother, and of the brother consigning him to storage. His only memory after that was of Anita hitting him with a hammer and of his turning her over to the police.

The little man remained thoughtful. 'Theoretically, that hammer blow could have damaged your programming, but that wouldn't explain your failure to leave here on the night you revealed who you were and gave her that sleeping potion. So I'd better check you.'

He proceeded to do so, but presently turned the android on again; now the psychiatrist was visibly shaken.

'Whoever tampered with you,' he said, 'was an expert. I've accordingly programmed you to kill that woman in some secret way, and I'll do the same for Peter III.'

'Kill Anita?'

'Yes. I suspected we were in danger when she broke out of all that conditioning and escaped from the hospital. I still can't figure that, but the simplest solution is' – he shrugged – 'death.'

He broke off. 'You'd better leave here right after I depart.'

With that, he turned and walked out of the camera's eye. A minute later, Peter II followed him.

Dan looked up presently from the film and said to Officer Sutter, 'At the time, it didn't occur to me to ask you, but who ordered the ambul-air that took my sister to the hospital? Did you?'

'No, the android had already phoned for it. Why?'

Dan did not reply at once. In his mind a lot of things were falling into place.

The dozen men in the dark room watched silently as the film unrolled. After the lights went on, everyone waited; all eyes, including Dan's, fixed on the thoughtful countenance of a stern-looking man who appeared to be in his mid-forties. His name was Edward Jarris, and he was the assistant chief of National Security.

This individual presently straightened in his chair and shook his head.

'We can't get away with it,' he said with finality. He turned to Dan. 'A very good effort,' he said, 'but that film could too easily have been doctored; it wouldn't stand in a court.'

Dan waited. He had attended similar meetings in the past where evidence was reasoned to nothing by a process of legal logic.

The great man addressed him again: 'Who else has actually seen one of these super – as you call them – androids?'

Dan parted his lips to identify officers Sutter and Black, and Peter and Anita.

But something in the other's tone of voice stopped that instant answer. He said, after a moment, courteously, 'Why don't I prepare a report for you, sir, listing such details?'

'Yes, of course,' was the testy reply. 'That's the proper method.'

Whereupon Assistant Chief of National Security Jarris stood up and strode from the room without a backward glance.

Dan's immediate superior came over and shook his hand admiringly. 'I think you made a big impression,' he said. 'Jarris isn't usually interested in such details.'

Dan thanked him, hurried to the projection room to secure his film, and departed. Once outside, he ran most of the way to his combo, and did not feel safe till he was in the air again.

But he had been up only a minute when there was a call from his boss. 'Hey, Dan, Mr Jarris just asked for that film, and the projectionist said you took it.'

Dan pretended to be surprised. 'I need it to prepare my

report,' he said. 'I'll submit it at that time – tomorrow.'

'All right,' was the cheerful, unsuspicious reply, 'I'll relay that.'

Shuddering, Dan broke the connection. Then he shot over to his bank, placed the film in his personal deposit box, and got into the air again. He now contacted Officer Sutter.

'I'm going over to the Center Hospital. Tail me.'

'Going to talk to Schneiter?'

'Yes.'

'Do you think these people know about me?' asked Sutter.

'Only my immediate boss knows,' said Dan. 'Such details have not been of interest to anyone else' – he paused – 'until now.'

It was a short time later. As Dr Schneiter emerged from his office, Dan slipped into step beside him, pushed a gun into him in the direction of his right kidney, and said, 'I'm Anita's brother. I'm going to have an interview with you if it's the last thing you ever do.'

And so, presently, they were in the psychiatrist's office, and Dan at the beginning pretended he was merely a brother who was concerned about a mentally ill sister.

'Couldn't you have held her?' he asked peevishly. 'Isn't there some law governing would-be suicides?'

The psychiatrist shook his head. His initial tension was gone, and he was smiling genially. 'It seems reasonable that she should make the attempt to kill herself in those first few minutes after discovering what had happened.' He eyed Dan brightly. 'Right? But no further suicide attempt – right?'

And that, with added details, was the level of voluntary reply Dan evoked from Dr Schneiter.

So a woman was promiscuous? Statistically, she would presently become fixated again on one man, and the promiscuity would end. Dan was disturbed by it? An infantile reaction. Grow up.

Objective, cool, amused – that was the outward appearance of the man who was undoubtedly a leading human figure in the secret android rebellion.

Dan had been curious. He had wanted to look over the psychiatrist before precipitating the crisis.

That he had now done.

And so –

He raised his gun. 'Doctor,' he said, 'I don't want to listen any longer to your phony talk. You have fifteen seconds to make your first statement of truth.'

There was a long pause. The face in front of him grew pale, but the eyes remained bright and watchful. Finally Dr Schneiter spread his hands with deceptive mildness.

'What do you want to know?'

'Why did you have my sister brought here? And I don't want any denials. Start talking.'

This time the pause was briefer. 'In spite of all her conditioning, she was going out of our control. I wanted to find out why.'

'What conditioning did she have?'

'The three stages. Complete android simulation.'

'In what way was she out of control?'

'We merely wanted to use her – as we have other women – to force her husband to buy an expensive android. That's how we get funds. But, somehow, Anita got out of control and became a threat.'

'A threat – how?'

Since she was out of control, we couldn't be sure of her.'

'Did she know she was supposed to simulate an android and respond only to programming?'

'Normally they know it only when it's being done, but the memory fades; but we began to believe that she did know. Whether she did or not, she resisted it, and we couldn't take a chance with her.'

'Did you find out why?'

'No, she got out of the hospital before I could determine the problem. I have a theory – ' His gaze questioned Dan.

Dan said, 'Yes, tell me.'

' – The only comparison I can think of,' said Dr Schneiter, 'is the "running-amok" situation which we had in most recent historical times in Asia, but prior to that it occurred among slaves and other abused persons.'

'Yes?' said Dan.

'It suggests to me,' continued the doctor, 'that a certain kind of rebel personality should not be subjected to android simulation. They must be won over on the basis of the ideal.'

Dan looked straight into those glittering eyes. 'What ideal?' he asked, softly.

'I'm a supporter of GALS,' said Dr Schneiter in a quiet

voice, as if that explained everything.

He took a deep breath and said earnestly: 'You're in a battle you can't win. Almost everybody has some use for an android – as a perfect servant, to keep from being lonely, as a protector – there's almost no limit. Of course, at present they're still purchased like dogs or objects, but the next step will be that you can buy one on a basis that he must be freed after you have got some equivalent of your money back in terms of service.'

He shrugged. 'I hope you realize you're not going to escape from this building with what I've told you.'

'Jarris called you?'

'Yes,' said Schneiter simply.

Dan said, 'I can't believe you've had time to take precautions.'

Schneiter said, 'This hospital, except for the doctors, is operated by androids. The nurses, the maintenance people – ' He broke off. 'It was when I gradually realized how tireless, uncomplaining, undeviating, and, oh, all good things, the androids were that I became a complete supporter of their civil rights.'

Dan said, 'Let me tell you my strengths. I have the film.'

'That's your greatest strength. Where is it?'

'If anything happens to me,' said Dan, 'people who are against GALS will get it.'

'What are your weaknesses?' asked the inexorable, calm voice.

'Undoubtedly, Jarris is a secret GALS supporter, so that means I'll be taken off the case. Knowing that, I should tell you that I'm really here on a personal matter and willing to bargain. My sister – '

'Yes,' said Dr Schneiter softly. 'What about your sister?'

'I want androids Peter II and III reprogrammed not to kill her.'

'It shall be done,' said the psychiatrist.

Dan stared into those bright eyes and said, 'Let me put it like this: *You* figure out how to convince me that you mean that – and that'll be the end of the matter. I'll get in touch with you within twenty-four hours. And now, just so you *don't* act against me in the next few minutes – '

He fired three times into the small body in front of him.

Since his gun was a gas injector unit constructed to

134

resemble a bullet-firing automatic, the shots consisted of anesthetic gas, which induced unconsciousness. The psychiatrist slumped in his chair.

Dan walked out of the same private entrance, where he had originally caught Dr Schneiter, and headed rapidly down the corridor to the elevators.

One of the two men who entered the elevator with Dan was first at the controls. This individual turned and asked Dan politely, 'Which floor, sir?'

Fingering the gun in his pocket, Dan told him.

He was alert to danger, and so he had a minimum of thoughts.

But a simple awareness underlay them.

It was an accident that he, the principal government agent investigating the android conspiracy, had proved to be the brother of someone being manipulated. And an even bigger accident that that someone was Anita.

But as a result, he, an expert, had seen a superandroid.

These supers were, for the most of their behavior, normally programmed; thus Peter II and the others lived in the human society, their identities concealed for one reason or another by their owners.

The conspiracy would continue to develop in the same substantially unnoticed fashion only if his film were destroyed, and a few people killed or disposed of.

Among the people who would have to be dealt with were the two police officers, Black and Sutter – at least, Sutter – plus Anita, all the security people who had seen the film, and of course, Dan Thaler.

His analysis ended as he grew aware that the elevator had stopped and that the door was opening.

Dan Thaler made a move to step out, but stopped when he saw that a combo-cruiser was in the act of pulling up opposite the elevator, so close that it barred his way. At that moment the two men inside the elevator stepped to either side of him and grabbed him with an inhuman speed of movement.

'Hey!' said Dan Thaler.

He was lifted toward the combo, the door of which slid open. The two men hoisted him effortlessly inside and climbed in with him.

The door slid shut behind them.

Belatedly, as he felt the combo-cruiser begin its forward

135

glide, and when it was already far too late, Dan started to struggle.

As the ship lifted to the 1,100-foot lane going west, Dan discovered that in the tussle his wrists had been tied to the chair arms and his ankles were similarly held by steel bands attached to the legs of the seat.

One of the two men took over the controls of the ship. The other settled down opposite Dan and regarded him with a faint, mocking smile.

'So we finally got you.'

Dan considered how it had been done and said, 'I can't see that it was so difficult.'

'Well,' said the man, 'our problem is different from what it seems. Androids, with the help of a few enlightened human beings, are engaged in taking over this planet from an inferior race. But our true potentialities have been cunningly limited by our lesser group. When you accidentally saw an advanced type android like myself and my friend' – he indicated his companion – 'you became – when we discovered who you were – a problem. Only the fact that you have a film restrains us from killing you at once, and indeed it makes necessary what might be called a more lenient solution.'

Dan found his voice. 'How far has this take-over gone?' he asked.

The man held up his hand. The cynical smile was on his face again. 'I don't have time to go into details.' He glanced out of the transparent plate beside him. 'We're about to land. But, very briefly, our first task is to reverse the entire process, that is, to free the androids from restriction and place proper restrictions on human beings.'

Dan said earnestly, 'In order for you to have such a goal, it means that a human being programmed you to have it.'

'The free androids,' was the retort, 'all have such thoughts, and it was, of course, a learned process – which, after all, is the way human beings also get their training.'

'What about human creativity?' Dan asked.

The android gave a ridiculing laugh. 'A logical process, in the final analysis, which, even before androids as such were constructed, was largely turned over to computers, the pre-cursors of androids.'

'But those computers were programmed by human beings,' Dan pointed out.

136

'Who cares how it all started?' was the contemptuous answer.

The android shrugged and went on, 'But we recognize that there will be setbacks in this early stage of the take-over. Eventually thousands, and then millions of us will be free, and all human beings will be living drugged existences. Then we can dominate. But right now, we want two things from you. One is your sister –'

Dan blinked. 'Anita!' He added, 'And what is the second thing?'

'You'll see,' was the reply.

The android had taken what looked like a syringe from his pocket. He pointed this at Dan's face. A fine spray shot out from it.

And it was not exactly then that Dan lost consciousness. But the next thing he knew clearly, he was sitting.

For a while he kept making a body effort of resistance, and he kept thinking he was in an air-ground combo, and that the two men were holding him.

Now he grew aware of something. He was sitting, yes. He was inside somewhere, yes.

But it was not an air-combo.

And there was no one holding him.

In front of him was glass. In front, behind, to either side, above, below. He was surrounded by glass.

A remote part of his brain registered his awareness of this environment as an impact: astonishment, dismay, shock. But these were shadowy feelings, like echoes of reactions rather than the reactions themselves.

Time passed. And he had another awareness: There were people on the other side of the glass.

Not-easy-to-see people. The glass distorted them, somehow. Parts of bodies and hands could be glimpsed at odd moments, as if for an instant a piece of face or cloth, or a hand or leg, had come opposite a peephole.

The peepholes were of different sizes and shapes. Some stretched long, some were vertical, others horizontal, diagonal, and curved. Several times an eye – each different – peered at him. In every instance, the eyes were inquisitive and wondering.

Somewhere in the course of this observational period, Dan

137

had a thought of his own: I seem to be living at a retarded speed.

Having had the thoughts, he continued to sit.

He had ceased his body effort of resistance, and so he was receptive when what seemed to be a voice said into his mind: 'You are now, as you have observed, turned on. You have observed that, haven't you? Say yes.'

'Yes,' said Dan.

'Are you ready for programming?' said the voice. 'Say yes.'

'Yes,' said Dan.

'Very good,' said the voice. 'You want to be programmed, do you not? Say yes.'

'Yes,' said Dan.

'Programming,' said the voice, 'consists of you receiving specific instructions regarding your behavior and response. You will always and invariably respond and behave exactly as the programming indicates. You agree to respond and behave exactly as programmed? Say, yes, I agree.'

'Yes, I agree,' said Dan.

'The initial programming,' said the voice, 'is simple. You stand up. Stand up!'

Dan got to his feet.

'Sit down!'

Dan sat.

'There, that was easy, wasn't it? Say yes, it was easy.'

'Yes, it was easy,' said Dan.

'Splendid,' said the voice. 'Your next programming will be to stand up, walk forward two steps, then back up two steps, then sit down. You agree to do this, do you not? Say yes.'

'Yes.'

Dan now had his second personal thought. 'Hey,' he thought, 'no.'

Even as he made the mental objection, he got up, took two steps forward, two steps backward, and sat down again.

And, as time went by and more programming took place, he sat, walked, lifted objects, put them down, responded to commands with verbal answers or actions as required by the voice, which continued to speak directly, so it seemed, into his brain.

Finally: 'You are now ready,' said the voice, 'to come out of your training cabinet.'

He was commanded to walk straight ahead. As he did so,

an opening appeared in the glass; a moment later Dan emerged into a room where several dozen human beings behind a rope barricade were evidently waiting for him. As he came out and moved along – which he was now commanded to do – inside of his part of the rope barrier individuals among these watchers asked questions about him, and the same voice that had spoken into Dan's head answered the questions through a wall speaker. They all seemed to take it for granted that he had volunteered to simulate an android.

'But I didn't volunteer,' Dan said. 'I don't want to be like an android.'

He did not say that aloud.

He was not programmed to speak such a sentence.

He stood there and waited for his next command.

The people began to disperse. Some went out of what seemed to be a front door; others went through a side door.

Behind Dan, a door opened, and there were footsteps; then a man came into view.

'Walk out of that door!' He indicated the front entrance with a curt gesture. It was the same voice that had given him his training.

Dan walked as directed and found himself on *Queer Street!*

He recognized in that distant way that this was unquestionably what Anita had been referring to.

The street where the robots came, headquarters of GALS: Give Androids Life Society.

The GALS had androids donated to them, willed to them, bought for them. And here, on this strange street, was a city within a city. Here these 'free' androids 'lived' without anyone to give them orders. The GALS reprogrammed them according to a systematic idea, which had in it, first of all, a delimiting concept.

The concept was: I can refuse to be turned off.

In addition, several consciousness-expanding ideas were programmed into the free android.

One of these, in essence, gave the android permission to learn.

Dan walked along, held in his android-mental frame by some inner force beyond his control, and only vaguely conscious of his past.

He saw an android-enticing sign: GET JUICED UP HERE.

He saw a for-androids-only theater, whose marquee

featured a double bill. 'Remember,' it said, 'you see both pictures at once, because an android can – '

A billboard showed a towering android beside a puny human. 'An android,' it said, 'is stronger, more logical, better in every way.'

Another billboard showed a male and a female figure. The legend was: 'Human note – Androids make perfect wives and husbands.'

From somewhere deep in Dan's own mind came his own thought: The day will come when every human being has been treated as I am now being treated; first, this present stage one, then stage two, then the final permanent stage of total control. On that day, life on earth will be – what?

He walked on, the thought fading into a shadowy region of his mind.

Officer A. Sutter wrote in his notebook: 'On leaving Dan Thaler, earlier, I put a tracer on him and followed him to the Central City Hospital, hovered above this structure until tracer line swung over, indicating tracer line was moving away from hospital. Located source in a combo with number 8-283-746-A and followed to free-robot area, sometimes called Android City. With spy ray observed Dan Thaler being carried out by two superandroids into GALS headquarters. Consciousness-diminishing drug injected immediately; spy ray showed human audience observing stage-one induction. At this point called for reinforcements, and then, shortly after Thaler came into street for his initial walk, and as raid began, rescued him. Am now waiting for effect of drug to wear off. Believe this to be first time pictures taken of actual enforcement of android simulation by human. Thus suspicion that such simulations were not always voluntary confirmed.'

Dan sat for four hours in Sutter's police combo, and then he felt normal.

But he was in a meditative mood.

'The lines are drawn for battle,' he said. 'And the secret of the superandroids is out; so that's a gain. I may have to give up the film to save my sister, but I'll leave her in jail while I think about that.'

He shook his head. 'It's strange to think that that mad woman is in a position where she can't do anything nutty. In fact' – he frowned – 'maybe you'd better check to see if she's still there.'

Sutter turned back presently from his phone. 'Yes,' he said, 'she's still there – and it's over my time to go off duty. My wife will be expecting me –'

The following morning, Sutter noted that on his visual tape were three reports: (1) Dan Thaler's sister still in custody; (2) GALS board of directors deny knowledge of use of GALS headquarters for coerced simulation of androids; board fires on-premises manager, who is under arrest; (3) Apparently all quiet on Thaler-Copeland front. Signed: INSPECTOR INGRATH.

Sutter couldn't quite believe that last item, so he put through an A-plus call to Dan Thaler's apartment.

No answer.

He then called Peter Copeland I at his private number.

No reply.

He zoomed over to the Copeland factory and insisted on going into the private office.

No sign of Peter I.

And Peter III was not in the building.

He flew to the original Copeland home.

Unoccupied.

The container in the storeroom, where Peter II was supposed to be kept when turned off, was not there. And no sign of Peter II.

At his next stop, where Peter I had been living with Anita II, there was no answer to his ringing. And the apartment manager refused him entry without a warrant.

Officer A. Sutter was beginning to have a strange, empty feeling when he received a call from Dan Thaler.

'I'm over at the prison, getting Anita out. Join me.'

Sutter said, 'But –'

And at that point realized he was talking into a dead line.

On inquiring at the desk of the jailhouse, Officer Sutter was directed to one of the anterooms. Inside, he found Dan and the woman. Dan had taken her shoe off and had slit her stocking, and as Sutter watched, he reached into a hole in her heel and began to make adjustments on a set of dials.

Sutter stared, then hastily stepped into the room and closed the door. For once he was too taken by surprise to write anything either in his real *or* mind's-eye notebook.

Sutter found his voice. 'You mean – that woman yesterday ... was your sister?'

Dan said, 'I couldn't raise anybody anywhere today; so I hurried down here.'

Sutter said, 'I couldn't find anyone, either.'

Dan made a shushing gesture. 'I'm going to turn her on.'

He closed the opening in the heel, slipped the shoe back on, steadied the woman, and drawing a gun-shaped instrument from his pocket, pointed it at the heel and pulled the trigger.

The Anita duplicate turned and evidently finished a thought she must have been about to speak before being turned off.

'Yes, I'm the android who has been living with the real Peter Copeland.'

'Why did you not report this to the police yesterday?'

'I am not programmed to handle that kind of situation that developed yesterday.'

'What was that situation?'

'She pretended to be an android – me.'

Dan glanced at Sutter and shrugged. 'Well?' he said.

Sutter said, 'What would she want to do that for?'

Dan said, 'How would I know what goes on in that woman's skullcase!' His tone was sharp.

Sutter's thought had leaped back to the previous morning. 'That was *her*, here?' When Dan did not reply, Sutter persisted, 'But she did it so well. So polite. What's she up to?'

This time Dan replied, 'We'd better get over there and check.'

'Over where?'

Dan glanced significantly at Anita II and said, 'I think we should leave her here and get organized for a raid, based on all the silence we ran into this morning when we tried to locate people.'

Officer Sutter had his first glimmering of understanding. The empty feeling returned. Somebody was in danger. He said, 'Uh!'

He wrote rapidly in an imaginary notebook, 'It would seem that in some circumstances Inspector Ingrath's is the only appropriate remark.'

142

On the way over to Peter I's apartment, Sutter asked, 'What did you program Anita II to do?'

'To obey only me in future.'

'Uh!' said Sutter.

They came to N-12, or rather, to where they could see the front entrance of the Copeland apartment. A wide hallway, a staircase, then more hallway – that was the view from the elevator. The front door of N-12 was ornate, showing a design which obviously cost money.

Dan led the way to the rear entrance, drew a short-circuiting device from a pocket, and inserted it into the electronic lock. The device detected the exact pattern of the electronic flow by a sensitive feedback system, adjusted itself, and soundlessly unlocked the door.

Officer A. Sutter raised his eyebrows as the door silently swung open. But he made no comment as he tiptoed after Dan into the corridor beyond.

Dan gestured with one hand. Sutter softly closed the door.

And they were inside.

The interior alcove was surprisingly large, and three doors led from it: one to a half-open door which showed a kitchen; another, directly opposite, either a bathroom or the rear entrance to a bedroom.

The third door was also slightly open – inches only – and from beyond it there was audible and muffled sound of voices. Dan moved in that direction, Sutter close at his heels.

Dan reached the door, flattened himself against one wall, and peered through the three-inch opening.

He saw the backs of two men. Both resembled Peter Copeland. Peter II and Peter III – he deduced.

And as he watched, one of the men said, in Peter's voice, 'There's got to be a way you can help us get your wife out of jail, so we can kill her.'

'Go to hell,' said Peter's voice from somewhere out of sight.

'It's you or her,' said the android.

And Peter said, 'We've been over this twelve hundred times. I've told you I'm not going to do it.'

'It's you or her,' repeated the android.

Standing there, Dan realized what had happened here.

Somebody must have programmed these two to believe that for humans personal survival was an ultimate motivation. Whoever had programmed that had forgotten to add, 'Except

143

when a mother is defending her baby, or a man's maleness is somehow at issue, or his honor – or something.'

As a result, they were stuck in a circular thought process: The threat, the unexpected response – for which they were not programmed – then back to the threat – timelessly repeating. Dan divined that this had been going on now for a long time – what was it Peter had said? Twelve hundred times.

At least since early morning.

And Peter must be answering in the repetitive way because he did not understand the situation.

Dan felt relief. The danger he had divined had been real. But now that his circular madness had been started, Sutter and he need only wait. Make no sudden moves. Wait for the arrival of the police goon squad that Sutter had called.

Standing there, realizing, Dan experienced a vague pity, a sadness, a strange regret for androids and their bid for freedom.

He thought: On one level, I'm not really against androids achieving freedom.

But the problem was fantastically difficult. For, basically, androids had to be programmed for everything they thought or did.

These two didn't realize that the real Anita was in the room with them.

What kind of a chance did such beings have to be free?

As he had these thoughts, he had been edging forward, his intention being to catch a glimpse of Anita's or Peter's foot or hand, so that he would have them mentally located.

These androids had the superspeed response ability of electronic devices; and there would be violence when the goon squad arrived; for that would break the stereotype that now held them.

Dan suspected that no attempt would be made to kill Peter I when the raid began.

So where was Peter I, *exactly?*

He bent his head, angled inches farther into the room – and saw Anita.

She was looking up. Their gaze met.

Her eyes widened, and she came to her feet.

'Time for lunch,' she announced.

She walked rapidly out of Dan's range of vision – easy to do, for he had more inches of visual leeway.

144

Dan cursed silently. For Peter II and Peter III turned and looked at each other.

'Lunch,' they said simultaneously. 'But he never eats lunch at home.'

Dan was thinking violent, vituperative language at his mad sister. At the same time, he was backing away from his position at the doorway. There was a faint, ever so faint, muffled sound from Sutter.

Dan turned and saw that Sutter was staring at the kitchen door. Dan glanced in that direction. And froze.

Anita stood there.

In her hand was an automatic pistol.

'All right,' she said. 'You two – inside.'

She gestured toward the living room with the weapon.

Dan restrained an impulse to scream at his sister as he complied. His restraint was based on a bit of knowledge of which she was apparently unaware: that the two Peter androids would, after the manner of programmed machines, kill her instantly if they discovered she was the real Anita.

As he entered the living room, he was aware of Sutter's dragging foot following him. And behind Sutter was the click of Anita's high heels on the gleaming floor.

He was too dazed by the unexpected turn of events to think clearly. In a single act of madness, Anita had converted what had been completely under control into a deadly, dangerous situation. And there was nothing he could do about it.

His purpose, and, in a different way, Peter's had been concentrated on saving her. As usual, everyone protecting Anita, and she protecting no one.

'Tie them!' Her voice came from behind him. And when that had been skillfully done by Peter II and III, she gave the equally inexplicable command, 'Gag them!'

As the duos of Peters completed this latter task, Anita raised her gun and fired at them. Twice.

The two androids fell almost simultaneously; and Dan noticed that in the death act their motions were not human.

There was no struggle, no twitching of limbs, with thousands of cells and muscles and nerves clinging desperately to life. Peter II and Peter III simply fell like inanimate objects.

Anita untied Dan first. As she undid his gag, she said in a low, fierce whisper, 'Don't you say one word to Peter that I'm not an android. , , . And see to it that the policeman shuts his mouth, too.'

A light lit in Dan's mind. So that was it. All this danger had been incurred to further some scheme she had in connection with her husband.

Seething, Dan whispered the required admonition a minute later as he released Sutter. He was aware of Anita untying Peter I; and still he could not quite let his mind examine the implications of what he had said.

That didn't come until later.

There was an interlude, while Peter said to Anita, 'Let me see that gun.'

She handed it to him, and he stood staring down at it; and what he was thinking was not clear, for he finally slipped it into his pocket and said in an even tone, 'I didn't know you were programmed to protect your owner.'

'Oh, yes,' said Anita.

'And what about tying and gagging these two?' He indicated Dan and Sutter.

'That was part of the pattern of getting the gun.'

The police raiding party now, belatedly, arrived; ended the questioning. The two dead – though of course, reparable and reprogrammable – Peters were carted off, with Peter I's permission, to Dan's office.

Dan found himself unwilling to depart. He finally found himself standing in the doorway of the apartment, silently staring at his beautiful sister and her husband. It was at this point that he caught a glance from Anita's eyes. They flashed blue rage at him.

'Get out of here, you lunkhead!' that blue glance telegraphed.

Dan got.

It was another day. Shortly after noon.

Officer A. Sutter landed his combo in a suitable parking place in Android City, walked to the street, and presently espied Dan, Peter II, Peter III, and Anita II coming toward him.

At least Dan had said, when he called, that he was with these three persons. The two male androids had been repaired and reprogrammed.

They all stopped, and Dan said to the woman loudly, 'Well,

146

my dear sister, since I can't make you change your mind, I'll say good-bye, and wish you luck.'

He held out his hand. The woman ignored it. She walked off, followed by the male androids.

When they had gone, Dan said, 'I'm pretty sure I convinced the two Peters that the woman with them is Anita I. And if that raid on GALS broke up the local ring, then no one is, at least for the moment, monitoring any of the superrobots in this city.'

Sutter said, 'Why would you want to have them think it was actually your sister?'

'Well, I got a call from Anita late yesterday, and she gave me my instructions.' Dan laughed ruefully and looked embarrassed as he continued, 'Anita has a woman's outlook on things, and she thought it would be a good idea if I programmed Anita II to feel deep love for Peter II and Peter III, and vice versa.' He went on, apologetically, 'As I picture it, something in that strange head of my sister's gets pleasure out of thinking that Peter I is going to be believing that Anita I is living with Peter II and Peter III, and of course all the time it's Anita II.'

'But why would you do such a meaningless thing? Why do what your sister wants?'

'Well,' Dan confessed, 'she threatened to have the two male supers dismantled, and I may need them later as tools in my continuing assignment. Now that Mr Jarris has been removed from his high post, and Dr Schneiter is facing serious charges, everything is fine, but . . . ' He left the sentence hanging.

'Do you think your sister knew consciously that she had been subjected to an android simulation?'

'No.'

'But then how did she break out of it?'

Dan was silent. Part of the answer must lie in the concept – intimated by Dr Schneiter – that she had 'run amok'. But it was more than that, much more. Something in a human being resisted enslavement.

Not in all situations, of course. Not if it were subtle, not on the level of conformity – which the majority of all times and places did not even think of as slavery.

Yet the moment that a human being actually considered that enforcement was taking place, his resistance began.

The realization relieved Dan in a basic way. Human beings

would survive the android fight for freedom. Women, particularly, would hold their own.

Officer A. Sutter was also silent, startled. He was visualizing two male Peter androids and a female Anita android, each programmed for deep love, endlessly making love to each other.

He was vaguely aware of Dan Thaler saying, 'Kind of makes you wonder about life.'

Sutter nodded absently.

'Just imagine,' said Dan, 'a woman having to spend the rest of her life pretending to be a completely programmed android. I refer to my real sister, as she is now, living with Peter.'

'Uh!' said Sutter, startled. 'That!'

For a few seconds he put his attention on Anita I living with her husband under such conditions – a little enviously, he realized as he considered what a difficult female his own wife had become recently.

They had arrived – as Sutter had these thoughts – at his combo. From it there came the sound of a double buzzing.

'Just a moment,' he said, 'my wife is on the line.'

He walked in and pressed the switch for the – he estimated – tenth time since he had gone on the job that morning. He said resignedly:

'Yes, dear – of course I love you. I've already told you that nine times today. . . ,'

Laugh, Clone, Laugh

A. E. VAN VOGT and
FORREST J. ACKERMAN

Now men may wither, age and go,
Yet live anew, twinned Blueprint Men,
When doppelgangers in
The Phoenix Gardens grow,
> – CHON GRAYSTARK,
> First Poet of the Clone Age

A miracle had happened with his birth.

The impossible.

The xillion-to-one deviation.

Incredibly, into the royal family a Good Guy at last had been born.

This was the secret that had burgeoned now within –

Himself.

Juniko, sole son of Erstava, Tator of Phernophalia.

He had such humane thoughts, such ennobling aspirations, so many plans for the betterment of the world. He found it almost unbelievable that someone like himself, so close to the throne, should have a predictable chance of eventually being in a position to bestow and dispense and achieve so many many perfections.

Unlikelihood of near infinite order – yet there was no doubt: here he stood, self-realized, the only son, one step from the pinnacle.

The universe of man quivered and waited, a throbbing heartbeat away from its ultimate destiny.

From very early in his youth Juniko had a plan based on a scientific development whose real implications had never seemed to occur to his father: the discovery of perfect cloning.

Take a few cells from a man and regrow his whole body. Create a total twin of the original. It could even be with the

149

same thoughts and attitudes: *duplicata exactica*. Although it didn't have to be. Already subtle methods which did not interfere with the basic abilities of the individual in any way had produced successful modifications.

His father's plan was to project a clone of himself, endlessly into the future. The Tator had a narrow view of cloning and intended to limit its benefits to himself and as a reward for loyal service to his person. Cloning was costly, he emphasized. Obviously, the great mass of the people could never afford its price. Accordingly, since it was automatically limited in application, it followed that other necessary limitations could be applied, on the principle that law and order must be served.

Juniko shrugged and smiled to himself whenever he heard his father expound on the price and realities of politics. Who cared about cost? Such problems could be worked out. Juniko felt even more scathing of the short-sighted biologists who were enthralled by the restricting concept of cloning future Shakespeares and other geniuses, which the Tator said he was willing to have done in all instances where it would serve the public interest.

'Naturally, *that*, also,' Juniko thought to himself, smiling with scorn.

But *his* goodness, his ideal, transcended all such minuscule imaginations.

Let there come an end to sorrow! – to needless suffering, deprivation of body, mutilation of mind, starvation of soul.

Let sad things cease! – and in their place, a smile upon each human face!

And so, to begin – subtly, cautiously – the change must come in circles around the throne, spiraling downward through the nobility to the fringe group and finally, systematically, to the great mass of the People themselves.

The heartbeat – his father's – that stands between the slave. Now world and the brave New world to come must not be allowed to clone endlessly into the future. One day that heart will falter, and when it does, the Tator will call for his eldest son, for he trusts no one to perform the cloning act but his smiling, loyal Juniko.

An assassin's ray! The heat sears the flesh of the Tator from the waist up, scorches the hair from his head, evaporates

150

one eye. More dead than alive, Juniko's writhing father screams for his son and is rushed to the secret laboratory.

The Tator dies with a smile on what is left of his crisped and contorted face as his last conscious feeling is of the knife slice that will preserve the necessary portion of his flesh to ensure his rebirth. He will be back!

But black, eternal oblivion is his fate. Smiling sorrowfully, royal Juniko feeds the fatal piece of his father's flesh to the Palace piranhas. . . .

The new regime begins.

Curiously, some people actually resent cloning, resist self-duplication, not realizing it will be beneficial for them. They go so far – too far! – as to try to escape from Phrenophalia, to flee to Zarnocopia to the west or seek asylum in Megatropolis to the east.

(Of course, to go north or south would be unthinkable.)

The robopo always bring them back, of course: 'The Metal Police always get their man.' Or woman.

And 'afterward', all clones admitted how wrong they had been and how right Juniko.

From the beginning Juniko had one personal thought, one small concession to ego: There should be a tiny differentiation between the created and the creator. Not much, nothing overtly egotistical – Phroide forbid! – but . . . instead of laughing like all the rest, he would . . . smile. Simply – smile.

Thus, the ever-laughing people would be able to recognize their benefactor. And, recognizing, love him.

Since, from birth, he had always been a smiler; had smiled perhaps with a little fear, perhaps even propitiatingly when his father stormed; had smiled with secret joy over his great plans and had smiled with pleasure as those deific dreams came to fruition – accordingly, there was no need for a Juniko clone. Juniklone – and he added one more smile to his life total as the portmanteau crossed his mind for the first time.

After his father's death and his ascendancy to Tatorship, he bit by bit came to realize a strange phenomenon: There were a few *natural* laugh-prones around the Palace, people who always had, they confessed to him, had an innate desire to laugh and laugh all day long but had restrained themselves because of his father. Juniko was glad to spare such individuals the expense of cloning. He even felt better because such natural rictal stock existed. Natural-born laughers were the automatic answer to any criticism from pre-clones who otherwise might dare to cavil at the idea that everybody but Juniko needed a clone.

In fact, thank God for the naturals! He welcomed them all with his warm heart; treated them like personal cloneys.

It was beautiful. Juniko even had to laugh to himself occasionally. There he would be among a group of happy laughers, and all of a sudden his own perpetual smile would break and rictivate, elevate to laughter, and he would laugh uncontrollably along with the rest.

Phrenophalia became a funderful world of laughing people – until one day the Secretary of Offense (soldiers now laughed all the way to the wars) was laughingly telling something to Juniko and Juniko caught a strange look in the man's eyes.

The face was laughing. The eyes were not.

A fantastic, shattering reality struck Juniko: *He's not laughing with me, he's laughing at me!*

Juniko fought off a bad feeling, the feeling of, *shek!* – people are really no damn good after all.

Juniko, Tator of Phrenophalia, continued to smile before his people, of course, but it was a Pagliacci smile, for inside him now grew a grief ineffable, a sadness beyond name. And an awareness that he had actually noticed the phenomenon from the beginning but had valiantly forced himself to blindness, mentally blotting out the fact that the human race was really rotten.

As he thought these dark thoughts, he walked like a zombie along a corridor of the Palace. As everywhere else, it was bedecked with a multiplicity of mirrors. Reflected in one of these he saw that his smile had taken on some of the old fixed quality that had been there so often when his father was alive.

The silent, internal conflict ended in what he finally decided had to be a win for the world. It was necessary, he realized, to learn to distinguish between the people who were laughing for the joy of it and those whose laughter was ill-meant.

Juniko was not immediately able to decide what should be done with those evil subjects whose abuse of laughter had despoiled his idyll. And that was his fatal mistake, for his paranoia began to become evident to those close to him, who remembered the example of Caligula, the Roman emperor who married his sister and performed an enormous number of crimes. Nobody wanted another Caligula, except perhaps Caligula's sister; but the problem was not complicated, as Juniko did not have a female sibling.

All admitted that Juniko the Original did have some good points, so his joint executioners agreed to reincarnate him via clonage and, opting for a nonparanoid Juniko the Second, a part of him was preserved and regrown after his assisted demise.

The world held its breath; watched and waited and wondered.

Here, in the twenty-second century, Phrenophalia of course is no longer on the map. Some of our senior citizens remember when it was laughed right off it. That was the first time Juniko Two had a rebirthday party with all his little happy, joyous, laughing friends, all hollers and horns and serpentine and games and goodies and funny hats and candy and cake and ice cream and –

Suddenly!

Inexplicably!

Juniko Two was not laughing, was not even smiling, was not even crying. Juniko Jr was –

Screaming!

It would have been comical if it hadn't been tragical.

You intuit what had happened, of course.

He was the first *I Scream Clone!*

The end (of a shaggy clone story).

Research Alpha

A. E. VAN VOGT and
JAMES H. SCHMITZ

I

Barbara Ellington felt the touch as she straightened up from the water cooler. It was the lightest of touches, but quite startling – momentary, tiny flick of something ice-cold against the muscle of her right arm at the shoulder.

She twisted quickly and rather awkwardly around from the cooler, then stared in confusion at the small well-dressed, bald-headed man who stood a few feet behind her, evidently awaiting his turn for a drink.

'Why, good afternoon, Barbara,' he said pleasantly.

Barbara was now feeling embarrassment. 'I . . . ' she began incoherently. 'I didn't know anyone else was near, Dr Gloge. I'm finished now!'

She picked up the briefcase she had set against the wall when she stopped for a drink and went on along the bright lit corridor. She was a tall, lean-bodied girl – perhaps a little too tall, but, with her serious face and smooth brown hair, not unattractive. At the moment, her cheeks burned. She knew she walked with wooden, self-conscious stiffness, wondering if Dr Gloge was peering after her, puzzled by her odd behavior at the water cooler.

'But something *did* touch me,' she thought.

At the turn of the corridor, she glanced back. Dr Gloge had had his drink and was walking off unhurriedly in the opposite direction. Nobody else was in sight.

After she'd turned the corner, Barbara reached up with her left hand and rubbed the area of her upper arm where she had felt that tiny, momentary needle of ice. Had Dr Gloge been responsible for – well, for whatever it had been? She frowned and shook her head. She'd worked in Gloge's office for two weeks immediately after she'd been employed here. And Dr Henry Gloge, head of the biology section at Research Alpha, while invariably polite, even courteous, was

154

a cold, quiet, withdrawn character, completely devoted to his work.

He was not at all the kind of man who would consider it humorous to play a prank on a stenographer.

And it hadn't, in fact, been a prank.

From Dr Henry Gloge's point of view, the encounter with Barbara Ellington in the fifth-floor hallway that afternoon had been a very fortunate accident. A few weeks earlier he had selected her to be one of two unwitting subjects for Point Omega Stimulation.

His careful plans had included a visit to her bedroom apartment when she was not there. He had installed equipment that might be of value later in his experiment. And it was not until these preliminaries were accomplished that he had headed for the steno pool, only to find that Barbara had been transferred out of the department.

Gloge dared not risk inquiring about her. For if the experiment had undesirable results, no one must suspect a connection between a lowly typist and himself. And even if it were successful, secrecy might continue to be necessary.

Gloge chafed at the delay. When on the fourth day of his search for her he suddenly recognized her walking along a hallway fifty feet ahead of him, it seemed as if fate was on his side after all.

As the girl paused at a water cooler, he came up behind her. Quickly he made sure that no one else was in view. Then he drew the needle jet gun and aimed it at her shoulder muscles. The gun carried a gaseous compound of the Omega serum, and the only sign of a discharge, when he fired it, was a thin line of mist from the needle end to her skin.

His task then accomplished, Gloge hastily slipped the instrument into the holster inside his coat and buttoned his coat.

Barbara, still carrying her briefcase, presently came to the offices of John Hammond, special assistant to the president of Research Alpha, which lay on the fifth floor of what was generally considered the most important laboratory complex on Earth. Alex Sloan, the president, was on the floor above.

Barbara paused before the massive black door with Hammond's name on it. She gazed possessively at the words

Scientific Liaison and Investigation lettered on the panel. Then she took a small key from her briefcase, slipped it into the door lock, and pressed to the right.

The door swung silently back. Barbara stepped through into the outer office, heard the faint click as the door closed behind her.

There was no one in sight. The desk of Helen Wendell, Hammond's secretary, stood across the room with a number of papers on it. The door to the short hall which led to Hammond's private office was open. From it Barbara heard Helen's voice speaking quietly.

Barbara Ellington had been assigned to Hammond – actually, to Helen Wendell – only ten days before. Aside from the salary increase, part of her interest in the position had been the intriguing if somewhat alarming figure of John Hammond himself, and an expectation that she would find herself in the center of the behind-the-scene operations of *Scientific Liaison and Investigation*. In that, she had so far been disappointed.

Barbara walked over to Helen Wendell's desk, took some papers from her briefcase, and was putting them into a basket when her eye caught the name of Dr Henry Gloge on a note in the adjoining basket. Entirely on impulse – because she had seen the man only minutes before – she bent over the paper.

The note was attached to a report. It was a reminder to Hammond that he was to see Dr Gloge today at three-thirty in connection with Gloge's Omega project. Barbara glanced automatically at her watch; it was now five minutes to three.

Unlike most of the material she handled, this item was at least partly understandable. It referred to a biological project. Point Omega Stimulation. Barbara couldn't remember having heard of such a project while she was working under Dr Gloge. But that was hardly surprising – the biological section was one of the largest in Research Alpha. From what she was reading, the project had to do with 'the acceleration of evolutionary processes' in several species of animals, and the only real information in the report seemed to be that a number of test animals had died and been disposed of.

Was the great John Hammond spending his time on this sort of thing?

156

Disappointed, Barbara put the report back into the basket and went on to her own office.

As she sat down at her desk, Barbara noticed a stack of papers which hadn't been there when she had left on her errand. Attached to them was a note in Helen's large, clear handwriting. The note said:

Barbara,
This came in unexpectedly and must be typed today. It obviously will require several hours of overtime. If you have made special arrangements for the evening, let me know and I'll have a typist sent up from the pool to do this extra work.

Barbara felt an instant pang of possessive jealousy. This was *her* job, *her* office; She definitely did not want some other girl coming in.

Unfortunately, she did have a date. But to keep an intruder from taking her place in John Hammond's office, even if only for a few hours, was the more important matter. That was her instant decision, needing no second thought. But she sat still a moment, biting her lip; for that moment she was a woman considering how to put off a male who had a quick temper and no patience. Then she picked up the telephone and dialed a number.

For some months now, Barbara had settled her hopes for the future on Vince Strather, a technician in the photo lab. When his voice came on the telephone, she told him what had happened, finished contritely, 'I'm afraid I can't get out of it very well, Vince, so soon after starting here.'

She could almost feel Vince absorbing the impact of the denial she was communicating; she had discovered quickly in their brief romance that he was trying to move her toward premarital intimacy, a step she was wholly determined not to take.

She was relieved now, when he accepted her explanation. She replaced the receiver, feeling very warm toward him. 'I really do love him!' she thought.

It was a few moments later that she suddenly felt dizzy.

The feeling was peculiar, not like her usual headaches. She could feel it build up, a giddy, light swirling which seemed both within and without her, as if she were weightless, about to drift out of the chair, turning slowly over and over.

Almost simultaneously, she became aware of a curious exhilaration, a sense of strength and well-being, quite unlike anything she could remember. The sensations continued for perhaps twenty seconds; then they faded and were gone, almost as abruptly as they had come.

Confused and somewhat shaken, Barbara straightened up in her chair. For a moment she considered taking aspirin. But there seemed no reason for that. She didn't feel ill. It even seemed to her that she felt more awake and alert.

She was about to return to her typing when she became aware of a movement out of the corner of her eye. She looked up and saw that John Hammond had paused in the doorway of her little office.

Barbara froze, as she always did in his presence; then slowly she turned to face him.

Hammond stood there, staring at her thoughtfully. He was a man about six feet tall, with dark brown hair and steel-gray eyes. He seemed to be about forty years old, and he was built like an athlete. Yet it was not his appearance of physical strength but the fine intelligence of his face and eyes that had always impressed her during the ten days since she had been assigned to his office. She thought now, not for the first time: This is what really great people are like.

'Are you all right, Barbara?' Hammond asked. 'For a moment, I thought you were going to fall out of your chair.'

It was highly disturbing to Barbara to realize that her dizzy spell had been observed. 'I'm sorry, Mr Hammond,' she murmured shyly. 'I must have been daydreaming.'

He gazed at her a moment longer, then nodded, turned, and walked off.

II

On leaving Barbara, Gloge went down several floors and stationed himself behind a pile of shipping crates. These were in a passage across from the locked door of the main photo-lab storeroom. On the dot of 3.15, a door farther along the passage opened. A lanky, scowling, redheaded young man wearing a stained white smock over his street clothes, pushing a loaded handtruck ahead of him, appeared

158

and turned down the passage toward Gloge and the laboratory storeroom.

It was the end of the lab shift. Gloge had discovered that one of the regular duties of Vincent Strather, Barbara Ellington's boyfriend, was to return certain materials to the storeroom at this hour.

Peering through the slats of a crate, Dr Gloge watched Strather's approach. He was, he realized, much more tense and nervous now than he had been when he had given Barbara the injection. Of himself, Vincent Strather was not the kind of subject Dr Gloge would have chosen – the young man was too angry, too bitter. But the fact that he was Barbara's friend and that they spent their spare time together should be useful in the further steps of the experiment – so it seemed to Dr Gloge.

Sliding his hand under his coat, where the jet gun rested, he moved quickly out into the passage and across it toward Vince Strather. . . .

Even as he pressed the trigger, he knew his nervousness had betrayed him.

The needle tip of the gun had been too far away from Strather; a foot; almost two feet too far. At that greater distance the jet stream, emerging from the needle at nearly a thousand miles an hour, had time to spread and slow down. It caught Strather high up on the shoulderblade and tugged at his skin as it entered. For Strather, the sensation must have been that of a sharp impact. He jumped and cried out, then stood shuddering, as if in shock – long enough for Gloge to slip the little gun back into its holster and close up his coat.

But that was all. Vince Strather whirled. His hands caught Gloge by the arms, and his angry face glared down into the doctor's.

'You damn jerk!' he shouted. 'What did you hit me with just now? Who the hell are you, anyway?'

For a moment Dr Gloge felt appalled. Then he tried to twist out of Strather's hard grip. 'I don't know what you're talking about!' he said breathlessly.

He stopped. He saw that Vince was gazing past his shoulder. The young man's grip relazed suddenly, and Gloge was able to free himself. He turned and looked behind him. He felt a stunned, incredulous dismay,

John Hammond was coming along the passage, gray eyes fastened questioningly upon them. Gloge could only hope desperately that he had not been in sight when the gun was being fired.

Hammond came up and said in a tone of easy authority: 'Dr Gloge, what's going on here?'

'Doctor!' Vince Strather repeated, in a startled voice.

Gloge put puzzled indignation in his tone: 'This young man appears to be under the impression that I struck him just now. Needless to say, I did nothing of the kind and don't understand what gave him such an idea.'

He looked frowningly back at Strather. Strather's gaze shifted uncertainly between them. He was obviously abashed by John Hammond's presence and Gloge's title, but not yet over his anger.

He said sullenly, 'Well, something hit me. At least it felt that 'way! When I looked around, he was standing there. So I thought he'd done it.'

'I was passing you,' Dr Gloge corrected him. 'You exclaimed something and I stopped.' He shrugged, smiled. 'And that's all I did, young man! I certainly had no reason to strike you.'

Strather said grudgingly, 'I guess I was mistaken.'

Dr Gloge said promptly, 'Then let's call it an error and forget it!' He held out his hand.

Strather reached out reluctantly and shook it, then looked at Hammond. When Hammond remained silent, he turned away in obvious relief, took one of the boxes from the truck, and disappeared into the storeroom with it.

Hammond said, 'I was on my way to your office, Doctor, where I expect to have an interview with you in a few minutes on the Omega project. I presume you were heading in that direction.'

'Yes, yes.' Gloge fell into step beside the bigger man. He was thinking: Did he see anything?

His companion gave no sign.

A few minutes later, as he gazed across the gleaming desk of his private office at John Hammond, Gloge had the uneasy feeling of a criminal confronted by the law. It had always amazed him that this man – Hammond – could make him feel at very least like a small boy.

Yet the discussion that now developed began with a re-assuring statement from the bigger man:

'This is a completely informal conversation, Doctor. I am not representing President Sloan at the moment — even less the Board of Regents. That has been deliberately arranged. It will make it possible for both of us to speak quite frankly.'

Dr Gloge said, 'Have there been complaints about my work here?'

Hammond nodded. 'You can't have remained entirely unaware of it, Doctor. You've been asked to amplify your project reports, make them more detailed and specific, three times within the last two months alone.'

Gloge was reluctantly deciding that he would have to tell some of his data.

He said with apparent openness, 'My reluctance to communicate has been due to a strictly scientific dilemma. Things were happening in the experiment, but their meaning was not clear to me until very recently.'

'There is a feeling,' said Hammond in his steady voice, 'that your project is failing.'

Dr Gloge said sharply, 'The accusation is unworthy!'

Hammond looked at him, said, 'No accusations have been made — as yet. That's why I'm here today. You have reported no successes within the past six months, you know.'

'Mr Hammond, there have been many failures. Within the limited framework of the present stages of the project experiments, that is exactly what should be expected.'

'Limited in what way?'

'Limited to the lower, less complicated forms of animal life.'

'That,' said Hammond mildly, 'is a limitation you yourself have imposed on the project.'

Dr Gloge agreed. 'True. The conclusions I've been able to form at such lower levels have been invaluable. And the fact that the results of the experiments have been almost invariably negative, in the sense that as a usual result the subject animals evolved into nonviable forms, is completely unimportant.'

'As a usual result,' Hammond repeated. 'Then not all of them died quickly?'

Gloge bit his lip. That was not an admission he had in-tended to make at this initial stage in the discussion.

He said reluctantly, 'In a respectable percentage of the cases, the subject animals survived the first injection.'

'And the second?'

Gloge hesitated. But there was no turning back. 'The survival percentage drops very sharply at that point,' he said. 'I don't recall the exact figures.'

'And the third?'

He was really being forced to make revelations. Dr Gloge said, 'To date, three animals have survived the third injection. All three were of the same species – *Cryptobranchus*.'

'The hellbender,' said Hammond. 'Well! a large salamander. . . . Now, the third injection, according to your theory, should advance an animal along the evolutionary line stimulated in it to a point which might be reached through half a million years of natural evolution. Would you say such a result was achieved in these three cases?'

Dr Gloge said, 'Since *Cryptobranchus* might be considered with some reason to be a species in which evolutionary development is at a practical standstill, I should say that much more was achieved.'

'What were the observable changes?'

Gloge had been bracing himself as he made one admission after another. He was striving to decide exactly when he could start resisting the interrogation.

Now! he thought.

He said aloud, trying to appear frank, 'Mr Hammond, I'm beginning to realize that I was in error in not making more positive reports. I can't believe that you are really interested in these superficial accounts. Why not let me summarize my observations for you?'

Hammond's gray eyes were calm and steady. 'Go ahead,' he said in an even tone.

Gloge outlined his conclusions then. The interesting features were twofold, probably equally important.

One of these was that there remained in all life forms a wide evolutionary choice. For reasons that were not yet clear, the Omega serum stimulated one of these potential developments, and no subsequent stimulation could alter the mutational direction. Most of these developments led to extinction.

'The second feature,' said Gloge, 'is that the chances for

success increase as the life form becomes more highly evolved.'

Hammond said, interested, 'What you're saying is that when you finally start working with the more active mammals and eventually monkeys, you expect more and better results?'

'I have no doubt about that,' said Dr Gloge firmly.

A secondary aspect – Gloge continued – was that brain areas which controlled the inhibition of simple reflexes often seemed to be the source of new neural growth and of sensory extension. The serum apparently intensified these effort points, increasing their operational flexibility. What went wrong was that all too often such one-sided inhibitory amplification ended in nonsurvival.

However, in *Cryptobranchus*, the roof of the mouth developed small functional gills. The hide thickened into segmented, horny armor. Short, grooved fangs were acquired, and connected to glands that produced a mild hematoxic venom. The eyes disappeared, but areas in the skin developed sight-level sensitivity to light.

Gloge shrugged, finished: 'There were other changes, but these would seem the most dramatic ones.'

'They sound sufficiently dramatic,' said Hammond. 'What happened to the two specimens which were not dissected?'

Dr Gloge realized that his diversion had not worked. 'They were given the fourth injection, of course,' he said resignedly.

'The one,' Hammond asked, 'which was to advance them to a point a million years along the evolutionary line they were following – '

'Or,' Dr Gloge said, 'to the peak-point of that evolutionary line. The equating of the four stages of the stimulation process to the passing of specific periods of normal evolutionary development – twenty thousand years, fifty thousand, five hundred thousand, and one million years – is, of course, hypothetical and generalized. My calculations indicate that in many species of which we have knowledge in that area the two points might be approximately the same.'

Hammond nodded. 'I understand, Doctor. And what happened after your evolved *Cryptobranchus* received the fourth injection?'

'I cannot give you a precise answer to that, Mr Hammond. In appearance it was a very rapid breakdown of the entire structure. Within two hours, both specimens literally dissolved,' Gloge answered tensely.

'In other words,' Hammond said, 'Point Omega Stimulation directs *Cryptobranchus* and, in fact, every species to which it has been applied into one of the many blind alleys of evolution.'

Dr Gloge said curtly, 'So far it has done that.'

Hammond was silent; then: 'One more point,' he said. 'It's been suggested that you might consider taking on a sufficiently qualified assistant in this work. Research Alpha probably could obtain Sir Hubert Roland for a project of such interest.'

Dr Gloge said coldly, 'With all due respect to Sir Hubert Roland's accomplishments, I would regard him as a meddler here! If the attempt is made to force him on me, I shall resist it.'

'Well,' Hammond said easily, 'let's not make any unalterable decisions at the moment. As I mentioned, this has been a completely informal discussion.' He glanced at his watch. 'I'm afraid we'll have to terminate it now. Would you have time to see me in my office one week from today at ten o'clock, Doctor? I wish to carry this matter a little further, and that will be my first free time.'

Dr Gloge had difficulty restraining his feeling of triumph. Today was Wednesday. He had selected it as his starting time because he had wanted his subjects to be away from their place of work over the weekend.

Between now and Saturday, he could undoubtedly accomplish the first two injections on the young couple.

By the following Wednesday, the third, perhaps even the fourth shot would have been administered and all strong reactions either taken care of or the experiment terminated.

To cover up his elation, Gloge said in the tone of one making a concession, 'As you wish, Mr Hammond.'

III

Dr Henry Gloge was awake much of the night, vacillating between hopes and fears of what he would find when he went to check on the first results of Point Omega Stimulation in human beings. If they were obviously negative, he would have only one choice.

It could be called murder.

Dr Gloge approached that subject in a detached, undisturbed frame of mind. He had several times in his work secretly carried on a more advanced experiment while, ostensibly, following the step-by-step scientific method. Thus fortified by special knowledge, he had in the past been able to plan lower-step work with the sometimes intuitive insights gained from his unpublicized private investigation.

The importance of the Omega project to him justified a similar expedient. Objectively considered, in the light of such a goal, the lives of the two young people he had chosen for the experiment were of no value. Their destruction, if it became necessary, would be in the same category as the slaughter of other experimental subjects.

With human beings there was, of course, an element of personal risk involved for himself. It was the realization that troubled him, now that he had made the first injection. Time and again, Dr Gloge awakened out of a nightmare-riddled half-sleep, to quail anew at the knowledge and to lie sweating with anxiety until he slid back into exhausted slumber.

When four o'clock came, it was almost with relief that he arose, fortified himself with several tablets of a powerful stimulant, made a last check of his preparations, and set out across town toward the house where the Ellington girl had a room. He drove in a black panel truck that he had bought and equipped for his experiment.

He arrived at his destination about a quarter past five. It was a quiet residential street, a tree-lined avenue in one of the older sections of the city, approximately eight miles west of the Research Alpha complex. Two hundred yards from the house, Dr Gloge pulled the small truck up to the curb on the opposite side of the street and shut off the motor.

For the past week, a miniature audio pickup-recorder, inserted under the bark of a sycamore tree across the street from the house, had been trained on Barbara Ellington's second-floor room, its protruding head cunningly painted to resemble a rusty nail. Dr Gloge now took the other part of the two-piece instrument from the dashboard compartment of the truck, inserted the plug in his ear, and switched it on.

After perhaps half a minute of twisting the tuning dial back and forth, he felt his face whiten. He had tested the instrument at night on two occasions during the past week. It was quite sensitive enough to pick up the sounds of breathing and even the heartbeat of anyone in the room; and so he knew with absolute certainty that Barbara Ellington's room had no living occupant at this moment.

Quickly, he attached the recording playback mechanism to the little device, turned it back one hour, and put the plug into his ear again.

Almost at once, he relaxed.

Barbara Ellington had been in that room, asleep, an hour ago, breath even and undisturbed, heartbeat strong and slow. Dr Gloge had listened to similar recordings of too many experimental animals to have the slightest doubt. *This* subject had moved up successfully, unharmed, to the first stage of Point Omega Stimulation!

The impact of his triumph after the ghastly fears of the night was very strong. Dr Gloge needed several minutes to compose himself. Finally, he was able to move the recorder by ten-minute steps to a point where the Ellington girl obviously was awake and moving about the room. He listened with absorbed fascination, feeling almost able to visualize from moment to moment exactly what she was doing. At one point, she stood still for some seconds and then uttered a low, warm laugh which sent thrills of delight through the listening scientist. Perhaps a minute later, he heard a door being closed. After that, there was only the empty, lifeless silence which had startled him so badly.

Barbara Ellington had awakened that Thursday morning with a thought she had never had before. It was: 'Life doesn't have to be serious!'

She was contemplating this frivolous notion with the beginning of amazement when a second thought came, which she had also never had in her entire previous existence. 'What is this mad drive to enslave myself to a man?'

The thought seemed natural and obviously true. It had no general rejection of men in it. She still – it seemed to her – loved Vince . . . but differently.

Thought of Vince brought a smile. She had already noted in one of numerous, quick, darting glances around the room that it was nearly two hours before her usual rising time. The sun was peering through her bedroom window at that almost horizontal angle which, in the past, had seemed to her a horrifying threat that she would be robbed of precious sleep.

Now it struck her: 'Why don't I call Vince, and we'll go for a drive before I have to go to work?'

She reached for the phone, then considered and drew back. Let the poor man sleep a little longer.

She dressed swiftly, but with more than usual care. When she glanced at the mirror, it occurred to her that she was better-looking than she had realized.

. . . Very much better-looking! she decided an instant later. Intrigued, for a moment amazed, she went up to the mirror, studied the face in it. *Her* face, familiar. But also the face of a radiant stranger. Another awareness came, and the bright, glowing, blue mirror-eyes holding hers seemed to widen.

'I feel twice as alive as I ever have before!'

Surprise . . . pleasure . . . and suddenly: 'Shouldn't I wonder *why?*'

The mirror-face frowned slightly, then laughed at her.

There had been a change, a wonderful one, and the change was not yet complete. There was a sense of shifting deep inside her, of flows of brightness along the edges of her mind. Curiosity had stirred, but it was light, not urgent or anxious. 'When I want to know, I *will* know!' Barbara told herself; and, with that, the trace of curiosity was dismissed.

'And now.'

She glanced once more around the little room. For over a year it had held her, contained her, sheltered her. But she didn't want shelter now. The room couldn't hold her today!

She decided, smiling, 'I'll go and wake up Vince.'

She rang Vince's doorbell five times before she heard him stirring inside. Then his voice called harshly, thickly, '*Who* is that?'

Barbara laughed. 'It's me!'

'Good God!'

The lock clicked back and the door opened. Vince stood staring at her with bloodshot eyes. He'd pulled a robe on over his pajamas, his bony face was flushed and his red hair tangled.

'What are you doing up at this hour?' he demanded as Barbara stepped past him into the apartment. 'It's half-past five!'

'It's a wonderful morning. I couldn't stay in bed. I thought I'd get you to go for a drive with me before I went to work.'

167

Vince pulled the door shut, blinked at her incredulously. 'Go for a drive!' he repeated.

Barbara asked, 'Aren't you feeling well, Vince? You look almost as if you're running a fever.'

Vince shook his head. 'I don't feel feverish, but I sure don't feel well, either. I don't know what's the matter. Come on and sit down. Want some coffee?'

'Not especially. I'll make some for you, if you like.'

'Nah, don't bother. I'm sort of nauseated right now.' Vince sat down on the couch of the little living room, fished cigarettes and matches from a pocket of his robe, lit a cigarette, and grimaced. 'That doesn't taste too good either!' He scowled at Barbara. 'Something pretty damn funny happened yesterday! And I'm not sure –'

He hesitated.

'Not sure of what, Vince?'

'That that isn't why I'm feeling this way.' Vince paused again, shook his head, muttered, 'Sounds crazy, I guess. You know that Dr Gloge you worked for once?'

It seemed to Barbara as if whole sections of her mind lit up in brilliance at that instant. She heard Vince start to tell his story. But – except for John Hammond's intervention – it was something she already knew.

Part of a much bigger story. . . .

She thought: Why, that impudent little man! What a wild, wonderful, terrific thing to do!

Excitement raced through her. The paper she had seen lying on Helen Wendell's desk flashed into her mind, every word sharp and distinct – and not only the words!

Now she *understood*. What they meant, what they implied, the possibilities concealed behind them – for herself, for Vince.

Another feeling awoke. Sharp wariness.

There was danger somewhere here! John Hammond . . . Helen . . . the hundreds of little impressions she'd received all suddenly flowed together into a picture clear but puzzling – of something supranormal, she decided, amazed.

Who were they? What were they doing? In a dozen different ways, they didn't really *fit* in an organization like Research Alpha. But they had virtually complete control.

Not that it mattered immediately. Yet she was certain of one thing. They were opposed to what Dr Gloge was attempting through Point Omega Stimulation, would stop it if they could.

'But they can't!' she told herself. What Dr Gloge had begun was right. She could feel the rightness of it like a song of triumph in every aspect of her being. She would have to make sure that it wasn't stopped at this point.

But she would need to be careful – and act quickly! It was incredibly bad luck that John Hammond had arrived almost while Dr Gloge was giving Vince his first shot.

'Do you think I should report it?' Vince asked.

'You'd look a little foolish if it turned out that you were coming down with the flu, wouldn't you?' Barbara said lightly.

'Yeah.' He sounded hesitant.

'What does it feel like, aside from the nausea?'

Vince described his symptoms. Not unlike her own – and she'd had a few bad moments before she went to sleep last night. Vince was going through an initial reaction period more prolonged and somewhat more severe than hers.

She was aware of a fond impulse to reassure him. But she decided it would be unwise to tell him what she knew. Until he came out of his physical distress, such information might disturb him dangerously.

She said urgently, 'Look, you don't have to go to work until tonight. So the best thing for you is to get a few more hours of sleep. If you start feeling worse, and would like me to take you to a doctor, give me a call and I'll come and get you. Otherwise, I'll phone at ten.'

Vince agreed immediately. 'I'm really awfully groggy. That's a big part of it. I'll just stretch out on the couch instead of going back to bed.'

When Barbara left a few minutes later, her thoughts quickly turned away from Vince. She began to consider various methods she might use to approach Dr Gloge this very day.

Gloge reached the street where Vincent Strather lived and was looking for a parking place, when suddenly he saw Barbara Ellington emerge from the area of the apartment building and start across the street ahead of him.

The girl was perhaps a hundred yards away. Dr Gloge braked the panel truck hastily, pulled it in to the curb, rolled up behind another car parked there, and stopped. He sat there, breathing hard at the narrow margin by which he had avoided being seen.

Barbara had hesitated, glancing in the direction of the approaching truck, but now she was continuing across the street. Watching her swift, lithe stride, the proudly erect carriage of her body – comparing that picture with the frozen awkwardness he had observed in all her movements the day before – Dr Gloge felt his last doubts resolve.

It was in the human species that Point Omega Stimulation would achieve its purpose.

His only regret now was that he had not arrived even as much as ten minutes earlier. The girl obviously had come to see Strather, had been with him until now. If he had found them together, examination on a comparison basis could have been made of them simultaneously.'

The thought did not in the least diminish the tingling excitement that filled him as he watched Barbara's brown car pull out into the street and move away. He waited until her car was out of sight, then drove the truck down to the alley beside the apartment building and turned in to it. His intention was to give Strather a careful physical examination.

A few minutes later Dr Gloge watched a pointer in the small instrument he was holding drop to the zero mark on the dial. Pulling off the respirator clamped over his mouth and nose, he stood looking down at the body of Vincent Strather sprawled on the living-room couch.

Vincent Strather's appearance was much less satisfactory than he had expected. Of course, the young man's reddened face and bloodshot eyes might be due to the paralyzing gas Dr Gloge had released into the apartment as he edged open the back door. But there were other signs of disturbance: tension, distended blood vessels, skin discoloration. By comparison with Barbara Ellington's vigor and high spirits, Strather looked drab and unimpressive.

Nevertheless, he had survived the first shot.

Gloge straightened, studied the motionless figure again, then went about the apartment quietly closing the window he had opened exactly one minute after releasing the instantly effective gas. The gas had dissipated now. When its effect on Strather wore off an hour or so from now, there would be nothing to tell the subject that anything had occurred here after Barbara Ellington had left.

Tomorrow he would return and give Strather the second shot.

As he locked the back door behind him and walked over to the panel truck, Dr Gloge decided that he would have to come back and check both his subjects that night.

He felt extremely confident. It seemed to him that before anyone found out that it had been started, the Point Omega Stimulation experiment on human beings would have run its course.

IV

Hammond heard the bell sound as he was shaving in the bathroom of his living quarters, which were located behind his office. He paused, then deliberately put down his razor and activated a hidden microphone in the wall.

'Yes, John?' Helen's voice came.

'Who came in?'

'Why – only Barbara.' She sounded surprised. 'What makes you ask?'

'The life-range indicator just now registered an over-six read.'

'On *Barbara!*' Helen sounded incredulous.

'On somebody,' said Hammond. 'Better have Special Servicing check the indicator out. Nobody else came in?'

'No.'

'Well – check it.' He broke the connection and finished shaving.

The buzzer sounded in Barbara's office a little later – the signal that she was to report with her notebook to Hammond's office. She went, curious, wondering if he would notice any change in her. Much more important was her own desire to take a closer look at this strange, powerful man who was her boss.

She walked into Hammond's office and was about to sit in the chair he motioned her to, when something in his manner warned her. Barbara made an apologetic gesture.

'Oh, Mr Hammond – excuse me a moment.'

She hurried out of the office and down the hall to the washroom. The moment she was inside, she closed her eyes

171

and mentally relived her exact feelings at the instant she had sensed – whatever it was.

Not Hammond at all, she realized. It was the chair that had given forth some kind of energy flow. Eyes still closed, she strove to perceive what within herself had been affected. There seemed to be an exact spot in her brain that responded each time she reviewed the moment she had started to sit down.

She couldn't decide what the response was. But she thought: 'I don't have to let it be affected now that I know.'

Relieved, she returned to Hammond's office, seated herself in the chair, and smiled at Hammond where he sat behind his great, gleaming, mahogany desk.

'I'm sorry,' she said. 'But I'm ready now.'

During the half-hour that followed, she took shorthand with a tiny portion of her mind, and with the rest fought off a steady, progressively more aware battle against the energy pressure that flowed up at her in rhythmic waves from the chair.

She had by now decided it was a nerve center that reacted to hypnotic suggestion, and so when Hammond said suddenly, 'Close your eyes, Barbara!' she complied at once.

'Raise your right hand!' he commanded.

Up came her right hand, with the pen in it.

He told her to place it back in her lap; and then swiftly put her through several tests – which she recognized as being of a more important kind.

What interested her even more was that she could let the center respond and monitor the parts of the body that he named – without losing control. So that when he commanded her hand to be numb and suddenly reached over and stuck a needle into it, she felt no sensation; and so she did not react.

Hammond seemed satisfied. After normalizing the feeling in her hand, he commanded: 'In just a moment, I'm going to tell you to forget the tests we've just been doing, but you will remain completely under my control and answer truthfully any questions I ask you. Understand?'

'Yes, Mr Hammond.'

'Very well, forget everything we've done and said since I first asked you to close your eyes. When the memory has completely faded, open your eyes.'

172

Barbara waited about ten seconds. She was thinking: 'What roused his suspicions so quickly? And why would he care?' She suppressed an excited conviction that she was about to discover something of the secret life that went on in this office. She had never heard of a hypnotizing chair.

She opened her eyes.

She swayed – an act – then caught herself. 'I beg your pardon, Mr Hammond.'

Hammond's gray eyes regarded her with deceptive friendliness. 'You seem to be having problems this morning, Barbara.'

'I really feel very well,' Barbara protested.

'If there's anything in your life that has changed recently,' he said quietly, 'I want you to confide in me.'

That was the beginning of an intensive questioning into her past history. Barbara answered freely. Apparently Hammond was finally convinced, for he presently politely thanked her for the conversation and sent her off to type the letters he had dictated.

As she sat at her desk a few minutes later, Barbara glanced up through the glass and saw Helen Wendell walking along the hall toward Hammond's office, disappear into it.

Hammond greeted Helen: 'All the time I talked to Barbara, the life-range indicator showed eight-four, above the hypnotizable range. And she told me nothing.'

'How is it registering for me?' Helen asked.

He glanced down at his right to the instrument in an open desk drawer.

'Your usual eleven-three.'

'And you?'

'My twelve-point-seven.'

'Perhaps only the middle ranges are out of order,' Helen said, and added, 'Special Servicing will make their check after daytime office hours. All right?'

Hammond hesitated, then agreed that there seemed to be no reason for breaking the rules of caution by which they operated.

During the lunch hour Barbara experienced a brief return of the dizziness. But she was alert now to the possibilities. Instead of simply letting it happen, she tried to be aware of every nuance of the feeling.

There was a – shifting – taking place inside her.

She sensed a flow of energy particles from various points in her body to other points. A specific spot in her brain seemed to be monitoring the flow.

When the pulsations ceased – as abruptly as they had started – she thought: 'That was more change taking place. I grew in some way in that minute.'

She sat very still there in the restaurant, striving to evaluate what had changed. But she couldn't decide.

Nonetheless, she was content. Her impulse had been to seek out Dr Gloge sometime during the day in the hope that he would be wanting to give her a second injection. That ended. Obviously, all the changes from the first shot had not yet taken place.

She returned to *Scientific Liaison and Investigation*.

The bell sound, as Barbara entered, caused Hammond to glance at the indicator. He stared at it for a long moment, then buzzed Helen Wendell.

'Barbara now reads nine-point-two!' he said softly.

Helen came to the door of his office. 'You mean her reading has gone up?' She smiled. 'Well, that settles it. It is the instrument.'

'What makes you say that?' Hammond seemed strangely unsure.

'In all my experience,' Helen said, 'I've never seen anyone change for the better. There's the slow drop as they grow older, but – ' She stopped.

The strong face was relaxing. Yet after a moment Hammond said, 'Still – we never take chances, so I think I'll keep her with me tonight. Do you mind?'

'It's a nuisance,' she said, 'but all right.'

'I'll give her the conditioning that overwhelms twelve-point-oh and higher. She'll never know what hit her.'

v

It was shortly after dark when Dr Henry Gloge parked his black van near Barbara's home. He promptly turned in on the audio device attached to the tree and adjusted the volume for pickup.

After thirty seconds of silence, he began to frown. 'Not again!' he thought; then, wearily, 'Well, maybe she's over at her boyfriend's.'

174

He started the motor and presently drew up at the curb opposite Strather's apartment. A quick check established that the lanky redhead was there – but alone.

The young man was awake and in an angry state. As Gloge listened in, Vince savagely picked up the phone and dialed what must have been Barbara's number, for presently he slammed the receiver down and muttered, 'Doesn't she know I've got to go to work tonight? Where can that girl be?'

That, in rising alarm, was a question which Gloge asked himself as the evening wore on. He returned to the vicinity of Barbara's boardinghouse. Until eleven p.m. the phone in her room rang periodically, testifying to Vince's concern.

When it had not rung for an hour, Gloge presumed that Strather had gone off to night duty. It was not a fact that could be left to surmise. He drove back to Vince's apartment. No sounds came from it.

Gloge accordingly returned to the street where Barbara lived.

He was tired now, so he rigged up an alarm system that would buzz him if Barbara entered her room; then, wearily, he crawled onto the cot in the back of the van and quickly fell into a deep sleep.

Earlier, as Barbara sat in her office a few minutes before closing time, she swayed and almost blacked out.

Greatly alarmed, she emerged from her office and reported the feeling to Helen Wendell. She did not question the logic of seeking the help of Hammond's blonde aide.

The secretary was sympathetic, and promptly took her in to John Hammond. By this time Barbara had experienced several more brief blackouts. So she was grateful when Hammond unlocked the door behind his desk, led her through a luxurious living room, and into what he called the 'spare bedroom'.

She undressed, slipped under the sheets, and promptly went to sleep. Thus, subtly, she was captured.

During the evening, Hammond and Helen Wendell took turns looking in on her.

At midnight the Special Servicing expert reported that the life-range indicator was working properly, and he himself checked the body of the sleeping girl. 'I get nine-two,' he said. 'Who is she? New arrival?'

175

The silence that greeted his remark abruptly startled him. 'You mean she's an Earther?'

'At least,' said Helen Wendell after the man had departed, 'there's been no further change.'

Hammond said, 'Too bad she's above the hypnotizable stage. Mere conditioning is actually a sorry substitute for what we need here – truth.'

'What are you going to do?'

Hammond did not make up his mind about that until after daybreak.

'Since nine-two is no real threat to us,' he said then, 'we merely return to routine and keep aware that maybe somebody is doing something that we don't know about. Perhaps we might even use a little ESP on her occasionally.'

'Here – at Alpha?'

Hammond stared thoughtfully at his beautiful aide. Normally, he trusted her reactions in such matters.

She must have sensed what he was thinking, for she said quickly, 'The last time we used extended perception, about eighteen hundred Earthers tuned in on us. Of course, they thought of it merely as their imagination, but some of them compared notes. It was talked about for weeks, and some awfully important things were close to being revealed.'

'We-l-l-l, okay, let's be aware of her then.'

'All right. On that basis I'll wake her up.'

As soon as she was in her office, Barbara phoned Vince. There was no answer. Which was not surprising. If he had worked the night shift, he would be dead to the world. She hung up and checked with the photo lab, and was much relieved when the night work list showed that Vince had signed in and out.

As she sat at her desk that morning, Barbara felt extremely grateful to Hammond and his secretary for having been so helpful to her. But she was also slightly guilty. She suspected that she had been affected again by the injection that Gloge had given her.

It was disconcerting to have been so *strongly* affected. 'But I feel all right now!' she thought as she typed away at the pile of work Helen Wendell had put in her basket. Yet her mind was astir with plans. At ten o'clock Helen sent her out with the usual morning briefcase full of memos and reports.

Elsewhere –

Gloge had awakened shortly after seven. Still no Barbara. Baffled, he shaved with his electric razor, drove to a nearby business thoroughfare, and ate breakfast.

He next went back to the street where Strather lived. A quick check established that the man was home. Gloge triggered his second charge of gas – and a few minutes later was in the apartment.

The young man had changed again to his pajamas, and he lay stretched out once more on the settee in his living room. If anything, the angry expression on his face was more pronounced.

Gloge, needle in hand, hesitated. He was not happy with this subject. Yet he realized that there was no turning back at this stage. Without further pause, holding the point almost against Strather's body, he squeezed the trigger.

There was no visible reaction.

As he headed for his office at Research Alpha, Gloge's thought was on the girl. Her absence was unfortunate. He had hoped to inject the serum into his two subjects at approximately the same time. Evidently that was not going to happen.

VI

A few minutes after he returned to his office, Dr Gloge's phone rang. His door was open, and he heard his secretary answer. The woman looked up over the receiver.

'It's for you, Doctor. That girl who worked here for a while – Barbara Ellington.'

The shock that went through Gloge must have shown as disapproval, for the woman said hastily, 'Shall I tell her you're not in?'

Gloge quivered with uncertainty. 'No.' He paused; then, 'I'll take the call in here.'

When he heard the clear, bell-like voice of the girl, Dr Gloge felt tensely ready for anything.

'What is it, Barbara?' he asked.

'I'm supposed to bring some papers over to you,' her voice trilled in its alive, vital way. 'I'm to give them to you only, so I wanted to make sure you would be there.'

... Opportunity!'

It seemed to Gloge that he couldn't have asked for a more

12

177

favorable turn. His other subject would now come to his office, where he could fire the second injection into her and deal personally with any reaction.

As it developed, there was no reaction that he could detect. She had turned away after delivering the papers to him, and that was when he fired the needle gun. It was a perfect shot. The girl neither jumped nor swung about; she simply kept going toward the door, opened it, and went through.

Barbara did not return to Hammond's office. She expected a strong physiological disturbance from the second injection, and she wanted to be in the privacy of her own room when it happened. It had cost her an effort not to react in front of Gloge.

So she stayed in her bedroom, waited as long as she thought wise, and then phoned and told Helen Wendell that she was not well.

Helen said sympathetically, 'Well, I suppose it was to be expected after the bad night you had.'

Barbara answered quickly, 'I began to have dizzy spells and nausea. I panicked and rushed home.'

'You're home now?'

'Yes.'

'I'll tell Mr Hammond.'

Barbara hung up, unhappy with those final words. But there was no way to stop his learning about her condition. She had a feeling she was in danger of losing her job. And it was too soon. Later, after the experiment, it wouldn't matter, she thought uneasily.

Perhaps she had better take the 'normal' precautions of an employee. 'After all,' she thought, 'I probably show symptoms.' She called her doctor and made an appointment for the following day. Barbara replaced the receiver, feeling a strange glee. 'I ought to be in foul shape by tomorrow,' she thought, 'from the second injection.'

What Hammond did when he returned to his office late that afternoon was to sit in thought for a while after Helen reported to him Barbara's situation.

Then: 'It doesn't add up. Helen. I should have asked you before. Have you examined her file?'

The blonde young woman smiled gravely. 'I can tell you everything that's in it, right from the top of my head. After all, I security-checked her. What do you want to know?'

'You mean there's nothing?'

'Nothing that I could find.'

Hammond hesitated no longer. He was accustomed to trusting Helen Wendell. Abruptly he threw up his hands. 'All right. She's got the whole weekend to be sick in. Call me when she comes in to work again. Did that report arrive from New Brasilia?'

'It was sent to Manila Center.'

'Are you serious? Let me talk to Ramón. There must be a reason!' Quickly he was absorbed in his new tasks.

Barbara slept. When she awakened, her clock said twelve after seven.

It was daylight, early morning. She found that out in a sensational fashion. She went outside and looked . . . without moving from the bed!

There she was lying in her bedroom; and there she was out in the street.

Simultaneously.

Involuntarily, she held her breath. Slowly, the outside scene faded, and she was back in the bed, wholly indoors.

With a gasp, she started breathing again.

By cautious experimentation, she discovered that her perception extended about a hundred yards.

And that was all she learned. Something in her brain acted like an invisible eye stalk that could reach through walls and bring back visual images to the light-interpretation centers. The ability remained completely stable.

Presently she became aware that a small black van was parked down the street and that Dr Gloge was in it. She realized that he had an instrument with an earplug with which he seemed to be listening in on her.

His face was intent, his small eyes narrowed. Something of the determination of this little bald-headed scientist seeped through to her, and Barbara suddenly felt uneasy. She sensed remorselessness, an impersonal quality that was entirely different from her own lighthearted participation in his experiment.

To Gloge – she realized suddenly – his subjects were like inanimate objects.

In human terms the viciousness of it was infinite.

As she continued to perceive him, Gloge shut off his instruments, started the motor of his car, and drove off.

Since Vince was again on the night shift, presumably Gloge was heading home.

She phoned Vince's apartment to make sure; when there was no answer, she called the photo lab.

'No, Strather didn't come in last night,' the administrative assistant of that department told her.

Barbara replaced the receiver unhappily, recalling that Vince had not responded well to the first shot. She suspected the biologist had given him his second shot also, and that he was not responding favorably to it either.

She dressed and drove over to his apartment. As she came near, she could see him inside, so when he showed no sign of replying to her ring, she let herself in with her key – and found him on the living-room couch, tossing and turning. He looked feverish. She felt his forehead; it was dry and hot to the touch.

He stirred and opened his eyes, looked up with his sick brown eyes into her bright blue ones. She thought unhappily: 'I'm so well and he's so ill. What can be wrong?'

Aloud, anxiously, she said, 'You need a doctor, Vince. What's the name of that man who gave you a checkup last year?'

'I'll be all right,' he mumbled. He sank back to sleep.

Sitting there on the settee beside him, Barbara felt something in her lungs. Her instant, amazed thought was: 'Gas!' But she was too slow.

She must have blacked out instantly, because her next awareness was of lying on the floor, and of Gloge bending over her.

The scientist was calm, efficient, seemed satisfied. Barbara caught his thought: 'She'll be all right.'

She realized that he was stepping past her to Vince.

'Hmmm!' Gloge seemed critical and unhappy. 'Still not good. Let's see if tranquilizer will help him.'

He made the injection, then straightened, and there was a strange, hard thought in his mind: 'By Monday night, it'll be time for the third injection, and I'll have to decide what to do.'

So clear was the thought that came from him, it was almost as if he spoke aloud. What his thought said was that he intended to kill them both, if either failed to develop as he desired.

Shocked, Barbara held herself very still; and at that

moment an entirely different growth process occurred in her.

It began with a veritable flood of suppressed information suddenly rising to the surface of her mind.

. . . About the reality of what people were like . . . the dupes, the malingerers, and the weaklings on the one hand, and, on the other, the angry and the distorted, the worldly wise and the cynics. She recognized that there were well-meaning people in the world who were strong, but she was more aware of the destructive at this instant . . . by the million, the swindlers and betrayers – all self-justified, she saw now. But she realized also that they had misread their own bitter experiences. Because they were greedy and lustful and had lost their fear of punishment, earthly or unearthly; because they resented being thwarted in their slightest whim; because –

A forgotten scene flashed into her mind from her own past, of a minor executive in her first job, who had fired her when she refused to come up to his apartment.

All her life she had been taught, and she had tried not to be aware of such things. But now, at some level of neural computation, she permitted all *that* data to be calculated into the mainstream of her awareness.

The process was still going on a few minutes later when Gloge departed as silently as he had come.

After he had left, Barbara tried to get up and was surprised that she could not even open her eyes. The realization that her body was still unconscious presently enthralled her.

What a marvelous ability!

As time passed, it began to be disconcerting. She thought: 'I'm really quite helpless.' It was early afternoon before she was finally able to move. She got up, subdued and thoughtful, warmed a can of soup for Vince and herself, and forced him to drink it from a cup.

Immediately after, he stretched out again on the couch and fell asleep. Barbara left the apartment to keep her appointment with her own doctor.

As she drove, she could feel a stirring inside her. More change? She decided it was. Perhaps there would be many such between now and Monday. Yet her intuition was that she would not be able to dominate this situation with the changes from the first and second shots only.

'Somehow,' she thought, 'I've got to get that third shot.'

VII

At noon Monday, after he had dictated some letters to a girl from the steno pool, Hammond came out of his office.

'What's the word from Nine-two?'

Helen looked up with her flashing smile. 'Barbara?'

'Yes.'

'Her doctor called in this morning at her request. He said he saw her Saturday. She appears to have a mild temperature, is subject to dizzy spells and a variety of unmentionable ailments like diarrhea. However, there's one unexpected thing, the doctor said – evidently his own comment. Interested?'

'Of course.'

'He said that in his opinion Barbara has had a major personality change since he last checked her about a year ago.'

Hammond shook his head slowly. 'Merely confirms our own observation. Well, keep me in touch.'

But about four o'clock, when the long-distance screen was finally silent, he buzzed Helen Wendell. 'I can't get that girl out of my mind. It's premonition-level stuff, so I can't ignore it. Phone Barbara.'

She called to him a minute later: 'Sorry, there's no answer.'

'Bring her file to me,' said Hammond. 'I've got to assure myself I'm not missing something in this unusual matter.'

As he scanned the typed pages a few minutes later, he came presently to the photograph of Vince Strather. He uttered an exclamation.

'What is it?' Helen asked.

He told her what had happened the previous week between Dr Gloge and Vince Strather.

He finished, 'Of course, I didn't connect Barbara with that young man. But this is his picture. Get Gloge's file.'

'Apparently the change started when his sister died two months ago,' Helen Wendell said presently. 'One of those sudden and dangerous shifts in personal motivation.' She added ruefully, 'I should have watched him on that. The death of a near relative has often proved important.'

She was seated in the main room of Hammond's living quarters at Research Alpha. The door of Hammond's private office behind them was closed. Across the room, a large wall safe had been opened, revealing a wide double row of thin, metal-bound files. Two of the files – Henry Gloge's and Barbara Ellington's – lay on the table before Helen. Hammond stood beside her.

He said now, 'What about that trip he made back east early in the month?'

'He spent three days in his hometown, purportedly to make arrangements to sell his sister's and his property there. They had a house, complete with private laboratory, untenanted, on the grounds of an old farm. The perfect location for unsupervised experimentation. On primates? Not likely. They're not easy to obtain secretly, and except for the smaller gibbons, they should make potentially quite dangerous subjects for Dr Gloge's project. So it must be humans he planned to work on.'

Hammond nodded.

There was an almost sick expression on his face.

The woman looked up at him. 'You seem very anxious. Presumably, Barbara and Vince have now had two injections each. That will take them to fifty thousand years from now on some level. It doesn't seem desperately serious to me.'

The man smiled tautly. 'Don't forget that we're dealing with one of the seed races.'

'Yes – but only fifty thousand years so far.'

He stared at her sympathetically. 'You and I,' he said, 'are still far down on the ladder. So it's hard for us to conceive of the evolutionary potential of the genus *Homo galacticus*.'

She laughed. 'I'm content with my lowly lot –'

'Good conditioning,' he murmured.

' – but I'm willing to accept your analysis. What do you intend to do with Gloge?'

Hammond straightened decisively. 'This experiment on humans has to be stopped at once. Call Ames and have him put special security men at every exit. For the next hour, don't let Gloge out of this building. And if Vince or Barbara try to enter the complex, tell him to hold them. When you've done that, start canceling my appointments for the rest of the day and evening.'

He disappeared into his bedroom, came out presently dressed for the street.

Helen Wendell greeted him with: 'I called Ames, and he

183

says "Check!" But I also phoned Gloge's office. He left about an hour ago, his secretary says.'

Hammond said quickly, 'Sound a standby alert. Tell Ames to throw a guard around the homes of both of those young people!'

'You're going where?'

'First Barbara, then Vince. I only hope I'm in time.'

A look must have come into Helen's face, because he smiled tensely and said, 'Your expression says I'm getting too involved.'

The beautiful blonde woman smiled with understanding, said, 'Every day on this planet thousands of people are murdered, hundreds of thousands are robbed, and countless minor acts of violence occur. People are struck, choked, yelled at, degraded, cheated – I could go on. If we ever opened ourselves to that, we'd shrivel away.'

'I kind of like Barbara,' Hammond confessed.

Helen was calm. 'So do I. What do you think is happening?'

'As I see it, Gloge gave them the first injection last Wednesday and the second on Friday. That means the third one should be given today. That I've got to stop.'

He departed hastily.

VIII

Gloge had become nervous. As Monday wore on, he kept thinking of his two specimens; and what bothered him was that he did not have them under observation on this last day.

What a ridiculous situation, he told himself. The greatest experiment in human history – and no scientific person watching it through to a conclusion of the key second injection.

There was another feeling, also.

Fear!

He couldn't help but remember the young man. It seemed to Gloge that he had seen too many animals show in their fashion the symptoms he had observed in Vince. Failure to respond well to the serum, the signs of internal malaise, the sick appearance, the struggle of the cells visibly reflecting defeat in the efforts and chemistry at the surface of the skin.

And there was – he had to admit it – a further anxiety. Many of the unsuccessful animal specimens had developed

184

tough fight-back characteristics. It would be wise to be prepared for emergencies of that nature.

He thought grimly: 'No use fooling myself. I'd better drop everything and take another look at those two.'

That was when he left his office.

He took it for granted that Barbara was all right. So he drove to Vince's apartment, and first checked with his audio pickups to make sure he was there and alone.

He detected at once movements; the sound of labored breathing, an occasional squeak of the springs of the couch. These noises came screeching through the hypersensitive receiver, but Gloge had the volume on them turned down so that they were not actually painful in his ears.

Gloge's spirits had already dropped even more, for the sounds he was hearing confirmed his fears.

Suddenly, all the justified scientific attitude that had motivated him until now came hard against the reality of the failure that was here.

By his previous reasoning, he would now have to kill Vince.

And that meant, of course, that he would also have to dispose of Barbara.

His state of funk yielded, after what must have been many minutes, to a strictly scientific thought: Mere sounds were not enough data for so basic a decision, it seemed to him.

He felt intense disappointment.

Now he must go and make his decision from an actual meeting with Vince. It would be improper to dispose of his two human subjects without a face-to-face interrogation.

As Gloge climbed out of his car and headed for the apartment building, Vince had a dream.

He dreamed that the man – what was his name? – Gloge, with whom he had quarreled a few days before in the corridor at Research Alpha, was coming here to his apartment, with the intention of killing him. At some deep of his being, anger began. But he did not awaken.

The dream – product of his own disturbed, strange evolutionary development – continued.

From some vantage point, he watched Gloge approach his back door. He felt no surprise when the small bald-headed man produced a key. Tense with fear, Vince watched as

185

Gloge stealthily inserted the key into the lock, slowly turned it, and quietly opened the door.

At that point, Vince's body was impelled by his extreme anxiety to defensive action. Millions of tiny, shining, cream-colored energy bundles were emitted by his nervous system. They resembled very short straight lines. And they passed through the wall that separated the living room from the kitchen, and they struck Gloge.

Great masses of the energy units unerringly sought out nerve ends in Gloge's body and darted in their scintillating fashion up to the man's brain.

The energy units were not the result of conscious analytical thought. They were brought into being solely by fright, and carried pressor messages. They pushed at Gloge mentally, urging him to leave, to go back to where he had come from.

Dr Gloge came to his senses with a start. He was back in his van. He remembered running in precipitant flight. He had a vague recollection of complete panic.

He sat now, trembling, breathing hard, trying to recover from the most disgraceful act of fear that he had ever experienced in his whole life.

And he knew that he had to go back.

Twice more, the sleeping Vince emitted enough energy bundles to compel Gloge to run. Each time the power available was less and Gloge retreated a shorter distance before stopping and forcing himself to go back again to the apartment.

On Gloge's fourth approach, the brain mechanism in Vince was able to manufacture only a small energy discharge. Gloge felt the fear rise in him, but he fought it – successfully.

He moved silently across the kitchen floor toward the door of the living room.

He still did not realize that the sleeping body and he had fought a battle – which he had now won.

Moments later, Gloge looked down at the exhausted form of his male subject. The sleeping body had perspired excessively. It trembled and moaned, and, as Gloge watched, jerked fitfully.

Unmistakably – Gloge decided – a failed experiment.

He wasted no time. He had come prepared. He pulled a pair of handcuffs from his pocket, carefully slipped one over Vince's farthest-away arm, and softly clicked it shut.

He lifted the arm as carefully toward the other wrist and clicked that handcuff on also.

Gloge next successfully tied Vince's legs together, and then lashed together the hands and feet.

The victim continued his restless, feverish sleep.

Gloge brought out a gag. As he had anticipated, forcing it into the closed mouth was more disturbing. Under him, the body grew rigid. Wild eyes flicked open and glared up at him.

In a single, convulsive effort, Vince tried to bring up his arms and simultaneously struggled to get to his feet.

But Gloge had done his preliminary work well. The victim's intense effort subsided. Dr Gloge realized that his control of this situation was complete. He removed the gag and said: 'What I want to know is, how do you feel?'

The half-crazy, rage-filled eyes snapped with the impulse to violence. Vince cursed in a shrill voice. He kept this up for several minutes. Then he seemed to realize something.

'Y-you did something to me last week.'

Gloge nodded. 'I injected you twice with a serum designed to accelerate cellular evolution, and I've come here to find out how you are.'

His gray eyes were steady; his bald head gleamed in the reflection of the light he had turned on. His face was serious. 'Why not tell me exactly how you feel?' he asked earnestly.

This time Vince's cursing subsided after about a minute. He lay, then, staring at his captor, and something about the pale, tense face of the scientist must have convinced him. 'I feel – awful,' he said uneasily.

'Exactly how?' Gloge persisted.

Slowly, by dint of determined questioning, he drew from his reluctant victim the fact that he felt weak, exhausted, and numb.

It was the fateful combination that had so often shown in the animals; and Gloge knew that it was decisive.

Without another word, he bent down and started to force the gag into Vince's mouth. Vince twisted, wriggled, turned his head, and several times tried to bite. But inexorably Gloge pushed the gag all the way into the other's mouth and knotted it firmly behind his head.

He now went outside and drove the van into the driveway opposite the back door of Vince's apartment. Wrapping

187

the young man's body in a blanket, he carried him boldly outside and into the van.

A few minutes later he was heading for the home of one of his subordinates. The man was on loan to an eastern laboratory, and his house and yard were unoccupied.

If he had paused, if he had stopped moving, if he had even taken his foot off the accelerator, Gloge might have faltered in his grisly plan. But his only slowdown was when he finally brought the car to a stop at his destination. And that, in its real meaning, was a continuation of the plan.

Its final moments.

Laboriously, he dragged the gagged, handcuffed, and bound Vince across the sidewalk, through a gate, and over to the deep end of the swimming pool. And still without pausing, he shoved the tense body over the edge and into the water.

He straightened from his terrible act, stood there gasping for breath, exhausted, watching the trail of bubbles that roiled the dark surface. Abruptly terrified that he might be seen, he turned and staggered away.

As he half-fell, half-crawled into his car, the first opposing thought came, as much a feeling of horror as an idea: 'My God, what have I done?'

But there was no opposing motion in that reaction. He did not go back. Instead, he sat there, bracing to the realization that a few feet away a man was still in process of drowning.

When there was no longer any doubt, when the subject of his experiment was by all laws of life dead, Gloge sighed and stirred. There was no turning back. One gone, one to go.

Next – the girl!

From a phone booth a few blocks away, Gloge dialed Barbara Ellington's boardinghouse. The voice of an elderly woman answered and told him Barbara had gone out.

The voice added, 'She certainly is a popular girl today.'

Gloge said uneasily, 'How do you mean?'

'Several men came by a little while ago and asked for her, but of course I had to tell them also that she wasn't here.'

A sharp fear struck through Gloge. 'Did they give their names?' he asked.

'A Mr Hammond,' was the reply.

Hammond! The chill of that froze Gloge. 'Thank you,' he gulped, and hung up.

He returned shakily to his car, torn between two impulses. He had intended to return after dark to the pool, fish Vince's body out of it, take off all the bindings, and dispose of it. He had a strong feeling now that he should do that at once. On the other hand, he had a desperate conviction that he must return to his office and remove the rest of the serum from the safe there.

That last suddenly seemed the more important thing to do, and the safest at this hour. The sun had gone down below the western hills, but the sky was still bright blue. The dying day had too much light in it for the gruesome task of getting rid of a dead body.

IX

At ten minutes past seven, Dr Gloge unlocked the door that led directly from the corridor to his office in the biology section of Research Alpha. He went in, closed the door behind him, walked quickly around the big, bare desk in the center of the room, and stooped down to unlock the desk drawer where he kept a key to one of the safes.

'Good evening, Dr Gloge,' a woman's voice said behind him.

For an instant Dr Gloge seemed unable to move. The words, the tone, sent an electrifying hope through him. He could scarcely believe his luck: that the second person he had to dispose of had come to where he could best deal with her.

He straightened slowly, turned around.

Barbara Ellington stood in the open door to the adjoining library, watching him, face serious and alert.

At no time in what followed did Gloge have any other *conscious* awareness than that this was Barbara Ellington.

But the very instant that he saw the girl, at some depth of his being neural readjustments took place. Millions of them. And from that instant, subconsciously, she was his dead sister. But she was not dead anymore. She was reassuringly alive in the person of Barbara.

A look passed between them. It was one of complete understanding. It occurred to Gloge that it was scientifically wrong to kill this successful experimental victim. He even had a feeling that she was on his side and would cooperate with him. He suppressed a fleeting impulse to pretend not to know why she was here.

He said matter-of-factly, 'How did you get in?'

'Through the specimen room.'

'Did any of the night workers see you?'

'No.' Barbara smiled slightly.

Gloge was examining her with quick evaluative looks. He noted the way she stood, almost motionless, but lightly and strongly balanced – a pose of contained, absolutely prepared energy. He saw in her eyes bright, quick intelligence.

The thought came to him: Nothing quite like this was ever on Earth before!

Barbara said suddenly, 'You took a long chance on us, didn't you?'

The words that burst from Dr Gloge surprised him: 'I had to do it.'

'Yes, I know.' Again she spoke matter-of-factly, moved forward into the room. Dr Gloge felt a surge of alarm, a sharp, cold prickling of the skin. But she turned from him to the left, and he watched silently as she sat down in a chair against the wall and placed the brown purse she carried on the armrest of the chair. She spoke first.

'You must give me the third injection of the serum immediately,' she told him. 'I'll watch you do it. Then I'll take the instrument and a supply of the serum to Vince. He – '

She paused, blue eyes kindling with abrupt comprehension as she studied Dr Globe's expression. 'So you've drowned him!' she said. She sat there, thoughtful; then: 'He's not dead. I sense him to be still alive. Now, what is the instrument you use? You must still have it with you.'

'I do,' Dr Gloge admitted hoarsely. 'But,' he went on quickly, 'it is advisable to wait till morning before administering the third shot. The chances of a further favorable development would be increased by doing it. And you must stay here! Nobody should see you as you are. There should be tests . . . you will tell me . . . '

He halted, realizing he was stammering. Barbara's eyes hadn't turned from his face. And in the same way that her knowledge of Vince's fate had not disturbed him – somehow, he took it for granted that she realized and appreciated why

190

and what he had done – so now her expression reassured him.

She said quietly, 'Dr Gloge, there are several things you don't understand. I know I can assimilate the serum. So give me the shot – and the serum – at once.'

Barbara Ellington arose and started over toward him. She said nothing, and her face revealed no emotion, but his next awareness was of holding the jet gun out to her on his open palm as she came up.

'There's only one charge left.'

She took the gun from his palm without touching him, turned it over, studied it, laid it back in his hand. 'Where is your supply of the serum?'

Dr Gloge nodded at the entrance to the library behind her. 'The larger of the two safes in there.'

Her head had turned in the direction he indicated. Now she remained still for a moment, gaze remote, lips parted, in an attitude of intent listening; then she looked back at him.

'Give me the injection,' she told him. 'Some men are coming.'

Dr Gloge lifted the gun, put the point against her shoulder, pulled the trigger. Barbara drew her breath in sharply, took the gun from him, opened her purse, dropped the gun inside, and snapped the purse shut. Her eyes shifted to the office door.

'Listen!' she said.

After a moment, Dr Gloge heard footsteps coming along the narrow corridor from the main laboratory.

'Who is it?' he asked anxiously.

'Hammond,' she said. 'Three other men.'

Dr Gloge made a stifled sound of despair. 'We've got to get away. He mustn't find either of us here. Quick – through there.' He waved toward the library.

Barbara shook her head. 'This place is surrounded. All passages are guarded.' She frowned. 'Hammond must think he has all the evidence he needs against you – but don't help him in any way! Admit nothing! Let's see what I can do with my – ' As she spoke, she moved back to the chair on which she had been sitting. She settled into it, her face composed. 'Maybe I can handle him,' she said confidently.

The footsteps had reached the door. There came a knock.

Gloge glanced at Barbara. His thoughts were whirling. She nodded, smiled.

'Come in!' Dr Gloge said harshly, too loudly.

Hammond entered the room. 'Why, Mr Hammond!' Barbara exclaimed. Her face was flushed; she looked embarrassed and confused.

Hammond had stopped, as he caught sight of her. He sensed a mental probing. His brain put up a barrier, and the probing ceased.

Their eyes met; and there was a flicker of consternation in hers. Hammond smiled ironically. Then he said in a steely voice: 'Stay where you are, Barbara. I'll talk to you later.' His voice went up. 'Come on in, Ames!' he called.

There was threat in his tone; and Dr Gloge sent a quick, desperate, appealing glance at Barbara. She gave him an uncertain smile. The look of earnest, fumbling innocence with which she had greeted Hammond had left her face, leaving it resigned but alert.

Hammond gave no sign of being aware of the change.

'Ames,' he said to the first of the three men who came in through the library from the specimen room – Dr Gloge recognized Wesley Ames, the chief of Research Alpha's security staff – 'this is Barbara Ellington. Take charge of that handbag she's holding. Allow no one to enter this office. Miss Ellington is not to leave and is not to be permitted to touch any object in this room. She is to stay in that chair until I return with Dr Gloge.'

Wesley Ames nodded. 'Understood, Mr Hammond!' He glanced at his men, one of whom went to the office door and locked it, while Ames turned to Barbara. She handed him her purse without comment.

'Doctor, come with me,' Hammond said curtly.

Dr Gloge followed him into the library. Hammond closed the door behind him.

'Where's Vince?' he said in an inexorable voice.

'Really, Mr Hammond,' Gloge protested. 'I don't – '

Hammond stepped toward him abruptly. The movement seemed a threat. Dr Gloge cringed, expecting to be manhandled. Instead, the bigger man firmly caught his arm and pressed a tiny metal object against his bare wrist.

'Tell me where Vince is!' Hammond commanded.

Gloge parted his lips to deny any knowledge of Barbara's

192

boyfriend. Instead, the confession of what he had done poured forth from him. As he realized what he was admitting, Gloge tried desperately to stop himself from talking. He had already divined that the metal touching his skin was some kind of a hypnotic device, and so he tried to pull his arm from Hammond's grasp.

It was a vain effort.

'How long ago did you drown him?' Hammond asked.

'About an hour ago,' said Dr Gloge hopelessly.

At that instant shouts came from the adjoining office. The door was pulled open. Wesley Ames stood there, ashenfaced.

'Mr Hammond – she's gone!'

Hammond darted past him into the office. Dr Gloge hurried after, legs trembling. As he reached the door, Hammond already was coming back into the office with one of the security men from the hall on the other side. Ames and the other man stood in the center of the office, looking about with stupefied expressions.

Hammond closed the door, said to Ames, 'Quickly, now! What happened?'

Ames threw his hands up in a gesture of furious frustration.

'Mr Hammond, I don't know. We were watching her. She was there in the chair; then she was *not* there, that's all. He' – he indicated one of the men – 'was standing with his back to the door. When we saw she was gone, he was sitting on the floor next to the door! The door was open. We ran into the hall, but she wasn't there. Then I called you.'

'How long had you been watching her?' Hammond asked sharply.

'How long?' Ames gave him a dazed look. 'I had just taken my mother down the hall to the elevator –'

He stopped, blinked. 'Mr Hammond, what am I saying? My mother's been dead for eight years!'

Hammond said softly, 'So that's her little trick. She reached to that deep of the heart where the pure, unsullied dead are enshrined. And I thought she was only trying to read my mind!'

He broke off, said in a clear, commanding voice: 'Wake up, Ames! You three have been gone from the world for a couple of minutes. Don't worry about how Miss Ellington did it. Get her description to the exits. If she's seen approaching by a guard, tell him to keep her at a distance at gun point.'

As the three hurried from the office, he indicated a chair to Dr Gloge. Gloge sat down, senses swimming, as Hammond took a pencil-shaped device from his pocket, pressed it, and stood waiting.

On the fifth floor of the Research Alpha complex, Helen Wendell picked up the small private phone at the side of her desk, said, 'Go ahead, John.'

'Switch all defense and trap screens on immediately!' Hammond's voice told her. 'Gloge's drowned Strather – as an experimental failure. But the other one's awake and functioning. It's hard to know what she'll do next, but she may find it necessary to get to my office as a way of getting out of this building fast.'

Helen pressed a button. 'Not this way she won't!' she said. 'The screens are on.'

X

Outside, it grew darker on that tense Monday night.

At eight-eighteen, Helen Wendell again picked up the small phone purring at the side of her desk in the Research Alpha complex, glanced over at the closed office door, and said into the receiver, 'Go ahead, John.'

'I'm here at the pool,' John Hammond's voice told her. 'We've just fished his body out. Helen, the fellow is alive. Some reflex prevented any intake of water. But we'll need an oxygen tent.'

Helen's left hand reached for another telephone. 'You want the ambulance?' she asked, starting to dial.

'Yes. You have the street number. Tell them to pull up at the side gate. We have to act swiftly.'

'Police uniforms, also?' Helen asked.

'Yes. But tell them to stay in the cab unless needed. We're out of sight, behind a high fence. And it's dark. I'll come back with them. Has Barbara been apprehended?'

'No,' Helen said.

'I really didn't expect she would be,' Hammond said. 'I'll question the guards when I get there.'

Barbara had allowed Ames to escort her to the nearest elevator, while she continued to have him think that she was his mother.

194

Once in the elevator, she pushed the up-button and came out presently on the roof. As she had already perceived, a helicopter was scheduled to take off. And though she was not an authorized passenger, the pilot took her along believing her to be his girl friend. Her sudden arrival seemed perfectly logical to him.

A little later, he set her down on the roof of another building. And that, also, seemed the most natural act to him, her reason for going there obvious.

He flew off and promptly forgot the episode.

The hasty landing was an urgent necessity for Barbara. She could feel the new injection beginning to work. So in her scanning of the buildings flitting by below, she perceived one in which the upper floors were unoccupied.

'I'll try to make it down to some office,' she thought.

But she didn't get beyond the top floor. She actually began to stagger as she went down the first steps from the roof. And there was no mistaking the out-of-control state of her body. To her left, a door opened into a warehouse-like loft. She weaved through it, closed it behind her, and bolted it. Then she half-lowered herself, half-fell to the floor.

During that evening and night she never quite lost consciousness. Blackout was no longer possible for her. But she could feel her body changing, changing, changing –

The energy flows inside her took on a different meaning. They were separate from her. Presently they would be controllable again, but in another fashion entirely.

Something of Barbara seemed to disappear with that awareness.

'I'm still me!' the entity thought as it lay there on the floor. 'Flesh, feeling, desire – '

But she had the distinct realization that 'me' even in these early stages of the five-hundred-thousand-year transformations was ME PLUS.

Exactly how the self was becoming something more was not yet clear.

The slow night dragged by.

XI

Tuesday.

Shortly before noon, Helen Wendell came along the hallway that led from John Hammond's quarters to the main office. Hammond was sitting at the far side of her desk. He glanced up at her as she approached.

'How are the patients?' he asked.

'Gloge is role-perfect,' Helen said. 'I even allowed him to spend part of the morning talking to his assistants here. He's already had two conversations by Telstar with Sir Hubert about his new task overseas. I've put him to sleep again, but he's available. When did you come in?'

'Just now. How's Strather?'

Helen tapped the recorder. 'I checked with the MD machine on him twenty minutes ago,' she said. 'It gave me its opinion in detail. I took it all down. Do you want to hear it?'

'Sum it up for me.'

Helen pursed her lips; then: 'The MD verifies that he didn't swallow any water, that some newly developed brain mechanism shut off breathing and kept him in a state of suspended animation. Vince himself has no conscious memory of the experience, so it was evidently a survival act of the lower brain. MD reports other developments are taking place in Vince, regards them as freakish in nature. It's too soon to tell whether or not he can survive a third injection. He's under sedation.'

Hammond looked dissatisfied. 'All right,' he said after a moment. 'What else do you have for me?'

'A number of transmitter messages,' Helen said.

'About Gloge?'

'Yes. New Brasilia and Manila agree with you that there are too many chances of a revealing slip-up if Dr Gloge remains at Research Alpha any longer than is absolutely necessary.'

'You said Gloge is role-perfect.'

Helen nodded. 'At the moment. But he is a highly recalcitrant subject, and naturally I can't give him the kind of final conditioning he'd get at Paris center. That's where they want him. The courier, Arnold, will take him aboard the Paris-jet at five-ten tonight.'

'No!' Hammond shook his head. 'That's too early! Gloge is our bait to catch Barbara. His experiments indicate that she won't be able to function until sometime this evening. I calculate that somewhere around nine o'clock will be a good time to let Gloge out from behind the defense screens.'

Helen was silent a moment, then said, 'There seems to be a general feeling, John, that you're overestimating the possibilities of any really dangerous evolutionary developments in Barbara Ellington.'

Hammond smiled tautly. 'I've seen her. They haven't. Mind you, for all I know, she may be dead or dying of the effects of the third shot by now. But if she's capable of coming, I think she'll come. She'll want that fourth injection. She may start anytime looking for the man who can produce the serum for her.'

By Tuesday a new awareness had come to Barbara.

She had developed brain mechanisms that could do things with space – do them on an automatic level, without her conscious mind knowing what, or how. Fantastic things. . . .

As she lay there, a new nerve center in her brain reached out and scanned a volume of space 500 light-years in diameter. It touched and comprehended clouds of neutral hydrogen and bright young O-type stars, measured the swing of binaries, took a censuse of comets and ice asteroids. Far out in the constellation of Ophiuchus a blue-white giant was going nova, and the new, strange linkage in Barbara's mind observed its frantic heaving of spheres of radiant gas. A black dwarf emitted its last spray of infrared light and sank into the radiationless pit of dead star.

Barbara's mind encompassed it all, and reached farther . . . reached out effortlessly until it touched a specific Something . . . and withdrew.

Brimming with ecstasy, Barbara cried out in her mind, *What did I touch?*

She knew it had been something the brain mechanism was programmed to search for. But no conscious perception was involved. All she could be sure of was that the nerve center seemed satisfied, and ceased its scanning.

But she sensed, in an intensely happy way, that it remained aware of What it had contacted.

She was still savoring the joy a while later when she became aware that the shifting energy flows inside her had resumed.

Gradually, then, she permitted her body and mind to sink into a receptive state.

Midsummer heat built up over the city throughout the day. In the locked room on the vacant top floor of the multi-storied building three miles from Research Alpha, the heat grew stifling as the sun shifted overhead, began to beat in through closed, unshaded windows. Barbara, curled on her side on the dusty floor, did not move. Now and then she uttered a moaning sound. Sweat ran from her for a long, long time, as the heat increased; then the skin of her face dried and turned dirty white. She made no more sounds. Even a close study would not have been able to prove that she still breathed.

By four o'clock the sunblaze had shifted past the windows, and the locked room lay in shadows. But it was another hour before the temperature in it gradually began to drop. About six, the curled figure moved for the first time.

She straightened her legs slowly, then, with a sudden convulsive motion, rolled over on her back, lay flat, arms flung loosely to the sides.

The right half of her face was smeared grotesquely with thick dust caked in drying sweat. She breathed – lay quiet again. Several minutes later, her eyelids lifted. The eyes were a deep, brilliant blue, seemed oddly awake and alert, though they remained unfocused and did not shift about the room. After a while, the lids slowly closed and remained closed.

The day darkened; the city's lights awoke. The empty warehouse stood silent. More than an hour passed before the figure in the room on the top floor moved again.

This time, it was motion of a different order. She rose suddenly and quickly to her feet, went to the nearest window, and stood looking out through the dirt-stained glass.

The towering Research Alpha complex was a glow of white light to the west. The watcher's eyes turned toward it. . . .

A second of time went by. Then the mind that directed the eyes moved on an entirely new level of extended perception.

Night-shift activities in the research complex were not essentially different from those of the day; but there were fewer people around as the awareness that was Barbara drifted along familiar, lighted hallways, about corners, dropped suddenly to a sublevel which contained the biology section. Here she flicked through the main laboratory and up a narrow corridor, pausing before the door to Dr Gloge's office.

She moved through the door, paused in the dark and silent office, then moved on into the library. She remained a minute or two above the big safe in a corner of the library. Then she knew.

The safe was empty – and trapped.

The awareness flicked out of the library, shifted to the fifth floor of the complex, drifted toward a great black door showing the words: *Scientific Liaison and Investigation*. She stopped before it.

Minutes passed as she slowly and carefully scanned the outer walls of John Hammond's offices and living quarters. Here was something new . . . something that seemed very dangerous. Within the walls and doors, above the ceiling, below the flooring of this section, strange energies curled and crawled like twisting smoke.

She could not pass through that barrier.

But though she could not enter, her perceptions might, to some extent.

She must avoid, she decided, both the front entry door and the secret elevator which led directly to Hammond's living quarters in the rear of the section. As the most obvious points for an intruder to consider, they were also the most formidably shielded.

She shifted back along the hall to a point some twenty feet away from the massive black door, well back from the wall between her and the front office. She waited. Gradually a picture began to form. . . .

This was an unfamiliar room, the inner office of the section. There was no one in it, nothing of interest except a closed door across from the one which opened on the corridor.

The inner office disappeared . . . and what came next was no picture, but a surge of savage, demanding hunger.

Startled, shocked, already feeling the pull that in a moment would hurl her into the murderous barriers about the section, the searching awareness instantly broke the thread of visual perception, went inactive to allow herself to stabilize.

Nevertheless, she now knew where the serum was – in a strongroom of Hammond's quarters, heavily screened, seemingly inaccessible.

Perception cautiously opened again. Another section of the living quarters appeared, hazy with hostile energies. The other – the male counterpart – was here. Alive.

Here, but helpless. Here, but unconscious, in a cage of dark force which permitted no more than barest identification by the searcher. She was very glad he had been rescued.

Minutes later, she knew there was no one else in Hammond's locked quarters. She withdrew visual perception from there, and let the picture of the main office develop. The blurred image of a woman – Helen Wendell – now seemed to be speaking into an instrument connected with the apparatus before her.

A second band of perception opened, and voices became indistinctly audible.

Ganin Arnold, the New Brasilia courier, was making his final call from the city jetport, nine miles south of the Research Alpha complex.

'The doors are being secured,' he said. He was speaking into a disguised microphone clamped over his mouth and nose, which had the appearance of the tranquilizing respirators many of the other jet passengers were using now in the last moments before lift-off. Even to anyone within inches of him, his voice would have remained completely inaudible. In John Hammond's office, it emerged clearly from the device on Helen Wendell's desk.

'Lift-off for the nonstop jet to Paris,' Arnold went on, 'will follow' – he glanced at the watch on his wrist – 'in two minutes and thirty seconds. All passengers and every member of the crew have passed at least once through the measurement radius. Nothing which may have preceded or followed myself and our biologist aboard registers life-energy levels significantly above the standard Earther range – that is, of course, below six.

'To sum it up, we definitely are *not* being accompanied to Paris by any abnormally high human evolutionary form. Dr Gloge's behavior has been excellent. His tranquilizer has begun to take effect, and he is showing signs of drowsiness. Undoubtedly, he will sleep soundly throughout the trip.'

Arnold paused, apparently waiting for comment. When there was none, he resumed, 'As soon as the lift-field goes on, communication by this means, of course, will be impossible. Since nothing is likely to go wrong from this moment on, I suggest, if it's satisfactory to Mr Hammond, that I end my report now.'

Helen Wendell's voice, seeming to speak from a point just within the left side of the courier's skull, told him pleasantly, 'Mr Hammond prefers you to remain alert and available for final instructions until the lift has begun.'

<h1 style="text-align:center">XII</h1>

In the locked room on the top floor of the empty warehouse a few miles east of Research Alpha, the womanshape standing at the window stirred suddenly out of the tranced immobility it had maintained for the past minutes. The head lifted, gaze sweeping the softly glowing night sky above the city. A hand moved, touching the thick windowpane probingly. The glass fell away like a big drop of melting ice.

Dust swirled as cool air rushed in.

Barbara waited, then moved closer to the opening.

Her gaze swung to the west again, remained there. She listened. The myriad noises of the city were clear and distinct now. Overlying them was a thin fountain of skysound as, every thirty seconds – at this hour – a jet lifted vertically from the city port, cut in its engines, and vanished up into the night with a whistling shriek. Her head shifted quickly, briefly following the changing pattern of the sound. Then it steadied.

Her gaze rose slowly, slanting to the north, following a moving, distant point in the night, eyes narrowed with intentness.

On board the Paris jet which had left the city port a few minutes before, Dr Henry Gloge now had a very curious experience. Drowsily, almost on the verge of sleep, he had been contemplating the pleasant significance of his assignment today to Sir Hubert Roland's Paris project. Suddenly, then, there was a sensation of coming partly awake.

He gazed around him with a rising sense of alarm, looking first of all at his seat companion.

The fellow was big, heavily built. He looked like a police detective, and Gloge knew that the man was his guard. The curious thing was that he was slumped back in the seat, head lolling forward, eyes closed . . . typical indications of a tranquilizer stupor.

Gloge thought: 'Why is he asleep?' He had a strong conviction that it was he who should be unconscious. There was a clear memory of a device – an instrument totally unfamiliar to him – which the Wendell woman had used to implant a complete, compelling set of delusions in his mind. He had come willingly aboard the jet. And he had, at the suggestion of his guard, inhaled enough tranquilizing gas from the seat respirator to have kept him somnolent until the jet touched down in Paris.

Instead, minutes later, he had come awake, the delusions of the day slipping from his mind!

There must be an explanation for these apparently contradictory events.

The thought ended. A feeling of blankness held him for a moment. Then came a churning wave of terror.

Somewhere a voice had said: 'Yes, Dr Gloge – there *is* an explanation for this!'

Slowly, against his every inclination, but completely unable to withstand the impulse, Dr Gloge turned, looked back. There was someone in the seat behind him.

For an instant, it seemed to be a complete stranger. Then the eyes opened. They fixed on him, glowing brilliant demon-blue, even in the muted light of the jet.

The woman spoke, and it was the voice of Barbara Ellington. 'We have a problem, Dr Gloge. There seems to be a group of extraterrestrials on this planet, and I still do not have any clear idea of what they are doing here. That's our immediate task – to find out.'

'You are *where*?' Helen Wendell said sharply.

Her hand flicked to the right, snapped a switch. A small view-screen on the right side of the desk lit up. She said, 'John – quick!'

In the inner office, John Hammond turned, saw the lit screen on the desk behind him. An instant later he was listening to the words tumbling hoarsely from the telephone speaker on his left. He said to Helen's tense, pale profile in the screen to the right, 'Where is he?'

'At the Des Moines jetport! The Paris jet put down for emergency repairs. Now nobody seems to understand just what was wrong with it or what repairs are needed. But the passengers have been disembarked, are to be transferred to another jet. Arnold's in a state of confusion and shock. Listen to him!'

' – there was a woman with him,' the courier's voice

202

babbled. 'At the time, I thought it was one of the passengers who had come off the jet with us. Now I'm not sure. But I simply stood there and watched the two of them walk out of the hall together. It never occurred to me to ask myself why this woman was with Gloge, or to stop them, or even to wonder where they were going. . . .'

Hammond twisted a dial, dimming the voice. He spoke to Helen Wendell. 'When did the jet come down?'

'From what Arnold said first,' Helen told him, 'it must have been over half an hour ago! As he puts it, it didn't occur to him to call us about it until now.'

'Half an hour!' Hammond came to his feet. 'Helen, drop everything you're doing! I want an off-planet observer sitting in on this, preferably within minutes.'

She gave him a startled look. 'What are you expecting?'

'I don't know what to expect.'

She hesitated, began: 'The Wardens . . .'

'Whatever can be done here,' Hammond said, 'I can do myself. I don't need anyone else for that. The defense screens on the northern side will go off for exactly forty seconds. Now move!' He snapped off the screen, reached under the desk, threw over another switch.

In the main office, Helen Wendell stared at the blank screen for a moment. Then she jumped to her feet, ran across the room to the entry door, pulled it open, and slipped out into the hall. The door swung shut behind her.

Some moments later, John Hammond entered the room behind his private office where Vincent Strather lay enclosed by a trap screen. Hammond went to the wall, turned the trap controls there halfway to the off point.

The screen faded into smoky near-invisibility, and he stared for a few seconds at the shape stretched out on the couch within it. He asked aloud. 'There have been no further internal changes?'

'None within the past two hours,' the MD machine's voice said from the wall.

'This form is viable?'

'Yes.'

'He would awaken if I released the screen?'

'Yes. Immediately.'

Hammond was silent a moment, then asked, 'You have calculated the effects of a fourth injection of the serum?'

'Yes,' the machine said from the wall.

'In general, what are they?'

'In general,' the machine said, 'there would be pronounced changes, and at an again greatly accelerated rate. The evolutionary trend remains the same, but would be very much advanced. The resultant form would stabilize within twenty minutes. It would again be a viable one.'

Hammond turned the trap-screen controls full over to the left. The screen darkened once more into a dense, concealing shroud.

It was too soon to make the decision to give the fourth shot. Perhaps – mercifully – it would be avoided altogether.

XIII

At half-past ten, the long-distance signal sounded from the telephone screen. Hammond glanced around from the portable control box on the desk, simultaneously pressed the answer button and the stud which would leave him unseen if the caller's instrument was equipped with a view-screen, and said, 'Go ahead!'

The screen remained dark, but somebody made a gasping sound of relief. *'Mr Hammond!'* It was a reedy, quavering voice, but it was distinctly the voice of Dr Gloge.

There were two sharp clicks from one of the instruments lying on the desk – a signal from Helen Wendell, in the observer boat standing off Earth, that she was recording the conversation.

'Where are you, Doctor?'

'Mr Hammond . . . something terrible . . . that creature . . . Barbara Ellington –'

'She took you off the jet, I know,' Hammond said, 'Where are you now?'

'My home – in Pennsylvania.'

'She went there with you?'

'Yes. There was nothing I could do.'

'Of course not,' Hammond said. 'She's gone now?'

'I don't know where she is. I took the chance of phoning. Mr Hammond, there was something I didn't know, didn't remember. But *she* knew. I . . .'

'You had some Omega serum in that farm laboratory?' Hammond asked.

204

'I didn't think of it as that,' Dr Gloge's voice told him. 'It was an earlier experimental variant – one with impurities which produce a dangerously erratic reaction. I was under the impression I had destroyed my entire stock. But this being knew better! It brought me here, forced me to give it what was left of the serum. The quantity was small – '

'But enough for a standard fourth shot of the series?' Hammond said.

'Yes, yes, it was sufficient for the fourth injection.'

'And she has now taken it as an injection?'

Dr Gloge hesitated; then he said, 'Yes. However, there is reason to hope that instead of impelling the evolutionary process in what I now regard as a monstrous creature on to its next stage, the imperfect serum will result in its prompt destruction.'

'Perhaps,' said Hammond. 'But almost since you first launched Barbara Ellington into this process, she appears to have been aware of what was possible to her. I can't believe she's made a mistake now.'

'I . . . ' Dr Gloge paused again, went on: 'Mr Hammond, I realize the enormity of what I've done. If, in any way, I can help avert the worst consequences, I shall cooperate to the fullest extent. I – '

There was a sharp click as the connection was broken; a pause, then Helen Wendell's voice whispered into Hammond's ear, 'Do you think Barbara let him make that call, then cut him off?'

'Of course.'

Helen made no further comment, simply waited; and presently, softly, Hammond continued: 'I think she wants us to know that she's coming here.'

'I think she's there now,' said Helen. 'Good-bye.'

XIV

John Hammond glanced at the control box on the desk and saw the flickering indicators. He also saw a wholly unexpected reaction: a condition of nonenergy that actually canceled energy.

'Helen,' he said. 'This woman has gone up somewhere out of our reach! What you're seeing is energy trying to maintain itself against antienergy. I received recognition drilling on such things, but I've never seen it before in an actual situation.'

Helen Wendell, eyes fixed on a duplicate check screen in the distant observer boat, did not reply. A shifting electronic storm was blazing through the check-screen indicators; it showed that the defensive forces enclosing Hammond's office and living quarters were coming under a swiftly varying pattern of attack . . . presently that they were being tested almost to the limit.

It held that way for over a minute – every reading almost impossibly high, barely shifting.

'John Hammond!' the desktop said softly to Hammond.

He jerked slightly away, eyes flicking down to it.

'John Hammond!' the chair whispered beside him.

'John Hammond!' 'John Hammond!' 'John Hammond!' 'John Hammond . . .'

His name sprang at him from every part of the office, in a swirling, encircling pattern. Because of his special supervisory position, Hammond knew the pattern and its danger. It had never been considered probable, but nevertheless *they* had taken the possibility into account, and so he had outside power available to deal with this emergency.

He looked hurriedly about on the desk for an instrument he had laid down among the others there. For an instant he seemed unable to recognize it, and there was an icy touch of panic. Then he realized he already held it in his hand. He ran a knob up along its side with his thumb, locked it into place, laid the instrument back on the desk.

A rasping came from it. Not only a sound, but a vibration, a rough, hard shuddering of the nerves. The voice-ghosts sank to a whisper, flowed from the room. Helen Wendell's tiny, distant voice stabbed at Hammond's ear like a needle: 'The check screen! She's leaving!' Hopefully.

'You're certain?'

'Not really.' Alarm whipped at him through Helen's voice. 'What does *your* screen show?'

'A subjective blur at the moment. It's clearing.'

'What happened?'

'I think she felt above us, and so she took it for granted that she could walk all over us. Accordingly, she's just had the surprise of her brief existence as a subgalactic super-woman. She didn't realize we represent the Great Ones.'

'Is she damaged?'

'Oh, I wouldn't say that. She's learned too much. But . . . details later.' Hammond blinked at the check screen, swung around toward the door of the adjoining room, pulled it open.

'Administer the final injection to the subject!' he said sharply into the room. 'Acknowledge!'

'The fourth and final injection of the Omega Stimulation series will be administered to the subject,' the machine replied.

'Immediately!'

'Immediately.'

Helen's voice reached Hammond again as he drew the door shut and came back to the desk. 'At moments,' she said, 'the antienergies were holding the ninety-six point of overload. Within four of the theoretical limit. Did she get to you at the energy balance?'

'Very nearly,' Hammond told her. 'A very high-energy, pseudo-hypno trick that didn't quite work. And she'll be back. I still have something she wants!'

On his desk, the telephone screen blurred. When he turned it on, the voice of Dr Gloge sounded in his ears.

'We were cut off earlier, Mr Hammond.' The biologist's voice was strongly even and controlled.

'What happened?' Hammond asked warily.

'Mr Hammond, I have finally analyzed what evolution really is. The universe is a spectrum. It needs energies in motion at all levels. This is why those at the higher levels do not interfere directly with individual activities at the lower. But this is also why they are concerned when a race reaches the point where it can begin to manipulate large forces.'

Hammond said steadily, 'Barbara, if the purpose of this call is to find out if I'll let you in, yes, I will.'

A pause, then a click. Then there was a tiny, momentary flickering in one of the check-screen indicators. Then, in a different section, another.

'What's happening?' Helen asked tautly.

Hammond said, 'She's coming through the screens, with my permission.'

'Do you think it's a trick?'

'In a way. For some reason, she hasn't let herself reach that theoretical, final million-year point on Dr Gloge's evolutionary scale. That may come a little later.'

'And you're actually letting her in, believing that?'

'Of course.' Helen did not answer him.

A minute went past in silence. Hammond shifted so that he faced the door, moved a few steps away from the control box and the desk, and stood waiting.

A small light burned red in a corner of the check screen. Something had come into the main office.

The heavy silence continued for some seconds. Then, on the hard flooring at the far end of the corridor, Hammond heard footsteps.

He couldn't have said what he had been expecting . . . but certainly nothing so commonplace as the sound of a woman's high-heeled shoes coming briskly toward the inner office.

She appeared in the doorway, stopped there, looking at him. Hammond said nothing. All outer indications were that this was the Barbara Ellington he had seen sitting in a chair in Dr Gloge's office the night before. Nothing had changed either in her looks or in her clothing; even the brown purse she held in one hand seemed the same. Except for the air of radiant vitality, the alertness of her stance, the keen intelligence in her face, this also was, in fact, the awkward, over-anxious, lean girl who had worked in the outer officer for less than two weeks.

And therefore, Hammond thought it was a phantom! Not a delusion; he was protected now against any attempt to tamper with his mind in that manner by barriers which would break only if he died. The shape standing in the door was real. The instruments recorded it. But it was a shape created for this meeting – not that of Barbara Ellington as she was at this hour.

He was unsure of her intention in assuming it. Perhaps it was designed to throw him off guard.

She came into the room, smiling faintly, and glanced about. Hammond knew then that he hadn't been mistaken. Something had come in with her . . . something oppressive, spine-tingling; a sense of heat, a sense of power.

The curiously brilliant, blue eyes turned toward him; and the smile deepened.

'I'm going to have to test why you're still here,' she said carelessly. 'So defend yourself!'

There was no sound; but a cloud of white light filled the air between them, enveloping them; faded; flared silently;

faded again. Both stood unmoving, each watching the other. Nothing in the office had changed.

'Excellent!' the woman said. 'The mystery behind you begins to reveal itself. I know the quality of your race now, John Hammond. *Your* science could never control the order of energies that are shielding you mentally and physically here!

'There should be other indications then that in extreme necessity you are permitted to employ devices created by beings greater than yourself – devices which you do not yourself understand. And where would such devices be found at the moment? . . . Over there, I believe!'

She turned toward the door of the adjoining room, took three steps, and halted. A rose-glowing haze had appeared before the door and the surrounding sections of wall and flooring.

'Yes,' she said. 'That comes from the same source! And here –'

She turned, moved quickly toward the control box on the desk, checked again. A rose haze also enveloped the box now.

'The three points you must consider vital here!' she said, nodding. 'Yourself, the being in that room, and the controls of the section. You may safeguard these at the expense of revealing a secret you would otherwise least want to reveal. Now I think it is time for us to exchange information.'

She came back to Hammond, stopped before him.

'I discovered suddenly, John Hammond, that your kind are not native of Earth. You are superior to Earth's humanity, but not sufficiently superior to explain why you are here. You have an organization on this world. But it is a curious organization. It does not appear to serve the purposes of conqueror or exploiter. . . . But let's leave it at that. Don't try to explain it. It doesn't matter. You are to release the human male who was to have received the series of serum injections with me. You and the other members of your race stationed here will then remove yourselves promptly from this planet. We have no further use for you.'

Hammond shook his head.

'We might be forced off the planet,' he said. 'But that would make Earth an active danger spot. The Great Galactics whom I represent do have servant races who carry out military assignments for them. It would not be to your advantage if such a race were to occupy or quarantine Earth to make sure that the seedling race here continues to receive the necessary degree of supervision.'

'John Hammond,' the woman-shape said, 'whether the Great Galactics send military servants to Earth or come here themselves is a matter that does not concern me in the least. It would be very unwise of them to do either. Within hours from now, the Omega serum will be available in limitless quantities. Within days, every man, woman, and child of Earth will have gone through the full evolutionary sequence. Do you thing Earth's new humanity could still be supervised by any other race?'

'The Omega serum will never be used again,' Hammond said. 'I'll show you why. . . . '

Hammond turned, went to the control box on the desk. The rose haze faded before him, appeared behind him again. He threw a switch, and the haze vanished. He turned away from the controls. 'The energy fields that kept you out of that room are being shut off,' he said. 'In a moment, the door will open. So see for yourself – the barriers are off.'

Except for the blazing blue of the eyes, her face was a cold mask. Hammond thought she must already know what was there. But she turned, went to the open door, and stood looking into the room. Hammond moved to the side of the desk where he could look past her. . . .

The energy trap enclosing the couch in the room had vanished. The dark thing on the couch was just sitting up. It shook its head dazedly, rolled over, and came up on all fours.

Its huge, dull-black eyes stared at them for an instant; then it straightened, rose to its full height. . . .

To a full height of twenty-two inches! It swayed unsteadily on the couch – a hairy little figure with a wide-mouthed, huge-eyed goblin head.

Its eyes blinked in vague recognition. The mouth opened. It cried in a thin, bleating voice: 'Bar-ba-ra!'

xv

The woman wheeled, turning away. She did not look back at the grotesque little figure. But a faint smile touched her lips as she gazed at Hammond. 'All right,' she said, 'there goes my last tie with Earth. I accept what you said. I gather that the

Omega serum is a unique development and that it hasn't shown up elsewhere in the galaxy.'

'That is not a literal truth,' said Hammond.

She nodded toward the adjoining room. 'Then perhaps you can tell me what went wrong.'

Hammond told her Gloge's twofold theory: that at this stage of man's evolution many possibilities remained for evolvement, and that apparently the serum stimulated one of these and thereafter was bound by natural law to follow that line of development.

As he talked, he was watching her, and he was thinking: 'This problem isn't resolved. How are we going to deal with *her*?'

He sensed an almost incredible strength, an actual, palpable force. It poured from her in a steady stream of power.

He continued tensely: 'The Great Galactics, when planting their seed on a new planet, have never interfered with the basic characteristics of the various races that live there. They interject selected bundles of their own genes by grafting into thousands of men and women on every continent. As the generations go by, these bundles intermix by chance with those that are native to the people of the planet. Apparently, the Omega serum stimulates one of these mixtures and carries it forward to whatever it is capable of, which, because of the singularity factor, usually leads to a dead end.'

'The singularity factor – ?' Her words were a question.

Men, Hammond explained, were born of the union of a man and a woman. No one person carried more than a portion of mankind's genes. As time passed, the interaction and inter-relation of all the genes occurred; the race progressed because billions of chance intermixings of different bundles took place.

In Vince, one such bundle had been stirred, been whipped up to its ultimate point by repeated Omega Stimulation – but evidently that particular bundle had strictly limited possibilities, as would always be the case when a single person was bred, so to speak, with himself – the singularity factor.

And that was what had happened to Vince and herself. They were products of the most fantastic inbreeding ever attempted – life surviving through one line, a link of incest carried to some ultimate sterility, fantastic, interesting, freakish.

'You are wrong,' said the woman-shape softly. 'I am not a

211

freak. So what has happened here is even more improbable than I have realized. In myself, it was the galactic seedling bundle of genes that was stimulated. Now, I understand what it was I contacted out in space. One of them. And he let me. He understood instantly.'

She added, 'One more question, John Hammond. Omega is an unusual term. What does it mean?'

' . . . When man becomes one with the ultimate, that is Point Omega.'

It seemed to Hammond that, even as he finished speaking, she was growing remote, withdrawing from him. Or was it that it was he who was withdrawing? Not only from her, but from everything – drifting away, not in any spatial sense, but, in some curious fashion, away from the reality of the entire universe? The brief thought came that this should be an alarming and disturbing experience. Then the thought itself was forgotten.

'There is something occurring,' her voice was telling him. 'In the small thing behind the door, the Omega evolutionary process is completed, in its fashion. In me, it is not completed – not quite.

'But it is being completed now. . . .'

He was nowhere and nothing. New word impressions, new thought impressions, came suddenly and swept through him like the patter of rain.

The impressions took form. It was later in time. He seemed to be standing in the small room next to his office, looking down at the lanky, redheaded young man sitting groggily on the edge of the couch holding his head.

'Coming out of it, Vince?' Hammond asked.

Vincent Strather glanced uncertainly up at him, ran his hand over the jagged rent in the sleeve of his jacket.

'I guess so, Mr Hammond,' he muttered. 'I . . . what happened?'

'You went for a drive tonight,' Hammond told him, 'with a girl named Barbara Ellington. You'd both been drinking. She was driving . . . driving too fast. The car went off a highway embankment, turned over several times. Witnesses dragged you to safety minutes before the car burst into flames. The girl was dead. They didn't attempt to save her body. When

212

the police informed me of the accident, I had you brought here to Research Alpha.'

As he spoke, he had the stunning realization that everything he was saying was true. The accident *had* happened late that evening, in exactly that manner.

'Well . . . ' Vince began. He broke off, sighed, shook his head. 'Barbara was an odd girl. A wild one! I was pretty fond of her once,' Mr Hammond. Lately, I've been trying to break off with her.'

Hammond received the impression that much more had happened. Automatically, he looked back through the open door as the private telephone in the inner office signaled. 'Excuse me,' he said to Vince.

As he flicked on the instrument, Helen Wendell's face appeared on the phone screen. She gave him a brief smile, asked, 'How is Strather?'

Hammond didn't reply at once. He looked at her, feeling cold, eerie crawlings over his scalp. Helen was seated at her desk in the outer office. She was not in a spaceboat standing off the planet.

He heard himself say, 'He's all right. There is very little emotional shock. . . . How about you?'

'I'm disturbed by Barbara's death,' Helen admitted. 'But now I have Dr Gloge on the phone. He's quite anxious to talk to you.'

Hammond said, 'All right, Put him on.'

'Mr Hammond,' Dr Gloge's voice said a moment later, 'this is in connection with the Point Omega Stimulation project. I've been going over all my notes and conclusions on these experiments, and I'm convinced that once you understand the extraordinary dangers which might result if the details of my experiments became known, you will agree that the project should be closed out and my records referring to it destroyed at once.'

After switching off the phone, he remained for a while at the desk.

So that part of the problem also had been solved! The last traces of the Omega serum were being wiped out, would soon linger only in his mind.

And for how long there? Perhaps no more than two or three hours, John Hammond decided. The memory pictures were paling; he had a feeling that sections of them already had vanished. And there was an odd, trembling uncertainty about what was left . . . thin, colored mind-canvas being tugged by a wind which presently would carry it off.

He had no objections, Hammond told himself. He had seen one of the Great Ones, and it was not a memory that it was good for a lesser being to have.

Somehow, it hurt to be so much less.

He must have slept. For he awoke suddenly. He felt vaguely bewildered, for no reason that he could imagine.

Helen came in, smiling. 'Don't you think it's time we closed up for the night? You're working too long hours again.'

'You're right,' Hammond nodded.

He got up and went into the room next to the office to tell Vincent Strather he was free to go home.

Him

A. E. VAN VOGT

As all knew, everything came from Him.

Josiah Him, dictator of Earth – except for a few areas of resistance, consisting of a total of about eight hundred million scientific savages, a portion of whom were located in the western half of North America and the rest in the great mountain regions of Asia and elsewhere.

These barbaric remnants had, in their madness, declared a state of war on Him. As it developed, the counterattack from Him had included an initial surprise invasion – which was repelled. After the defeat, the word from Him was that every means of humanitarian warfare would be employed to defeat the savages, including – in severe emergencies – the planarian education plan.

This particular word from Him had come that morning to Edgar Maybank: ' . . . Your assistants, hereinafter to be called students, have been selected for planarian accelerated education. . . . Report July 12. . . . '

That was *next day!*

The man who had climbed onto the bar stool next to Edgar, and who had somehow drawn the anguished truth out of Edgar, was singularly unsympathetic. He was a big, gentle fellow, who jiggled a little to the music, but had all the correct attitudes instantly at the tip of his tongue.

' . . . The word from Him,' he said with quiet certainty, 'is that the planarian system should be used only in extreme emergencies. All truly patriotic educators should therefore be prepared for the supreme sacrifice. You are to be congratulated on this rare opportunity to serve Him, but, uh, don't you think that's rather an unusual get-up for an expert?'

He thereupon eyed Edgar's corduroys and formless shirt.

Edgar said, 'I came straight from work.'

'Oh, straight from the laboratory.'

'I guess you could call it that,' said Edgar absently.

He was admitting to himself, gloomily, that he had been very remiss in the past, when other people had been selected for the planarian program. In fact, his indignation against the plan had started belatedly that morning. What bothered him most was the feeling that he was the victim of a scheme.

'After all,' he said, 'we know that these decisions are not made by Him, but by administrators and subadministrators –'

The older man interjected quickly: 'But always from the highest motives, solely in the name of Him, responsible to Him –'

No question, that was the theory; and Edgar had given lip service to it for so long that he was now briefly silenced.

While the dancers writhed around him, and his barmate kept time by moving one portion or another of his body, Edgar sipped his drink and grimly contemplated the entire planarian idea.

Long ago, it had been discovered that planarian worms could be trained in simple condition responses. When these trained worms were ground up and fed to other planarian worms, these latter learned the same responses faster than worms not so fed.

During the great rebellion, at the command of Him, the truths thus scientifically established were applied to human beings. University professors, scientists, and other experts were ground up and fed to their students in an accelerated education program.

Edgar's lean face took on a bitter expression. 'There's a certain subadministrator who's been trying to make time with my girl,' he said darkly, 'and it's significant to me that it's this sub who has now selected me.'

He added hastily, 'Don't get me wrong. I'll be the first to admit that I've always been proud of my special ability to brew beer. It's a rare talent I have, attested to by the undoubted fact that my company are the official brewers for Him. As a result, I am the highest-paid employee in the beer business. Still, there are other beers. So where's the emergency?'

He became aware that his companion had stopped his

wiggling and was blinking at him. Something seemed to have sobered him.

'Beer!' said the man. He sipped from his glass, his heavy face oddly twisted. Then: 'It's an unusual emergency, as you say. What did you say was the name of this subadministrator?'

Edgar told him it was Ancil Moody.

The man took out his card and handed it to Edgar with a decisive thrust. It read:

STACY PANGBORN
Chief of Administration
PalGlomHim
Government Center

Edgar gulped and almost dropped the card. Everybody knew that PalGlomHim was – well, it was tops.

'You're a VIP?' asked Edgar.

'Extremely so,' acknowledged the man quietly. He added, 'Write your name on the back of that card and do not – repeat, do not – report to the Segmentation Plant tomorrow.'

Edgar was weaving a little from the way something inside his head was singing. 'W-what do you think will happen?'

'Read the papers!' was the enigmatic reply.

Whereupon the VIP walked out, swaying in a dignified way.

Edgar was more than a little disturbed next day when there was no report in the papers that seemed relevant. He began to feel unpatriotic. His conscience began to tug him toward his duty.

But before he could decide, the secret police roared down on him. ' . . . Your failure to report . . . gross sedition . . . special hearing.'

At the hearing, held in a chamber deep in the bowels of the earth, Edgar was shown photographs. One was of the VIP.

'That's him,' he said.

Great excitement among his interrogators. ' . . . The enemy leader himself . . . come down from the mountains . . . in a bar.'

It was decided that the people in the bar must have been involved. Therefore . . . extermination program. But first, anything to do with the opposition leader required a personal interview with Him.

And so there was Edgar in the Presence, surrounded by the private guards of the great man, and with one top official. All others were barred. Edgar lay face down on the glossy floor; a voice from above asked questions, and he answered from the corner of his mouth as best he could.

Presently the voice said, startled: 'Beer?' It asked querulously, 'My brand?'

'Apparently, your Super.'

Silence; then: 'Bring that subadministrator!'

The secret service had already embraced Ancil Moody in steel handcuffs, and he was brought in, pale, fleshy, anxious, and laid down on the floor at the feet of Him.

There was a pause; Edgar ventured a quick glance and saw that the eyes of Him were gazing at the cringing subadministrator. Abruptly, the voice of Him came: 'Is there any shortage of subadministrators of his class?'

The voice of the chief of protocol could not seem to say fast enough that the shortage was unquestionably acute.

Again, silence; but presently the judgment of Him was delivered: 'First, obtain a confession, then segmentation under the planarian plan.'

They were about to subject the unfortunate Ancil Moody to a special type of humanitarian torture – instant, extreme pain – when he said hastily, 'I'm willing to confess. But first remove my disguise.'

That caused a murmur of wonderment and some tension. The disguise – a flesh mask – came off in its gooey way, quickly.

The chief of protocol, who had knelt beside the prisoner's body while it was being unmasked, said in astonishment: 'Your Excellency, this creature's face bears a startling resemblance to you. . . .'

Something of the truth of this situation must have penetrated to the dictator's side at that instant. He surged to his feet from beside the bound man and looked around him, eyes wide and wild. He yelled hoarsely, 'Guards, your guns!'

Blasters glinted in response, in half a dozen hands. At that point, the head guard said, 'All right – Dickenson – Gray!'

Two blasters flashed their purple flame, and the chief of protocol went down, skin blackened, clothes burning furiously.

A moment later – while Edgar, still not daring to move,

218

watehed from the top of his eyes – six blasters pointed at Him. The dictator had started to run, but now he stopped and slowly put up his hands.

The head guard walked over and removed the handcuffs from the subadministrator. That young man climbed to his feet, and said in a voice of command. 'That was good work. All right, disguise Him.'

Rough hands grabbed the tense Him. Handcuffs clicked. A makeup box appeared, and an Ancil Moody mask was produced from it. In a few minutes, one of the guards had made up Him to resemble the subadministrator as he had been when he was brought into the room. The dead aide was dragged into a closet.

The voice of the new Him said to the old Him, 'We got our men in to be your guards long ago, but of course they couldn't just kill you. That would simply have started a struggle for power among your military and political commanders, with no real change. So our problem was to figure out how we could maneuver the man who resembled you superficially – myself – into your presence, wary as you have always been. It took wild figuring – as you can see – including making sure that our bait' – he indicated Edgar, who was beginning to stir – 'did not became suspicious – and, of course, taking it for granted that the planarian program was, on the one hand, a method of controlling the scientific community and, on the other, a way of getting rid of any important recalcitrant –'

He broke off, finished grimly, 'Since the method has such enormous propaganda acceptance, I order that the original sentence on Ancil Moody be carried out.'

Actually, what happened when the subadministrators gathered for their educational supplement, the segmentation machine accidentally – it was said – flushed the entire ground-up body of the dictator into a sewer.

The new power group did not really believe that planarianism worked on human beings. But – involved as its members were in a careful reintroduction of democratic procedures – no one among them wanted to take the chance that the peculiar abilities possessed by Him might be passed on to any group of bright young executives.

As a substitute, these latter were given an ample ration

from the private beer stock of Him. They were served by the brewmaster himself – Edgar Maybank – whose charming new bride assisted her in waiting on tables.

A real festive occasion, everyone agreed afterward.

THE SILKIE
by A. E. van Vogt

THE SILKIE – a living spaceship impervious to heat and cold, virtually indestructible, and capable of travelling at supersonic speeds – similar to a human being, but not the same. Highly intelligent. The Silkie – able to live under the oceans with the ease of a dolphin and the speed of a shark. The Silkie – a modern angel or a computerised demon? The Silkie – friend of Earth, or a pitiless, alien destroyer? Once again A. E. van Vogt demonstrates his mastery of the science fiction genre in the incredible adventures of THE SILKIE.

On sale at newsagents and booksellers everywhere.

NEW ENGLISH LIBRARY

STRANGER IN A STRANGE LAND

by Robert Heinlein

The most famous Science Fantasy novel of all time

Entertaining, perhaps shocking, STRANGER IN A STRANGE LAND attacks all the religious explanations of faith ... undermines the idea of sexual relations based on jealousy ... pokes a bitter satirical finger at the materialists and politicians.

Like '1984', like 'Brave New World', STRANGER IN A STRANGE LAND is a searing indictment of Western Civilisation, a staggering shocking, revealing look at the fundamental urges in our way of life.

Robert Heinlein, winner of both 'Hugo' and 'Nebula' awards, has rightly been called the 'Dean' of present day writers of science fiction.

NEW ENGLISH LIBRARY

NEL BESTSELLERS